Rapid Reading in 5 Days

RAPID
Reading in 5 Days

The Quick-and-Easy Program to Master Faster Reading

Joan Minninger, Ph.D.

A Perigee Book

A Perigee Book
Published by The Berkley Publishing Group
200 Madison Avenue
New York, NY 10016

Copyright © 1994 by Joan Minninger, Ph.D.

Book design by Irving Perkins Associates

Cover design by Bob Silverman, Inc.

Interior illustrations by Martha Milton Stookey

First Perigee edition: September 1994

Published simultaneously in Canada.

Library of Congress Cataloging-in-Publication Data

Minninger, Joan.
　　Rapid reading in five days : the quick-and-easy program to master faster reading /
Joan Minninger.
　　　　　p.　　cm.
　　ISBN 0-399-52131-3
　　1. Rapid reading.　I. Title.　II. Title: Rapid reading in 5 days.
　LB1050.54.M56　　1994
　428.4'3—dc20　　　　　　　　　　　　　　　94-16092
　　　　　　　　　　　　　　　　　　　　　　　　CIP

Printed in the United States of America

10　9　8　7　6　5　4　3　2　1

DEDICATION

To Christopher and Brian

Gratitude

To John Duff, my marvelous editor; to Eugene O'Sullivan and Jack Bettenbender, my superb first teachers of rapid reading; to Becky Gordon for her creative desktop publishing; to Eleanor Dugan, Ted Werfhorst and Dennis Briskin for their editorial contributions; to Charlotte Milton for unflagging moral support; to Chris Harrington, Christopher Putz, Kyra Minninger, Marlene Blavin, Keiko Hamamoto, Barbara Fumea, and all my students for experimenting with the material and reporting back.

Contents

How to Get What You Want From This Book

by Chris Harrington[*]

Originally this book was the text in small, intensive speed-reading seminars taught by the author at colleges and corporations. These structured seminars yielded dramatic results.

Recently the author asked me to read and work my way through *Rapid Reading* without any personal guidance, exactly the way you are probably about to do. I waded right in and quickly realized that I would get even more value if I structured my reading. I'd like to make suggestions to help you get the most out of this book.

Different Speeds for Different Needs

Anyone who has ever spent a little time at a busy library knows that there are as many different types of readers as there are books and magazines. Different people read different things for different reasons.

Then what do these readers have in common? They are all familiar with the desire—and for some, the need—to read faster. *Rapid Reading* is a helpful guide to all these readers.

Rapid Reading teaches you not to read faster all the time, but to read faster when you need to and especially when you want to. It teaches a sort of cruise control for reading—different speeds for different needs with plenty of room for a variety of interests.

[*] *Chris Harrington is a desktop publishing specialist.*

Cruising

But don't go cruising straight into the book yet. Some of you, like me, have a stubborn streak and can digest lengthy chunks of print in long strings of unbroken reading. Others may have no appetite for these long reading meals or can spare only short periods of time out of their busy schedules. Either way, you will get more out of this book with a planned, structured approach, using either an intensive, two-to-four-hour-a-day schedule for five days or a two-week plan with shorter reading sessions.

The Five-Day Plan

The first plan, reading two to four hours a day for five days, is for people who feel comfortable reading that long and who really want to move through this book.

A Two-Week Plan

If you concentrate best in short, intensive sessions or are pressed for time, try spending thirty to ninety minutes a day. This is especially good if you're one of those people who prefer to learn things piece by piece.

Find Out Who's Boss

People invented words. We use them so widely that they have great power. For instance, we don't dare skip over words, sentences, and even books we have no use for. This is the "don't miss a word" syndrome. But remember that words are our creations, so we have the power to choose when we need them and when we don't.

When you work through *Rapid Reading*, your clock or timer isn't an opponent you have to beat. It's just a measure of your speed when you want to read fast. Remember that you're learning to read for yourself, not that ticking machine. Happy reading!

To the Reader

Rapid reading requires concentration. On recent research on concentration, *New York Times* writer Daniel Goleman says, "The seemingly simple act of being fully absorbed in a challenging task is now being seen as akin to some of the extravagantly euphoric states such as those sought in drugs or sex or through the 'runner's high.'" It's partly a sense of timelessness that many enjoy when absorbed in print.

Distraction is the enemy of concentration. And sometimes our minds wander away from print because we are not actively asking questions. Wanting to know something new or experience what others have thought or felt or done can be riveting. We can exploit our desire to know by deliberately asking questions. What a difference between a reader who obediently and passively hears every word in his head as he reads and one who formulates his own questions while pursuing their answers. The exercises in this book will help you perceive the structure of nonfiction and turn the pattern parts—such as problem, effects, causes and solution—into questions by asking What's the problem? etc. when your own questions do not announce themselves.

When you first learn to drive a car, you can't concentrate on speed until you feel secure with the mechanism of starting and stopping the car and mastering the clutch. In word processing you can't move rapidly until you learn the commands. In rapid reading you can't move quickly until you learn to let your purpose generate questions for you to actively pursue answers. Your curiosity and your need to know will keep you focused so you overcome the distraction that sets in if you are reading word-for-word.

Teddy Roosevelt read a book before breakfast and John Kennedy read 1,200 words per minute. But comparing your speed with others may be self-defeating. The only intelligent score to compete with is your own. But I urge you not to push for speed during those readings where you are not asked to time yourself. At first you are urged to assimilate the five nonfiction patterns of organization, which are generic structures, without timing.

Comprehension will be measured by your grasping the main ideas, the generalizations that are the pattern parts of the five patterns of organization. Like many others, you may find that reading rapidly will positively influence your comprehension, if it is not already adequate. However, you may make trade-offs. I suggest you aim for 70% comprehension when you want to cover more articles and books. You will experiment with adjusting your speed/comprehension ratio. If asked how rapidly you read, the perfect answer would be "It depends." It depends on your purpose and the complexity of material to be read. Your reading speeds may not form a consistent upward spiral but resemble the normal learning curve, $\mathcal{N}$, because each new pattern has its own demands.

The reading selections have been chosen to represent a range of complexity. Do consider some selections as optional challenges. They are there for you to push against your current boundaries. But you will still gain enormous benefit even if you skip readings that are too removed from your needs and interests.

Rapid Reading in 5 Days

DAY 1

Blocks and Attitudes
Main Ideas
Fact Hunts
Comprehension Sprint

BLOCKS

Analyzing Everything

Arden was the only student I'd ever trained who hadn't begun to increase his speed by the second hour of instruction. In fact, after four hours he had still not advanced beyond 200 words per minute. I was puzzled.

"What did you do in high school?" I asked him.

"I never went to high school," he told me. That was a surprise. This was a quick-minded and articulate man who was the president of his own successful corporation. How could he have missed out on schooling?

"What were you doing instead?" I asked.

"I was in a concentration camp."

"How did you survive?"

"I analyzed everything."

This was the clue I needed. He was critically taking everything apart,

1

which is very time-consuming and only worth the time if analyzing is our purpose. I looked right at him and said, "Arden, the war is over!"

He was smart enough to see what I meant. His habit of analyzing everything had helped him to survive while in the camp. Applied to reading, however, it did nothing but slow him down. But how was he to change? he wanted to know.

"Tell me," I asked, "do you give the same amount of attention to everyone who talks to you?"

"Hell, no!" he said.

"So, you are selective about whom you listen to?"

"Of course. It depends on who is doing the talking and my need to know."

I encouraged him to discriminate among the words he read the same way he did among the words he heard. My guess was that, like many people who lack formal education, he had undue respect for the printed word and believed that he owed to every author the benefit of his best attention. He was relieved to be told that he could *choose* when to analyze closely and when to glide over material simply to get the gist or add to his stock of general information.

Arden's story exemplifies the sort of psychological block that serves well under crisis conditions but becomes an impediment in ordinary times. Since he was willing to recognize that his block had become obsolete, he was able to dispense with it quickly. He took heart from Sir Francis Bacon, who wrote in 1625: "Some books are to be tasted,/ others to be swallowed,/ and some few to be chewed and digested."

Premature Evaluation

Risa's complaint was that, as an adult woman, she was still reading aloud. Most such problems begin during school days, so I asked how school had been for her when she was younger. She uneasily confessed that she had liked it at first but began to feel different when her father lost his job and became seriously depressed. Her father obviously wanted her company, because anytime she would so much as sniffle, he would encourage her to skip school and stay home. She now realized that she stayed home so much, not to "take care of her health," but to take care of him.

The attraction of school could not compete with the feeling of being wanted and important that Risa got from staying home with her father. When she did go to school, she always felt "in a fog," because she was so behind in her work and owed so many assignments. Not surprisingly, she never developed reading competence. To cope with the pain of "failure," she decided that she just wasn't smart and "that's just the way it was." But now that her poor reading skills were holding her back in her adult career, she came to me for help. To decide that she was smart after all, and to become a good reader, took far less time than she would have thought possible.

When Words Must Be Said Aloud

Besides psychological blocks, some readers suffer through physiological blocks. A friend who is a brilliant doctor at a world-class medical center amazed me when he said he was a good speller but a terrible reader.

"But how did you ever get through medical school?" I asked.

"I listened intently and took copious notes."

"But what about reading?" I asked.

"I read slowly because my brain only makes meaning from words I can hear. I literally read out loud so I can hear the words to make sense of them."

My friend belongs to a small minority of readers who have exceptional intelligence but a vastly diminished capacity to read. Unless you are a member of that minority, much of this book will help you break through your school-induced habit of reading word-for-word.

In the Beginning Was the Word-for-Word

The human mind can process at least 800 words a minute. So, why do most intelligent people read about 250 words a minute? Because that's as fast as we can talk or say the words in our heads. Some of us were taught to read accurately and precisely, *word-for-word*.

If you went to school where the teacher had you read out loud long after she knew that you could pronounce the words, then you've had a long history of learning how to say each word aloud. Slower readers are still busy saying each word and hearing its sound echoing in their heads. Have you ever been running your eyes over print and suddenly noticed that you hadn't the slightest idea what the last few paragraphs were about? Your mind wandered. Chances are you spent years in school allowing your mind to wander. What else can a mind do when it thinks faster than it is informed? Reading slowly puts some people in a trance.

Fun with Dick and Jane

You will learn to read rapidly and with more lasting benefit if you first reexperience how you learned to read. Read the following in a trancelike state by visualizing as you go:

Picture yourself in kindergarten, first or second grade.
See where you sat. Was it in the first seat in the first row? Third seat? Last seat, last row?
Notice the advantages of sitting there.
Notice the disadvantages of sitting there.
If you sat in rows, nod your head.
If you sat in circles, nod your head.
If you read aloud as a way to learn to read, nod your head.
If reading aloud was sometimes a good experience, nod your head.
If reading aloud was usually a bad experience, nod your head.
If occasionally it was a bad experience, nod your head.
If you can picture yourself in a miserable moment reading out loud, nod your head.
If other kids laughed when you made an error, nod your head.
If you were ever embarrassed by mispronouncing a word out loud, nod your head.
If you liked being asked to read, nod your head.
If it took forever for a class to get through reading a story, nod your head.
If you were bored and restless a whole lot, nod your head.
If you remember hearing other children reading in a flat, slow, monotonous voice, nod your head.
If you ever read like that yourself, nod your head.
If you're feeling yourself as five or six years old right now, nod your head.

See yourself as a five- or six-year-old with a reader. Now read the following out loud with no expression, giving each syllable the same stress as all the others.

See Dick. See Dick run. Dick likes to run with Jane. They both like to run with Spot. See Spot run with Dick and Jane.

How easy it was to be embarrassed in front of the whole class. Like some of us, you may have "learned" that if you knew how to pronounce the alphabet's sounds, you could read anything. Try the following exercise.

Pronounce out loud: *word*. Now using the same sound of *ord* you made in saying *word*, pronounce *lord* so the sound rhymes (like *lurd*). There are so many simple sounds that are not consistent in English that there are frequent opportunities to make a mistake while reading out loud.

Say the word *though*. Now say *through*, repeating the same *ough* sound. "But, no, boys and girls," your teacher may have said, "*throw* is not spelled *through*." Say *though* again; now say *cough* (*coe* like the *oe* in *toe*). *Cough* pronounced like *coe*, while reading aloud, would induce giggles from your peers. Try the word *hiccough*. How amazed we must have been to find out that's how to spell a word that sounds like *hiccup*.

Now pronounce out loud the word *steak;* now pronounce the word *streak* to rhyme with *steak*. Do have respect for how inconsistent the English language is. All this is in the service of having you not underestimate how much reading out loud in class was fraught with occasions to be "wrong" and to be laughed at.

How many boys and girls were in your first-grade class? Possibly twenty-five or more. Now imagine reading out loud once every twenty-five times. Imagine hearing all the other boys and girls taking turns reading out loud as you just did. Do you remember wanting to kick the child who stumbled interminably before he said the next word? Do you remember how long it took all the other boys and girls to read before it was your turn? Do you remember rehearsing your lines so you could say all the words without stumbling instead of paying attention to the story? Do you remember floating away until it was your turn, because other kids took so long to read?

For some of us the sight of words on paper is a cue to go off into a trance as in those comfy years in grammar school where much of our focus was out the window, safe from the tedium of hearing others read out loud. Appreciate where you first heard the phrase "Don't miss a word."

If you were taught to pronounce each word out loud after the teacher knew you could pronounce words, you were hindered from becoming fluent. This process is actually the reverse of what you needed. Children need to read fluently, not to be corrected for reading the wrong word (like reading "house" instead of "home") as long as they keep the author's meaning intact. Slow readers are busy saying each word right and hearing its sound echoing inside their heads. Fast readers make predictions about what will follow as they read. They are looking for answers to their questions.

Arden had to realize that "the war is over." You may have to realize that "school is out." You don't have to go through life following your teacher's order not to miss a word. Obeying that order is probably the single most important barrier to rapid reading, given your urgency to find answers through managing print.

How Fast Should You Read?

There's only one answer to the question "How fast should you read?" That answer is "It depends." Most of the time, reading efficiently means reading quickly, being pulled along by curiosity, following one line of thought. Yet there are other times when slow reading will serve you better. Sometimes, as with poetry, love letters, contracts, wills, or an IRS return, you'll want to consider every nuance and detail. There are some novels you'll want to race right through, but others you'll want to savor. So there's no reason to feel guilty over any particular reading rate.

Unfortunately, the simple act of reading has the potential for providing many sources of guilt. We can feel guilty that we don't read more "meaningful" books or that we haven't read the latest best-seller that everyone is talking about. We can feel guilty that we spend too much time reading or that we don't spend enough. We can feel guilty that we don't get enough out of what we read, or that we can't remember it later as well as we would like, or that we simply can't understand the instructions that come with a new VCR or digital watch or answering machine.

ATTITUDES

Sometimes we feel guilty about what we "should" be reading and that we fill our shelves with unread magazines, journals, and books. Instead of feeling guilty about not reading all the publications we buy, we could regard them as expensive greeting cards to ourselves, reminders of the kind of person we are or want to become. That they were not seductive enough to grab us from more compelling priorities is less important than their role in supporting our desire to know.

Success breeds confidence. All of us had an optimum time to learn to read. If you came to school already knowing how to read, you may have been forced to endure tedious exercises for those who hadn't yet learned. Boredom may have set in. You may have dealt with it by distracting yourself with other thoughts, then been accused of daydreaming or incompetence. You may have felt ashamed or angry when reprimanded.

Or you may have been pushed before you were cognitively ready, only to develop a sense of inferiority, not feeling smart. Even Albert Einstein and Thomas Aquinas were late starters. Our decisions about our intelligence are laid in childhood experiences. Before doing the exercises in this book, it's crucial that you know that there is no necessary connection between reading fast and intelligence. Professionals like lawyers and engineers are rewarded for precise, deliberate slow reading and may not know that they can develop a repertoire of different speeds and techniques.

Then there are attitudes that promote anxiety that grow out of school and family injunctions such as the following:

Old Injunctions	*New Permissions*
Don't miss a word.	Read for ideas, not words.
Start only at the beginning.	Begin wherever your interest takes you.
Don't skip ahead.	Take what you want, leave the rest.
Finish reading whatever you start.	Why read a book that doesn't interest you?
Don't mark up the book.	Mark your own books if you like. Try using Post-its.
Read only after you finish your chores.	Reading is thinking—read in prime time.
If you don't know a word, stop reading and look it up.	Rarely does a single word determine the whole meaning. It's usually better to keep going, wanting to know what's next, getting the strange word's meaning from the context.

How Useful Is Anxiety?

Let's do an anxiety check. What subjects do you feel obligated to read about to become a "better" person? Rate your anxiety level of these obligations.

	No Guilt	Some Anxiety	Lots of Anxiety
I should read more:			
1. _____	[ ]	[ ]	[ ]
2. _____	[ ]	[ ]	[ ]
3. _____	[ ]	[ ]	[ ]
4. _____	[ ]	[ ]	[ ]
5. _____	[ ]	[ ]	[ ]

If your mind is temporarily blank, here are some subjects frequently mentioned by participants in my seminars:

- job, business
- world events
- sports
- gossip (If this sounds frivolous, remember that gossip is social glue, the ambience of relationships, and a form of intimacy. Consider the Andy Warhol diaries: How terrible to be in them! How terrible *not* to be in them!)
- election issues
- new legislation
- retirement plans
- health issues (eggs, zinc in diet, eating fish and mussels, calcium, jogging, medical advances, etc.)
- the performing arts (who's good, who's new?)
- special interest action groups (civil rights, environmental issues, health, education, drug abuse, parklands, etc.)
- personal interests (gardening, stamps, quilts, cars, pets, etc.)

What do *you* choose to feel guilty about? Is this anxiety useful to you? That is, does it motivate you to find more efficient ways to process all this information? Or does it stall you and make you feel helpless, useless, totally overwhelmed?

Is it possible you have a choice about how you process information?   [ ] yes   [ ] no

Is it possible that you have a choice about how much you remember?   [ ] yes   [ ] no

If you answered yes to either of these questions, keep reading.

Reading Without Guilt

Processing printed words slowly also provides us with a way to shut out the world, to slow down, to go into a trancelike state of total absorption. There's even another benefit attached to reading slowly. What do some people do to fall asleep? Right. They read! Reading yourself to sleep is only a problem when that isn't your intention.

Comedian Woody Allen claimed he learned to speed-read *War and Peace* in twenty minutes. When someone asked him what it was about, he replied, "Russia." If you shudder when you encounter real-life versions of racing through fiction looking for facts, so do I. Fiction is meant to seduce. It is rarely created to provide clumps or sequences of useful, bare-bones information. Most of the reading we want to recall is nonfiction, which can be compared to K rations: relatively tasteless, but full of essential nutrients. Fiction, on the other hand, may be either rare wine or junk food; the best is meant to be tasted, not swallowed whole.

Beating Computers

Efficient readers get through the daily information onslaught by borrowing some techniques from computers. They learn to recognize common structures for information and to search for key words and ideas, soaring high over unrelated material and zooming down to focus on the desired bit. But computers don't have the ability to become bored. They just do mechanically what they've been told to do. People need both pleasure and purpose to work efficiently, and slow down considerably when they become bored.

Fortunately, efficient human information processors are rarely bored, because they are *active*. They make themselves curious and excited about the glut of facts, figures, and ideas they encounter by constantly asking questions, answering them, and then formulating new questions as they go. Their efficiency comes from racing ahead eagerly, not from being shoved from behind.

Remember that as an intelligent person, *you* are in charge of what you choose to miss. *You* decide what is reasonable to know. Of course, society and your teachers and employers are going to try to influence your choices, but you are the final judge. As long as you feel that others are making choices for you, you may resist and experience overload, no matter how small or simple the actual volume. When you see yourself in charge, energized by your inborn curiosity and able to decide what to notice and what to ignore, "overload" becomes unlikely.

School Is Out

Why are you reading? What do you expect to gain from a particular reading? If you don't pause to notice your own goals and purposes, you will be stuck back in third grade, reading to please the teacher and meeting the school's criteria for a good student. In some places the criteria included minute details that you would be tested on. After we were assigned *Silas Marner,* I can remember Miss Pratt testing us on "What did Silas say to Eppie in the snow?" To this day I am more familiar with rote answers than with the theme of *Silas Marner.*

Why were teachers so busy testing on detail? Because that's how they could be sure we had read assignments. Questions with verifiable answers were easiest to administer and test. Anyone who wishes to read rapidly must acknowledge that *school is out.* Otherwise, you will be heeding some archaic teacher's voice saying, "Don't miss a word," which, if followed, will cause you to miss worlds of ideas. The point is—*you* get to decide what you want from your reading and, yes, you can miss a lot. But what you gain will probably be more valuable because you will be in charge of what you want to know, as well as what you "miss," and your reading rate.

Frequently, the deal in school was "Read, then think about it; the 'Think-and-Do' questions are at the back of each chapter." Most of us got the notion that reading preceded thinking when what we needed to know was that *reading IS thinking!* The vital questions today are our own, not those made up by some textbook author.

Feeling Awkward

Reading faster is changing habits. You will tend to feel awkward at first, as with any change of habit, but a willingness to tolerate mild discomfort while you move faster through your reading will pay rich dividends later. Soon your mind will accustom itself to pushing through printed matter at faster speeds with the same or better comprehension.

WHAT TO DO

Now get your timer ready and time how long it takes you to read "SOS." Read the following article as you normally would this kind of material.

Be ready to answer a few questions when you're through. Start your timer. Go.

READ:

SOS— SAVE OUR SHORELINES

by Wesley Marx

Our barrier islands and mainland coastal beaches are the continent's protective bumper, advancing and retreating in perfect harmony with the ocean's relentless pounding. When we immobilize them with man-made structures, we invite catastrophe.

Recently I visited a Southern California beach of my boyhood. The sun was shining, and the sea sparkled. But the *beach was gone.* In its place was a foot-bruising strand of cobbles.

Reckless shoreside development by Americans who love beaches not wisely but too well threatens to devastate our magnificent coastlines. The barrier islands, sandbars and beaches of the Atlantic and Gulf coasts, the cliff-backed sands of California and Oregon, the unique shorelines of Alaska and Hawaii—all are at risk.

The risk, moreover, goes far beyond the loss of favorite leisure spots. A beach is more than a place to bask in sun and surf. It is a geological bumper, absorbing the attack of waves and currents that would otherwise erode coastal land.

How has our desire to enjoy the shore become a means of destroying it? Imperfect understanding of the dynamics of sea and beach is one reason. Beaches are lively landforms that survive by retreating and advancing in concert with the ocean. Yet people blithely build their dream homes in "active" zones. Some builders actually bulldoze view-blocking dunes. This is comparable to knocking down a river levee. Dunes serve as natural storm-surge barriers and provide beaches with a sand reserve. When they go, it isn't long before waves collide head-on with homes. And when large-scale development imposes immobility on a shoreline, as it has in such cities as Miami Beach, Galveston and Atlantic City, large-scale disaster is courted.

Barrier islands—low-lying strips of beach and dune—rim much of the Atlantic and Gulf coasts. In its natural state, a barrier island can "roll over" in response to sudden or steady rises in sea level, ensuring its continued existence and protecting the mainland shore. But when development deprives it of that resilience, the barrier island has no bumper to cushion the ocean's force. The resulting impact can be as violent as an auto colliding with a trailer truck—and as lethal.

The Town That Vanished. Even communities that keep a respectful distance from active beach zones can be thrust by selfish neighbors into punishing collisions with the ocean. Beaches are nourished by sand carried in currents running along the shore. On both our Pacific and Atlantic coasts the predominant direction of this "sand river" is north to south, so that sand from Georgia beaches, for example, helps sustain Florida beaches. When this vital sand flow is impeded, downcoast beaches starve; entire communities can be victimized.

In the 1930s South Cape May, N.J., rang with the laughter of summer visitors enjoying the beach. Today, fish school where the village once stood. Upcoast stands a sand-trapping harbor jetty that—in hindsight—could be considered South Cape May's grave marker. While a beach north of this jetty expanded, South Cape May's beachfront was shriveling. Block by block, the wave-battered village slipped into a watery tomb.

Similarly, dams, levees and man-made channels can disrupt the vital flow of shore-sustaining sand and soil that rivers carry down from their watersheds. Louisiana is rimmed by extensive coastal marshlands that were once sustained by massive silt-loads deposited by the Mississippi River. But since levees were constructed along the lower river in the 1920s, restricting flow to the marshlands, much of the silt is carried out into the Gulf of Mexico. As a result, according to the U.S. Fish and Wildlife Service, Louisiana is losing 33 square miles of coastal marshland a year. At this rate, Plaquemines Parish will be underwater in 52 years. Moreover, New Orleans is losing a natural buffer against hurricanes.

Towering Seawall. Such self-induced predicaments generate pressure for federal action to "stabilize" America's disaster-prone shores. Initially, the Army Corps of Engineers, the major federal agency involved in beach erosion control, adopted a fortification approach, building concrete seawalls, rocky groins (resembling jetties) and other artificial structures to hold beaches more or less in place. By 1970 Hawaii's Waikiki Beach was cluttered with 42 groins and 37 seawalls—many privately built. However, a seawall's steep face can foster a severe surf backwash that undermines whatever beach remains. Seawalls are now considered a major cause of the erosion that plagues Waikiki Beach. Moreover, the waves that undermine a beach may eventually undermine a seawall.

At Sea Bright, N.J., residents live in the shadow of a towering, prison-like seawall. "If you let nature take its course, Sea Bright will disappear," says Duke University geologist Orrin Pilkey. The present seawall, fronted by the rubble of its predecessors, is periodically washed over by storm waves. The shore, steepened by rising wave action, can no longer hold sand.

The Corps of Engineers now prefers to pour sand onto beaches rather than concrete into seawalls. But a beach denied its natural sand supply must be nourished again and again. In Southern California, Surfside-Sunset Beach, starved by upcoast jetties, is on its sixth synthetic beach; Waikiki imports sand from 30 miles away. To feed mainland coastal beaches, the Corps even mines offshore sand deposits—with mixed success.

In 1971 the Corps developed a $1.8 billion project to "halt significant erosion" along 2700 miles of shore. (Annual maintenance cost: an estimated $73 million.) But in 1975 a General Accounting Office study concluded that "no structural solution has been devised which will ensure the permanent preservation of the nation's shoreline and coastal areas."

Easy Money. Ironically, the U.S. government *encourages* destructive coastal development. Federal grants are available to help sewer, water, pave, bridge and otherwise urbanize hurricane-prone sand mounds. The Department of the Interior estimates that about half a billion dollars of public money was spent to aid barrier-island development between 1975 and 1978. Despite some recent modifications by Congress, the government continues to reimburse insured beach dwellers for storm losses that private insurers do not cover—at highly subsidized rates. Dinesh Sharma, a coastal planner in Fort Myers, Fla., in testimony before Congress in 1980, said that more than $60-billion worth of coastal property is covered, "making disaster relief the second-biggest liability of the federal government after Social Security payments."

With such generous government assistance, it is no wonder barrier islands are hot real estate. The Department of Interior reports that barrier islands are urbanizing at twice the national rate.

Once hit by disaster, even carelessly placed coastal communities are frequently eligible for federal disaster relief to rebuild for a return engagement. Alabama's Dauphin Island received a grant to rebuild a bridge wiped out by Hurricane Frederic in 1979. Cost: $39 million. Number of full-time island residents: 1600. Federal subsidy per permanent resident: $24,375—for the bridge alone.

Before long we may be counting the price of runaway shore development in lives as well as money and property. After a hurricane surged through Galveston, Texas, in 1900 and left more than 6000 dead in this barrier-island city, the United States began developing an elaborate warning and evacuation system. Thus, while Hurricane Frederic racked up $2.3 billion in property damage along the Gulf Coast in 1979, only five people died. An estimated half-million Gulf residents heeded warnings and went inland.

This system, however, is being pressed to the breaking point by the sheer intensity of coastal development. One mishap—an auto collision, a bridge closed for repair— could trap thousands of evacuees. According to the director of the National Hurricane Center, Neil Frank, the New Jersey coast, the Norfolk, Va., region, the Florida Keys, the Florida west coast, New Orleans and the Galveston Bay area are most vulnerable in terms of coastal populations having exceeded hurricane-evacuation routes and facilities. "This nation is more vulnerable to hurricanes than it has ever been," says Frank.

Turning the Tide. We can avert potential disaster—*if* we stop trying to control shifting beaches and learn to control careless urbanization instead. Prominent business and civic leaders—among them Frank Borman, Lady Bird Johnson, Anne Morrow Lindbergh, Laurance Rockefeller—have formed Americans for the Coast to promote reforms. As a critical first step, Sen. John H. Chafee (R., R.I.) and Rep. Thomas B. Evans, Jr. (R., Del.) want to ban most forms of federal assistance to undeveloped coastal barriers, which compose about one-third of our shoreline from Maine to Mexico. Without government grants, these islands will be less tempting to developers.

In developed beach areas, the emphasis should shift from rebuilding disaster-prone communities to relocating residents. After three punishing encounters with tsunamis, Hilo, Hawaii, relocated its bayfront commercial district on higher ground. At Cape Hatteras, N.C., and other national seashores, the National Park Service has reverted to a "strategy of submission." It will no longer build—or rebuild—permanent facilities in high-hazard coastal areas. New Jersey is considering restricting developments of all types in high-erosion areas of its coastline.

The National Flood Insurance Program should make federally subsidized coastal-insurance rates reflect actual dollar loss—and monitor local communities' enforcement of realistic safe-building standards. The current Federal Insurance Administration requires new homes to be elevated on pilings above anticipated storm-surge levels, but is only beginning to take into account wave heights atop the surge.

Coastal states and local communities must invoke more prudent land-use and building controls too. By comparing historical records with current surveys, scientists can often predict whether a coastal area will be above sea level 20 or 30 years hence. Banks in Massachusetts have denied loans for building projects that would not survive the terms of the mortgage. Florida, Rhode Island and North Carolina are establishing beach setback lines that require new buildings be placed a predetermined distance from the mean-high-tide line or dune zone.

After a damaging encounter with a 1962 winter storm, Avalon, N.J., decided to return to the most effective and cheapest storm protection device for its area, the natural dune system. Special pathways now pro-vide access to the shore while protecting the dune plant cover that anchors sand against sea winds. "Our beaches are for your enjoyment," declares a community sign. "The dunes are for our protection."

America has some 84,000 miles of coastline. Our beaches are among our most valuable and vulnerable assets. We simply cannot build seawalls tall enough to make up for careless development.

Wesley Marx, whose most recent book is The Oceans: Our Last Resource, *is a university lecturer and writer on ocean and coastal ecology.*

Write down your reading time in the blanks below. Then answer the questions and determine your comprehension level from your score, as calculated on p. 35. Length of article: 1,750 words. Use the table on page 35 to determine how many words per minute you read.

Mins. ____ Secs. ____ Words per minute ____ Comprehension ____ %

QUESTIONS

1. Check which of the following the author regards as POSITIVE.
    a. Increased development of our shorelines
    b. More levees, seawalls, and dams
    c. Federal funds to rebuild barrier islands following hurricanes
    d. An organization called Americans for the Coast
    e. Restricting mortgages in "active" coast areas
    f. Sand dunes
    g. The "Strategy of Submission"
    h. The policy of the Army Corps of Engineers to pour sand on beaches rather than build concrete barricades
    i. Urging people to buy vacation property on barrier islands
    j. Relocating residents away from coastal areas
2. Check the main PROBLEM as purported by Marx.
    a. Our efforts to protect our shoreline have had the opposite effect.

     b. The low budget of the Army Corps of Engineers is preventing them from maintaining our shorelines.

     c. Mortgage companies no longer offer loans on property along our shorelines.

     d. Sand drifts naturally from north to south.

3. Check the TWO CAUSES of shoreline destruction.

     a. Dams

     b. Hurricanes

     c. Reckless shoreline development

     d. Inaction by the Army Corps of Engineers

4. Check the THREE EFFECTS of shoreline destruction.

     a. Loss of leisure areas

     b. Loss of natural storm barriers

     c. An increase in sharks

     d. Increased erosion of inland areas

     e. An increase in hurricanes

5. Check the TWO SOLUTIONS to curb shoreline destruction.

     a. Public pressure on Congress to increase Corps budget and disaster aid following hurricanes and bad floods

     b. Refusal of banks to give mortgages in danger areas

     c. Public pressure on legislators to control careless urbanization and shoreline development

     d. Bulldozing all sand dunes

     e. More levees, seawalls, dams

Answers on page 35.

HUMPTY DUMPTY EXPERIMENT I

"When I use a word, it means just what I choose it to mean, neither more nor less."

               Humpty Dumpty in THROUGH THE LOOKING-GLASS

WHAT TO DO

Here's an experiment. Time how many seconds it takes you to read each of the columns on the following page. Jot the number of seconds it takes in the space below each column.

READ:

I.	II.	III.	IV.
L	list	Even though	Four score and seven years ago
K	send	major banks	our fathers brought forth
J	days	are extremely	on this continent
H	good	cautious	a new nation
G	foul	in making	conceived in liberty
F	tear	small	and dedicated to the
D	goat	business loans	proposition that
S	prod	and the rising	all men are created equal.
A	walk	interest rate	Now we are engaged
Z	sour	has excluded	in a great civil war
X	desk	most borrowers,	testing whether that nation
C	tree	the rate of	or any nation so conceived
V	fund	loan defaults	and so dedicated
B	show	has been rising	can long endure.
N	blip	steadily in	We are met on a great
M	Paul	the last few	battlefield of that war.
P	dash	years	We have come to dedicate
O	lamp	until	a portion of that field
I	fair	it is almost	as a final resting-place
U	spin	impossible to begin	for those
Y	lady	a new business	who here gave their lives
T	wind	without	that that nation might live.
R	both	sufficient capital	It is altogether
E	glue	from	fitting and proper
W	tiny	private sources	that we should do this.
Q	fend	or from	But in a larger sense
X	jump	the sale	we cannot dedicate
V	done	of a previously	we cannot consecrate
R	able	owned	we cannot hallow this ground.
J	gnat	enterprise.	The . . .

————	————	————	————
seconds	seconds	seconds	seconds

I has 30 letters	II has 30 words (120 letters)	III has 60 words	IV has 120 words

Notice that column II has four times as many letters as column I. Did it take you four times as long to read column II? Of course not. Many people read columns I and II in about the same time. How come? It's because we can read words as fast as or faster than letters, and sentences even faster than words. Notice that reading column III didn't take twice as long as reading column II, even though it has twice the number of words. Why? Because, again, it is easier to read for meaning, and there is even more meaning in column III. In fact, column IV may have gone faster because, in addition, you were more familiar with the material. Most likely, once you caught on that column IV was the Gettysburg Address, you just glanced at the whole thing to make sure it was there as you remembered it, or you slowed down to enjoy the poetry of the familiar.

Letters and words are only symbols for meaning. Your mind supplies that meaning, and the speed at which you do it is rarely affected by the number of symbols.

Convince yourself, especially the younger part of you that went to school, that you can read faster when you read for ideas than when you read isolated letters or words.

HUMPTY DUMPTY EXPERIMENT II

WHAT TO DO

You may remember this old party trick. Read the sign below out loud.

PARIS IN THE
THE SPRING

If you're like most people, you failed to read the extra "the." Everyone is susceptible to filling in the blanks with what they want to see or hear or skipping over what they find extraneous. Try the following exercise in which every fifth word has been dropped. Notice how your mind supplies the meaning even though 20% of the words are missing. Then answer the questions following the passage.

READ:

Her body was the _____ thing John saw as _____ entered the library. She _____ lying on the elegant _____ rug before the fireplace, _____ and limp and very _____ . A vague half-smile _____ on her cold red _____ as if she knew _____ terrible joke.

Beside her _____ a bloodstained poker, evidence _____ the anger that had _____ her murdered as he _____ in the wood-paneled _____ . Perhaps she taunted him _____ she died. Perhaps she _____ knew what happened.

John _____ beside her for a _____ minutes, then rose and _____ to the hand-cranked _____ in the hall. Fifteen _____ later, the house was _____ of police, going about _____ gruesome business with an _____ of efficiency.

Finally, after _____ questions and prying about, _____ departed with the body, _____ it off in an _____ gray mortuary van.

John _____ alone in the library, _____ into the fireplace. He _____ hard not to look _____ the new wet place _____ the rug, scrubbed almost _____ by the charwoman, Mrs. _____ .

A subtle uneasiness seized _____ . There was something he _____ forgotten, something terribly important. _____ racked his brains until _____ he remembered. With catlike _____ he bounded to the _____ bookcase and quickly pulled _____ the book he had _____ to get in the _____ place.

QUESTIONS

1. What type of story is this?_____

2. Where did it take place?_____

3. Who were the main characters?_____

4. Did John find what he was looking for?_____

Answers on page 36.

HUMPTY DUMPTY EXPERIMENT III

WHAT TO DO

Read the passage on the following page, allowing your mind once again to look for the main idea.

MEN WHO MADE THEIR MARK

There are a few groups of men that typify the American spirit, the dashing folk heroes who lived by their wits and conquered all obstacles with easy grace. The cowboys certainly, and the aviators of World War I with their leather helmets and boyish grins. Probably the junk salesmen and haberdashers who became the movie moguls in the early days of cinema. Horatio Alger and Barney Oldfield, Lindbergh and Tom Edison.

To thxs list, we shxuld add the cxlxrful eccentrix and ruggxd individxxlists who madx rubber stxmps possible. Txdxy, thxy are unknxwn, unpraised, unsxng, bxt thxx were jxst as tough xs thx cxwbxys, jusx as brxve as txe aviatxrs and xs innovxtive as the movxe mogxls. Their wxrkshops wxre in thxir bedrxxms, their pxrlours and thxxx barnx, xxd thxy combxned txx small scalx custom nxture of 18th cxntury cottxge indusxxx wxth txx complxx technoxxxx of txx 19th Cxxxxxx. They huckstered txxxx prodxxx wxtx txx zeal xx a medicxxx show pitchmxx and txx sophisxxxxxxx of a Madisxx Avxxxx ad mxx. Thxx trixd axx xried xxx trixx agxxx, lxsing mxney, famxxx and slxxp, bxt thxx didx'x gxvx xn. Thxxr descexxxxxx txdxy wxxk ix txx onxy majxx cottxxx indusxxx xo survxxx intxct xx txx 20xx Cxxxxxx.

QUESTIONS

1. Does the author admire his subjects? (_____) Yes (_____) No

2. How did rubber stamp makers promote their product?_____

_____

3. How persistent were they?_____

4. What is unique about today's rubber stamp makers?_____

_____

Did you surprise yourself by noticing how your mind, given a minimum of clues, kept right on making meaning? People who are deprived of sensory input make up meaning. They hallucinate. Given a few clues, you can trust yourself to make meaning without lingering on other words.

Answers on page 36.

MAIN IDEAS

WHAT TO DO

Read "Why Kids Read the Wrong Words," looking for the two main ideas. When you are finished, write them down on page 23.

READ:

WHY KIDS READ THE WRONG WORDS

A student learning to read comes upon the sentence, "The boy jumped on the horse and rode off." But instead of saying "horse," the boy substitutes "pony." Should the teacher correct him?

As far as Kenneth S. Goodman is concerned, the answer is a firm negative. "The child clearly understands the meaning," he said recently in an interview. "This is what reading is all about."

To Dr. Goodman, a professor of education at Wayne State University, mistakes such as substituting one word for another with similar meaning are not "mistakes" at all but perfectly healthy "miscues."

For more than a decade the 47-year-old professor has made "miscues" the focus of his research, and out of it has come a new theory of how children learn to read and new teaching methods that are beginning to make themselves felt in classrooms across the country.

The concept of "miscues" developed when Goodman, interested in figuring out how reading skills develop, began asking beginning readers to read unfamiliar materials aloud.

He noticed that many of the mistakes made by the young subjects were not "accidental" but quite logical and reflective of sophisticated reasoning.

"When a first grader substitutes 'the' for 'a' but not for other words, you realize there is a cause," he explained.

Teachers often confuse errors with healthy miscues

On the basis of his observations Goodman, who will move to the University of Arizona this September, began challenging a number of generally accepted notions about children learning to read.

First, he rejects the assumption that reading is a process of looking at words and sentences and then deciding afterwards what they mean.

Instead, he argues that reading is a process of taking in data, making informed "predictions" about what will follow, checking these predictions as you go along and, if necessary, making revisions.

Thus, in the example above, the student "predicted" on the basis of the words "jumped on," that "pony" might follow and, when he got to the verb "rode" saw no reason to change it.

"There is no way to process verbal data fast enough without make 'predictions,'" said Goodman. "The difference between a good reader and a poor one is that the good reader makes good predictions and checks them quickly."

Secondly, Goodman argues that reading is not the passive receipt of meaning from the printed page but rather an active process in which the reader actually constructs meaning.

He thus rejects the traditional distinction that most teachers make between "decoding"—or learning to translate letters into sounds—and the subsequent gaining of meaning from written words.

"The two processes are inseparable and dependent on the fundamental search for meaning," he said. Finally, he argues that children can learn to read in exactly the same way they learned to talk.

"After all, 95 percent of speech is saying things you've never heard before. And kids can do this, so why not teach reading the same way?"

For teaching, the consequences of Goodman's ideas are far-reaching. The basic rule, he said, is to begin with what the child has already taught himself and to continue to use materials that have "meaning" for his or her world.

Goodman cited the case of a 3-year-old who, while supposedly not able to read, could read the word "Bonneville" on a hub cap. "When he was shown 'Buick' he wasn't fooled," he said.

"Clearly it was something important to his world."

A second principle, according to Goodman, is to avoid correcting mistakes—such as the substitution of "pony" for "horse"—that do not interfere with the conveying of meaning.

"Accuracy will come with practice. It is the result of good reading, not the cause of it."

On the other hand, Goodman said he would question a child who substituted "house" for "horse" in the above example.

Goodman also has some tips for parents in helping their children to learn to read. The first is to encourage them to read everything they can—starting with cereal boxes and peanut butter jars. Another is to avoid pushing precocious children too fast.

"A lot of parents like to show off their children by having them read adult material," he said.

"But kids can become very good at reading stuff that they don't understand. When you do this, you suggest that reading is an end in itself, not a means of communication."

The New York Times

QUESTIONS

What are the main ideas?

1. _____

2. _____

3 (optional). _____

Answers on page 36.

Verbal Cues

Look at the verbal cues you were given: "First"—"Secondly"—"A second principle." From now on, watch for words that signal your attention, which shout above the others, "Pssst, over here."

Now that you've finished reading and have jotted down two or three key ideas you remembered, compare them with the following quotes:

> *First,* he rejects the assumption that reading is a process of looking at words and sentences and then deciding afterwards what they mean.
>
> *Instead,* he argues that reading is a process of taking in data, making informed "predictions" about what will follow, checking these predictions as you go along and, if necessary, making revisions.
>
> *Secondly,* Goodman argues that reading is not the passive receipt of meaning from the printed page but rather an active process in which the reader actually constructs meaning.
>
> A *second principle,* according to Goodman, is to avoid correcting mistakes—such as the substitution of "pony" for "horse"—that do not interfere with the conveying of meaning.
>
> "Accuracy will come with practice. It is the result of good reading, not the cause of it."

WHAT TO DO

How do you recognize the main idea? For starters, write down the number of the sentence that contains the main idea in the paragraph below.

READ:

JOGGING

1. Jogging has replaced tennis as the most popular participatory sport in America. 2. It can be done almost anywhere, almost anytime, and it requires a minimum of expensive equipment. 3. But doctors are concerned about the health aspects of the pastime. 4. Jogging without proper preparation and precautions can cause serious injuries and even permanent crippling. 5. Besides the usual cramps, blisters and sore muscles, incautious joggers can experience torn tendons and tendinitis, bone bruises, stress fractures, shin splints, heel spurs and a painful condition of the knee cap called chondromalacia patellae. 6. An enthusiastic novice may overdo and become subject to heart attacks, diabetes and stroke. 7. A dangerous drop in body fluids can result from failing to monitor water intake. 8. Joggers are also prone to dog bites, muggings and being struck by cars, three calamities that rarely occur on the tennis court.

QUESTIONS

The main idea is in sentence number _____.

Now ask yourself which statement the examples support. (Change your answer if it is now different from your first choice.) The three most popular responses are:

Sentence 1.   "Because it's the first sentence and I learned that the first sentence should be the topic sentence, right?" Answer: Not always!

Sentence 3.   "It's important." If you picked this sentence because "it's important," you're partly right. But it's important as a herald, saying, "Psst, over here," or "Ta-*dom*, announcing the star sentence." Ask yourself which sentence is the one the examples support: that doctors are concerned, or that jogging can cause serious injuries?

Sentence 4.   Hooray if you picked this one.

How come you picked sentence 4 as the main idea? Maybe good instinct, or you may already know you can tell the main idea by asking: "What idea do the examples support?"

When you learn to recognize the main ideas quickly, you can race from paragraph to paragraph, spotting what you want to know and reading the supporting examples only if you choose to.

All writing is composed of *generalizations* and *details*. For example:

Generalization: pasta

Details: spaghetti, macaroni, noodles, lasagna, cannelloni, linguine, vermicelli, fettuccine, mostaccioli, conchiglie, cappelletti, agnolotti, bucatini, fusilli, rigatoni, ravioli, tortellini, tagliarini, manicotti, gnocchi, farfalle, ziti

WHAT TO DO

Underline the sentence that expresses the main idea of each of the following short passages. Set yourself up to read each one in thirty seconds or less.

READ:

AMNIOCENTESIS

I. The most common reason given for not having children after the age of forty is the higher incidence of Down's syndrome (mongolism). During the last twenty-five years, a testing process called amniocentesis has been developed that reveals this condition before the baby is born and gives the expectant mother the option of terminating the pregnancy. By extracting a small quantity of amniotic fluid from the pregnant uterus and cultivating the extra cells thrown off by the developing fetus, it is possible to tell if the unborn child has any of a whole range of chromosomal disorders. These include Down's syndrome and spina bifida, both of which occur more frequently in the children of older mothers.

Answer on page 36.

READ:

MERRY-GO-ROUNDS

II. There are few things more pathetic than a broken-down merry-go-round. The few carousels that survive today are usually shabby and grim, mere ghosts or plastic replicas of the elegant creations of the nineteenth century. In the 1800s, wood carving had reached its peak as an art form and thousands of the finest European craftsmen spent their time creating unique and fantastical animals to inhabit the world's merry-go-rounds. These craftsmen were mainly German, but Italian, French and English masterworks have also survived. Their elegant poses of paw and hoof, the intricate flow of mane and tail, and the piercing glare of these man-made beasts have made them one of the most beloved of nineteenth-century artifacts.

Answer on page 37.

READ:

THE MARX BROTHERS

III. Irving Thalberg, popularly called MGM's "boy genius," was in-strumental in luring the Marx Brothers away from Paramount Studios. Thalberg did everything he could to keep the zany brothers happy. However, once when he was called away on an emergency during a story conference with the brothers, he returned to find his office door barricaded from the inside. When the door was finally forced open, there sat the three, naked and covered with shaving cream. They were roasting potatoes in his fireplace while the overflowing tub in the adjoining bathroom sent cascades of bubble bath onto Thalberg's expensive carpets. The Marx Brothers did not like to be kept waiting.

Answer on page 37.

WHAT TO DO

Practice looking for the main ideas. Check them off as you find them in this paragraph from the introduction to *The Golden Notebook.*

READ:

FROM *THE GOLDEN NOTEBOOK*

I say to these students who have to spend a year, two years, writing theses about one book: "There is only one way to read, which is to browse in libraries and book shops, picking up books that attract you, reading only those, dropping them when they bore you, skipping the parts that drag—and never, never reading anything because you feel you ought, or because it is part of a trend or a movement. Remember that the book which bores you when you are twenty or thirty will open doors for you when you are forty or fifty—and vice versa. Don't read a book out of its right time for you. Remember that for all the books we have in print, there are as many that have never reached print, have never been written down—even now, in this age of compulsive reverence for the written word, history, even social ethic, are taught by means of stories, and the people who have been conditioned into thinking only in terms of what is written— and unfortunately nearly all the products of our educational system can do no more than this—are missing what is before their eyes.

For instance, the real history of Africa is still in the custody of black storytellers and wise men, black historians, medicine men; it is a verbal history, still kept safe from the white man and his predations. Everywhere, if you keep your mind open, you will find the truth in words *not* written down. So never let the printed page be your master. Above all, you should know that the fact that you have to spend one year, or two years, on one book or one author means that you are badly taught— you should have been taught to read your way from one sympathy to another, you should be learning to follow your own intuitive feeling about what you need: that is what you should have been developing, not the way to quote from other people.

—Doris Lessing

WHAT TO DO

Jot down some of Doris Lessing's suggestions.

1. _____

2. _____

3. _____

4. _____

5. _____

Answers on page 37.

1. Name a book you read at the right time for you. _____

2. How old were you when you were engaged by a subject that captivated you? _____

3. What was the subject you felt excited learning more about? _____

_____

FACT HUNTS

"But how can I read longer, more complicated pieces quickly?" you are asking impatiently. It's a matter of wanting to know something and being willing to focus on meaning rather than on words.

You've explored how your brain perceives words, how it can grasp whole phrases and ideas as quickly as single words while remembering much more. Now discover how you perceive larger chunks of information. It's time to pick up some speed.

WHAT TO DO

Set your timer to go off in one minute. Read through the following with the intention of checking the answers before one minute is up. See if you can complete the answers before the buzzer goes off.

READ:

How to Clean Your Tiaras

Never soak diamonds in ammonia. It will cause dust and oils to stick to the surface, leaving a film. And don't use chemical cleaners. They will eat away your precious gems if you soak them too long. Instead use a very soft-bristled brush with toothpaste or a mild detergent. They're safer and less expensive than commercial cleaners.

Use cool water. Never dip your diamonds in very hot water and then put them in cold. Despite their reputation for imperviousness, they may crack.

Rubies, sapphires, topaz and jade can be cleaned in a similar manner, but pearls, opals, coral and lapis should only be cleaned by a professional jeweler because they scratch easily. Your pearls, of course, should be taken in every year for cleaning.

The gold and platinum portions should also be brushed, although silver can be rubbed gently with a professional polish. With proper care, your tiaras will give you many years of happy service.

QUESTIONS

1. You can clean your own diamonds if you do it carefully.   T   F

2. Diamonds should be scrubbed in very hot water.   T   F

3. Rubies are too soft to wash this way.   T   F

4. Some jewelry can only be cleaned by a professional jeweler.   T   F

5. Pearls never have to be cleaned.   T   F

Answers on page 38.

Score 20% for each correct answer.

% correct _____

READ:

MOVIE MEDICAL MILESTONES

Some people date old movies on TV by the cars or the clothes. But there is another sure test. Just watch what medical procedure saves the hero's little daughter.

In the early 1930s you could be sure it would be a (gasp) blood transfusion. No nonsense about blood types or Rh factor. The burly gangster flopped down on a cot next to the fading tot and made a poignant speech while the nurse hooked up the tubes.

Another big winner was the miracle serum. It usually had to be flown through a raging storm by the bravest pilot this side of the Rockies who had previously (a) cheated the hero or (b) refused to fly again after he had accidentally killed his co-pilot.

The 1940s brought reverent ceremonial administrations of sulfa and then of penicillin. Brain surgery in the early 1950s and heart surgery in the '60s were surefire climaxes.

Both medicine and movies have made giant strides since then. Hospitals and airplanes have gotten bigger. But nothing can ever beat the pure drama of the small-town doctor rolling up his sleeves, getting out his black bag and saying: "She's got to have a transfusion or she won't last the night."

QUESTIONS

1. The author dates old films on TV by looking at the cars.　　T　F

2. Blood transfusions were a popular medical miracle in films of the 1930s.　　T　F

3. Serums were used to establish the patient's blood type.　　T　F

4. Occasionally planes were used to transport serums to remote communities.　　T　F

5. Brain surgery and open-heart surgery were not portrayed in films until the 1970s.　　T　F

Answers on page 38.

Score 20% for each correct answer.
% correct _____

READ:

The Evolution of English

Whether we like it or not, all language is an evolutionary process and English is constantly undergoing changes. Some pass as quickly as they came. Some linger on.

The 1959 edition of *Guide to American English* by L. M. Meyers informs us that it is no longer necessary to use an apostrophe before 'phone or a period after ad. to denote the missing portion of the word. The book also advises that "cute" is a contraction of "acute" and should only be used as such, and it is now all right to use "people" as the plural of "person."

As quaint as these changes may seem to us, we wonder if the author of twenty-five years ago would be able to decipher some of today's argot. An executive sends a memo: "Reference my letter of January 5 and action. Copy me." A public official speaks of "mutually reinforcing conceptions" instead of ideas.

We now "conceptualize" instead of "conceiving" or "imagining." We "prioritize" and "manipulate" instead of rating and using. We conjugate the verbs "to impact," "to context" and "to decision."

Ironically, while the user sees these changes as more succinct and dynamic, the result may be longer and less clear.

QUESTIONS

1. Language is always changing.   T   F

2. Changes never last.   T   F

3. *Guide to American English*, printed just twenty-five years ago, lists many changes in English that now seem quaint.   T   F

4. "Mutually reinforcing conceptions" means a contractual agreement.   T   F

5. The author thinks the new business English is much clearer and more concise than standard English.   T   F

Answers on page 38.

Score 20% for each correct answer.

% correct _____

READ:

DOVE LOVE: FEMALES LAY EGGS ON COO

by Boris Weintraub

Oh, the romance of it all: Two doves billing and cooing at each other, joining to build a nest for the forthcoming egg.

Time to amend that romantic notion. Yes, the male coos at the female, and scientists had thought he thus stimulated glandular changes in the female that triggered egg laying. It now turns out that it is the female coo that causes follicles in the ovaries to grow and then burst to release an egg, according to psychobiologist Mei-Fang Cheng of Rutgers University.

Dr. Cheng devised painless experiments that rendered the female unable to coo. The male cooed as usual, but nothing happened. But when a female heard recordings of her voice, the result was an egg deposited in the glass nesting bowl.

The male's cooing still plays an important role, Cheng cautions. It "is a very powerful stimulus in inducing the female to call, but her own call is what triggers endocrinologic changes," Cheng says.

National Geographic Magazine

QUESTIONS

1. The male dove cooing at the female triggers egg laying.   T   F

2. The female coo causes follicles in the ovaries to grow and then burst to release an egg.   T   F

3. The male dove is irrelevant to the female's birth process.   T   F

4. The male cooing is a powerful stimulus in inducing the female to call.   T   F

5. The female dove's own cooing is what triggers endocrinologic changes.   T   F

Answers on page 38.

Score 20% for each correct answer.
% correct _____

COMPREHENSION SPRINT

"But how can I read longer, more complicated pieces quickly?" you may be asking impatiently. It's a matter of wanting to know something and being willing to focus on meaning rather than on words.

WHAT TO DO

You've explored how your brain perceives words, how it can grasp whole phrases and ideas as quickly as single words while remembering much more. Now discover how you perceive larger chunks of information. It's time to pick up some speed. Set your timer for two minutes. Challenge yourself by playing "Beat the Clock." Read "In Families That Have Two Children," looking for the two main ideas. Jot them down on page 34.

READ:

IN FAMILIES THAT HAVE TWO CHILDREN, REARING ISN'T DONE BY PARENTS ALONE

by Richard Flaste

There you are, raising two children, and doing the best you can. But the children are so different. One is intellectual, sensitive, even a bit introverted. The other is outgoing, independent, won't read a book unless coerced. And that second one seems a little harder to reach, off in some other world.

You wonder why, if so much of how children develop depends on the parents, the difference is so great.

For years, the usual explanation would have been something like this: With a first child parents are tense and demanding, also very loving, perhaps too loving, so the child becomes eager to achieve, but maybe somewhat anxious. With the second child, the parents relax and so does the child.

But that viewpoint strikes some professionals as being much too limited. It seems to ignore the power that children have over each other.

Among those trying to broaden the focus is Dr. Salvador Minuchin, the family therapist who is head of the department of child psychiatry at the University of Pennsylvania. He says that people who look at child-rearing are often "wearing blinders"; all they see is the parent-child relationship, with the parents "socializing," that is, teaching society's way to the children.

SYMPTOMS MAINTAINED

Take the blinders off, he said, "and it becomes self-evident that the parents socialize the children and the children socialize the parents. And the children also form their own sibling subsystem"—a system whose influence might even be beyond the reach of the parents.

Working with troubled children, Dr. Minuchin has found cases where the parents might be relating to a child in a warm, fine way, "but the siblings are scapegoating him and maintaining the symptom."

One psychologist who has been doing a lot of recent research on what brothers and sisters mean to each other and how that affects their relationship to the parents is Dr. Victor Cicirelli at Purdue.

He's been looking at two-child families, most of them in the middle-income and lower-middle-income brackets. And his findings point to the impact, for better or worse, of sibling rivalry—which is at its most intense when children are of the same sex—and of traditional sex roles.

ACCEPTS AND EXPECTS HELP

Dr. Cicirelli says that if a boy has an older sister, especially if she's from two to four years older, that boy is much more likely to be good at school—or any formal learning, including such things as taking instruction on how to tie a shoelace—than if he has an older brother.

The older sister is, for one thing, more inclined to help out around the house, including accepting some child-rearing chores. Her brother accepts that help, even expects it, and that predisposes him to accepting advice and instruction from others. It means his parents will be more effective with him.

If he had an older brother, however, the rivalry would be a prominent factor. The older brother is the last one in the world the younger boy would accept help from. Moreover, the older brother, because of the rivalry and because it is not his traditional role to help with "womanly" chores, wouldn't want to be bothered anyway.

The second child: a boy with an older sister will probably do better in school than if he had an older brother.

(Incidentally, Dr. Stephen Suomi, who has studied monkeys at the University of Wisconsin Primate Laboratory, says that the findings with monkey brothers and sisters are "consistent" with Dr. Cicirelli's conclusions about people—but he cautions that that doesn't necessarily mean the behavior is "either genetic or cultural" and that, in any case, these are generalizations that don't hold true for everybody.)

"One of the things we're bringing out," Dr. Cicirelli said, "is that the effectiveness of the parent on the second child partly depends on the older brother or sister."

Instead of taking instruction from parents, that boy with an older brother, in Dr. Cicirelli's view, would be more receptive to learning that is "informal"—at the ballpark, in the street or just among friends.

OTHER COMBINATIONS

What about the other combinations? With two sisters, Dr. Cicirelli says, the sibling rivalry would often work against the second girl's receptivity to formal learning and increase the amount of informal learning. But it wouldn't be as dramatic as with two boys. And the younger sister with an older brother wouldn't be as competitive with him nor would she find him as helpful as in the case when it's the sister who's the older.

Maybe all this smacks of too much sex-role stereotyping, and that may be exactly what you want to avoid in your family.

But Dr. Cicirelli points out that one possible result of the ongoing research could be a contribution to the breaking down of stereotypes when parents value intellectual development in younger children. "It might be," he said, "a matter of training the older brother to be more like an older sister."

The New York Times

WHAT TO DO

List two main ideas and any others if you remember more.

1. _____

2. _____

_____

_____

Answers on page 38.

DAY 1 ANSWERS

SOS

1. d–e–f–g–h–j   (5 points each)
2. a   (15 points)
3. a–c   (10 points each)
4. a–b–d   (5 points each)
5. b–c   (10 points each)

100 points equals 100 percent.

COMPUTE YOUR RATE FOR "SOS"
(Approximate number of words: 1,750)

Time	Wpm	Time	Wpm
1 min.	1750	5 min.	350
1 min. 15 sec.	1400	5 min. 15 sec.	333
1 min. 30 sec.	1167	5 min. 30 sec.	318
1 min. 45 sec.	1000	5 min. 45 sec.	304
2 min.	875	6 min.	292
2 min. 15 sec.	778	6 min. 15 sec.	280
2 min. 30 sec.	700	6 min. 30 sec.	269
2 min. 45 sec.	636	6 min. 45 sec.	259
3 min.	578	7 min.	250
3 min. 15 sec.	538	7 min. 15 sec.	241
3 min. 30 sec.	500	7 min. 30 sec.	233
3 min. 45 sec.	466	7 min. 45 sec.	226
4 min.	438	8 min.	219
4 min. 15 sec.	412	8 min. 15 sec.	212
4 min. 30 sec.	389	8 min. 30 sec.	206
4 min. 45 sec.	368	8 min. 45 sec.	200

Your rate is _____ wpm.
(Record this on page 224.)

HUMPTY DUMPTY II

1. This is a mystery story.
2. It takes place in the library of an old mansion.
3. The main characters are John, the dead woman, and the police, plus the charwoman.
4. After the body is removed, John finds the book he wanted.

HUMPTY DUMPTY III

1. The author admires his subjects.
2. The rubber stamp makers huckstered their product with the zeal of a medicine show pitchman and the sophistication of a Madison Avenue adman.
3. They tried and failed and tried again.
4. The unique thing about today's rubber stamp makers is that they work in the only major cottage industry to survive intact into the twentieth century.

WHY KIDS READ THE WRONG WORDS

1. Goodman says misread words can be positive, if they show logic and reflection.
2. Teachers should not correct misread words with similar meanings.
3. (optional). Parents should encourage children to read everything they can.

AMNIOCENTESIS

I. The most common reason given for not having children after the age of forty is the higher incidence of Down's syndrome (mongolism). During the last twenty-five years, a testing process called amniocentesis has been developed that reveals this condition before the baby is born and gives the expectant mother the option of terminating the pregnancy. By extracting a small quantity of amniotic fluid from the pregnant uterus and cultivating the extra cells thrown off by the developing fetus, it is possible to tell if the unborn child has any of a whole range of chromosomal disorders. These include Down's syndrome and spina bifida, both of which occur more frequently in the children of older mothers.

MERRY-GO-ROUNDS

II. There are few things more pathetic than a broken-down merry-go-round. The few carousels that survive today are usually shabby and grim, mere ghosts or plastic replicas of the elegant creations of the nineteenth century. In the 1800s, wood carving had reached its peak as an art form and thousands of the finest European craftsmen spent their time creating unique and fantastical animals to inhabit the world's merry-go-rounds. These craftsmen were mainly German, but Italian, French and English masterworks have also survived. Their elegant poses of paw and hoof, the intricate flow of mane and tail, and the piercing glare of these man-made beasts have made

them one of the most beloved of nineteenth-century artifacts.

THE MARX BROTHERS

III. Irving Thalberg, popularly called MGM's "boy genius," was instrumental in luring the Marx Brothers away from Paramount Studios. Thalberg did everything he could to keep the zany brothers happy. However, once when he was called away on an emergency during a story conference with the brothers, he returned to find his office door barricaded from the inside. When the door was finally forced open, there sat the three, naked and covered with shaving cream. They were roasting potatoes in his fireplace while the overflowing tub in the adjoining bathroom sent cascades of bubble bath onto Thalberg's expensive carpets. The Marx Brothers did not like to be kept waiting.

THE GOLDEN NOTEBOOK

1. Read only what attracts you.
2. Truth is not always written down.
3. Never let the printed page be your master.
4. Do not read a book out of its right time for you.
5. Browse.

HOW TO CLEAN YOUR TIARAS

1–T 2–F 3–F 4–T 5–F

MOVIE MEDICAL MILESTONES

1–F 2–T 3–F 4–T 5–F

THE EVOLUTION OF ENGLISH

1–T 2–T 3–T 4–F 5–F

DOVE LOVE

1–F 2–T 3–F 4–T 5–T

IN FAMILIES THAT HAVE TWO CHILDREN

1. The influence of the relationship existing between siblings may be as strong as or stronger than the influence of the parents.
2. The effectiveness of parent or child is influenced strongly by the child's relationship with an older brother or sister.
3. (Optional) Perhaps older brothers should be trained to be more like older sisters.

DAY 2

The Problem Pattern
The Instruction Pattern

We want to get more from newspapers, books, technical journals, newsletters, textbooks, and instructions the first time we read them, without having to go over and over them. The simple way to do this is to recognize the structure of what we are reading and then mentally sort and file informational chunks under the appropriate headings as we go. Edward de Bono, author of *The Use of Lateral Thinking*, says, "Once a pattern has been formed, then the mind no longer has to analyze or sort information. All that is required is enough information to trigger the pattern. The mind then follows along the pattern automatically in the same way a driver follows a familiar road."

One of the five patterns of organization is the Problem Pattern. To trust that an author understands what the problem is that he is presenting we look to his selection and treatment of the symptoms. It's the effects of a problem that lead us to know there is a problem. Then our mind wants to know what caused the problem. After that we are eager to know its solution. The structure of the Problem Pattern is:

Problem
Effects
Causes
Solution

WHAT TO DO

As you read the following article, turn the pattern parts into questions for which you look for answers. When you find them, draw an arrow from the pattern parts to the answers in the article.

READ:

THIS BUTTON SURVIVES THE LAUNDRY

by Stephanie Strom

Problem?

Buttons are the bane of the $2.5 billion men's shirt business. Never mind fine fabrics, microscopic stitching and exquisite tailoring: If shirt buttons crack under pressure or the heat of commercial laundering, that is what customers will remember.

Effects?

"The No. 1 complaint we get from customers is that the buttons on their shirts break when they have them laundered," said Jack Irving, executive vice president for Nordstrom's men's division.

Causes?

Enter Coors Ceramicon Designs Ltd., which makes components for cars, computers, radios and bulletproof vests. Joe Coors Jr., president of Ceramicon's parent company, asked Ceramicon to join the quest.

Solution?

The result was the Diamond button, which made its debut on Nordstrom shirts and shirts manufactured by men's designer Ike Behar. Made of sand transformed into zirconia and fired at 3,200 degrees, the buttons have more than twice the flexible strength of steel and resist cracking.

There is a drawback to the Diamond Z buttons. They cost 8 cents to 10 cents each for a shirt maker to buy, compared with roughly a penny for buttons made from ground shells and epoxy, or less than a penny for plastic buttons.

The New York Times

Answers on page 76.

If you want to process information efficiently, but you haven't yet decided exactly what you want to come away with for your effort, always start by analyzing the *structure* of what you're reading. When you walk into a strange house, you can usually find the kitchen or bedroom because you recognize a familiar structure. When you buy a new TV set or a new car, you can usually figure out how to operate it, even if the controls are in a different place. The details may be different, but the overall patterns are the same. In the same way, you can be in control of noticing and remembering what you read when you recognize the five nonfiction patterns.

Fortunately, most nonfiction information comes in one of the following five patterns or structures.

THE PROBLEM PATTERN

To spark action

Problem
Effects
Causes
Solution

THE OPINION PATTERN

To persuade

Opinion
Reasons
Significance

THE INSTRUCTION PATTERN

To instruct

Materials
  (optional)
Step 1
Step 2
Step 3, etc.

THE THESIS PATTERN

To prove something

Thesis
Proofs
Implications

THE INFORMATION PATTERN

To share information

Facet 1
Facet 2
Facet 3, etc.

By learning to recognize and identify these five patterns as you read, you can find what you are looking for quickly and remember it more easily. (Occasionally, you will run across a hybrid—a combination of two different patterns—or material that is so badly written you have no idea what the author intended. Strategies for dealing with both will be covered later.)

If you don't have a specific question, turning pattern parts into questions is a great way to scoop up the main ideas and to store them in a structure for easy retrieval.

THE PROBLEM PATTERN: To Move to Action

PROBLEM
EFFECTS
CAUSES
SOLUTION

Everything in an article, besides the Problem, Effects, Causes, and Solution, is just supporting detail for generalizations or entertaining asides. No matter which pattern you read, the strategy of turning pattern parts into questions will enable you to at least double your speed. Remember, you want to develop the habit of looking for answers rather than just to passively read. Be driven by your need to know the answer.

You read faster when you learn to vary your speed, flying high over what you already know, swooping down on the new and the different.

Buckminster Fuller said that to be easily understood and accepted by the general public, a book or article can only contain about 20% new material. The other 80% must be familiar or we have no framework for the new. If you doubt this, just remember how overwhelming a new Spanish text or employee manual seemed when you started and how simple it became later on.

Guess which of the nonfiction patterns is illustrated in the following heading and subheading.

IF YOU DON'T HAVE ENOUGH WOES, TRY FRETTING ABOUT BEES

They Are Eating Pesticides and Dying, Hurting Yields of Many Key Food Crops

WHAT TO DO

Sounds like a problem, doesn't it? Notice that you already know the problem, effects, and causes. They are given to you in the subheadline. Now read for what you don't know—the solutions. Gear yourself up to go in for the 25% you don't know. Find the answers to these questions:

What is the *problem*?
What are the *effects*?
What are the *causes*?
What are the *solutions*?

READ:

IF YOU DON'T HAVE ENOUGH WOES, TRY FRETTING ABOUT BEES

They Are Eating Pesticides and Dying, Hurting Yields of Many Key Food Crops

by Joseph M. Winski

Remember the old saying about how a horse and rider were lost because somebody neglected to tend to a small matter like a missing horseshoe nail?

Some scientists and agriculturists are worried that the same sort of ballooning consequences may stem from what many people probably consider to be a minor irrelevancy: The nation's honeybees slowly but steadily are being exterminated.

Not on purpose, of course. But as the honeybees forage for pollen and nectar they increasingly are gathering poison also—pesticides that farmers apply to protect their crops from destructive insects.

So there are 20% fewer honeybee colonies in the U.S. today than there were 10 years ago—about four million versus five million. (A colony contains between 25,000 and 60,000 bees.) In California, the leading bee state, as much as 20% of the state's honeybees have been killed in some recent years—a mortality rate double that of the early 1960s.

"All the indications are that it's going to get a lot worse," says Ward Stanger, an apiculturist at the University of California at Davis. "It's a serious situation," Mr. Stanger says—so serious that he's seeking to have the honeybee declared an endangered species.

BEE BENEFITS

It is even more serious in another respect: Nearly 100 crops with a farm value of $1 billion annually depend on honeybees for pollination; another $3 billion worth benefit from bee pollination in terms of higher and better-quality yields. Among these crops are apples, cherries, plums, broccoli, cucumbers, cabbage, melons—indeed, virtually all fruits and berries as well as many vegetables and even some livestock-forage crops such as alfalfa.

Thus, at a time when boosting food production is becoming a global priority, the fate of honeybees takes on some of the significance of the proverbial horseshoe nail.

Floyd Moeller, research leader at the North Central States Bee Laboratory at the University of Wisconsin, says that the economic value of honeybees as pollinators is twenty times their value as honey makers. Far from being an esoteric ecological concern, the dwindling number of honeybees bodes ill for the nation's food supply. "You just can't pollinate as efficiently with fewer bees," Mr. Moeller says.

(Bees pollinate inadvertently by dropping bits of pollen, which they gather for food, as they fly from plant to plant. This cross-pollination, which is also performed by other insects, the wind and hummingbirds, produces crops genetically superior to those produced by self-pollination. Nectar, the bees' other main food, is the one they make honey from.)

Some crops already are threatened by a lack of bees. Most notable is the California almond. Each of the 200,000 acres requires two colonies of bees for pollination, but there are now only 300,000 colonies in the entire state. Last year, almond growers had to import more than 100,000 colonies of bees, some of them hauled from as far away as Montana in big tandem-trailer trucks, to pollinate their fields. "This obviously isn't a very practical way to do things," says the University of California's Mr. Stanger. "I just don't know how long we can keep it up."

THE CRANBERRY CONNECTION

Researchers almost routinely are uncovering more evidence attesting to the honeybee's contribution. For example, Mr. Moeller and his colleagues at the University of Wisconsin discovered a few years ago that cranberry production could be tripled with efficient bee pollination—whereupon Wisconsin cranberry growers rushed out and rented 2,000 bee colonies and increased the cash value of their crop by $4 million. (Rental fees since have doubled to $30 per colony currently.)

An even more dramatic and significant breakthrough may lie in the potential effect of bee pollination of soybeans, the country's second most important fee crop and a critical source of protein. Some observers expect a new hybrid soybean that would double present yields to be in common use in several years. Unlike present varieties, however, the new hybrid will require honeybees for pollination. With all-out production, about two million colonies of bees—half of the country's present total—would be required for just this one crop.

In a way, it's surprising that honeybees are declining in numbers because they in effect have been a protected species for years. Their protectors have been the dedicated practitioners of the art of beekeeping, a form of animal husbandry whose beginnings are lost in antiquity.

But the economics of beekeeping have taken a turn for the worse in the last 10 years or so, largely because of the sharply increased possibility that a beekeeper's bees could be wiped out by pesticides. Changed farming practices (such as using chemicals for fertilizers instead of plowed-under legumes, which while in blossom are excellent sources of nectar) and the continuing spread of suburbia into what used to be open fields also have contributed. "The bee just doesn't have enough flowers she can visit," says John Root, whose family has been in the beekeeping supplies business in Medina, Ohio, since 1869. Another factor, until the last couple of years, has been a depressed honey market.

"There's just been no incentive for a guy to stay in the business," says Robert Banker, secretary-treasurer of the American Beekeeping Federation in Cannon Falls, Minn. The result, he says, has been "a steady decline" of full-time beekeepers to about 3,000 and of all beekeepers, including those with one or two colonies, to about 150,000. A rise in honey prices in the last two years appears to be attracting more people into beekeeping, though so far apparently not in substantial enough numbers to reverse the decline of either bees or beekeepers.

Researchers have suggested various protective measures to beekeepers, such as keeping bees in hives and feeding them pollen supplements when nearby sprayed crops are flowering, installing pollen traps that knock the poison-tainted pollen off the bee when she returns to the hive and even draping colonies with wet burlap when pesticides are being applied.

But there isn't a simple solution to the poisoning problem. "It's a complicated situation," Mr. Banker says. "We want to protect our bees but we fully recognize that a grower has a right to protect his crops" from legitimate threats. "Something's got to be done, but we're not sure what," says a spokesman for the National Wildlife Federation in Washington, D.C. He recalls that "last summer bees were dropping off like flies in Virginia."

All this doesn't mean that the honeybee faces extinction, however. They no doubt will be around as long as there are people who are intrigued by them. "I have several observation hives mounted in windows," says Mr. Root, the Ohio supplier of beekeeping equipment. "I can sit and watch them for hours."

Some people spend lifetimes watching bees. Foremost among them is Karl von Frisch, a professor at the University of Munich who has devoted virtually all of his working years to studying bees and other insects. Last year, Mr. von Frisch received a Nobel Prize for his work; it was the first time the prize was given to an animal behaviorist.

The bees' rigid social order (the females do all the work while the males do nothing but mate with the queen and die soon afterwards) and industry (a bee will make 30,000 trips, averaging up to 800 an hour, to gather enough nectar for a pound of honey) are well documented. But Mr. von Frisch found that bees also have a language facility for communication "which, as far as we know, has no parallel in any other animal."

Specifically, Mr. von Frisch found that a foraging bee can tell others in the hive when she has found food, how much, whether it's near or distant, and if distant how far away and in which direction her fellow workers should fly to find it. She does this by dancing—around in circles if the food is close, or with vigorous tail-wagging and varying rhythms if it's far away. (Bees frequently gather food a mile or more away from the hive.)

Later, a student of Mr. von Frisch's, Martin Lindauer, found that bees—again by dancing to communicate—are able to arrive at a community decision on a new home after they swarm from their existing one (usually because of overcrowding). Those bees who have inspected the best potential sites dance more vigorously than those who have examined mediocre spots; this causes more bees to inspect the site of the dancers, and if they agree they will return and dance in an equally vigorous manner. Eventually, a consensus is reached wherein the whole swarm is throbbing with ecstasy and they fly off to their new home. One swarm studied by Mr. Lindauer considered 21 possibilities and took two weeks to decide.

Though the research that led to these discoveries was conducted primarily for its scientific interest, the findings may have significant practical benefits. "When some day in the future food grows scarce," Mr. von Frisch writes, "people . . . should recall that in their own language bees can be aroused to greater industry and can be dispatched . . . in accord with the wishes of the beekeeper and the farmer."

Some scientists have poohpoohed such findings of what might be called intelligence in these "lower animals," as bees are categorized. But Donald R. Griffin, a biologist at Rockefeller University in New York and an early skeptic himself, duplicated the von Frisch experiments and came up with the same conclusions. Mr. Griffin says: "I am willing to entertain the thought that perhaps the bees know what they are doing."

QUESTIONS

1. The problem is _____

   _____

2. The effect(s) _____

   _____

3. The cause(s) _____

   _____

4. The solution(s) _____

   _____

Answers on page 76.

Reading Fast Is Different

You know how you feel when you read the slow way you used to do it. Reading quickly feels different. But remember: You can always read slowly when you want to. Make slow reading a choice, not a habit!

When you aggressively speed up, you are developing a different skill. If you have ever changed a habit like smoking or overeating, or, as a child, beginning each sentence with "You know what," you know how to tolerate the discomfort of the transition period. Ask the part of you that changed from one behavior to another how it made it through the transition. Make that part of you an ally when you read aggressively by asking questions. Decide to accept the healthy tension you feel as you push against your old 250-word boundary instead of being anxious.

Mope or Lope?

Those of you who ride horseback have an apt metaphor for what the transition from word-for-word reading to rapid reading is like. Word-for-word reading is like sitting on the horse, holding on, and letting the horse mope along with you while you sit there with minimum effort. Fast reading is like loping, a speed of sheer delight. You move swiftly and gracefully, as one with the horse, totally in charge of the direction and when to stop.

The difference between moping and loping on a horse is arduous training. Hugging the horse and keeping your heels down and close to it are definitely not "natural." So it is with fast reading. In fact, reading itself is not a natural behavior, but a highly developed, very sophisticated one!

More Time Not to Read

You are initiating a new behavior that will seem strange at first, but worthwhile in the long run. Rather than the womblike feeling that comes from reading word-for-word (just great if that is what you're after), you will enjoy the excitement of a rapid ride through many more books, magazines, journals, and reports or a quick journey through less print, leaving you more time not to read and therefore more time for something else.

Keep this enticing goal in mind as you whip yourself up to move through your reading rapidly. Remember, *asking questions is the way to move yourself from one concept to another.* The details are only there to support main ideas, not to be cherished for themselves, unless you find them entertaining—and that's what you want for some other purpose.

A Healthy Disrespect

To read quickly, you must cultivate a healthy disrespect for the printed word. Your need to know, your goals, must supersede those of the author. Of all the other communication skills, reading is most like listening. You don't hang on every word as most people talk to you. Be as selective when listening to an author talking to you through the printed page as you would be to someone speaking in person.

WHAT TO DO

Set your timer for one minute. Challenge yourself to scoop up the answers in one minute. Read "Speeding the Mails," looking for the problem, effects, causes, and solution. Keep these items in the front of your mind as you read.

READ:

SPEEDING THE MAILS

by U. Sedit

Miss Grinch dropped the morning mail on my desk with tight-lipped satisfaction. On the top, in a battered 9×12 envelope, was the million-dollar Higgleby contract that I had personally mailed last week.

Now it was back, callously stamped "Postage Due."

"You forgot the surcharge," sneered Miss Grinch. "The envelope is too large for the sorting machines. If they have to touch it, they charge extra." She departed to restamp the envelope and I turned in chagrin to my other mail.

A letter from Fiji made the trip in four days, but another from across town, mailed ten days earlier, had come via Spokane and Fort Lauderdale. It contained tickets for last Saturday's big game. Not only do postal employees hate to touch the mail, they also refuse to read what's written on it.

Muttering unprintable things about the post office, I turned to my paper and coffee. The front page announced another postal increase and a new 11-digit zip code. Just under this was an item that will one day revolutionize the American postal system.

It seems that the inhabitants of a tiny Pacific principality called Bubustan have just been thrown out of work by the closing of the island's only industry, an electric Frisbee factory. Riots are expected because the natives can no longer use their $1-a-day wages for American bubble gum.

Now here, I reasoned, are intelligent, hard-working people, not afraid to touch envelopes. We can solve our mail crisis once and for all. Let's export our mail!

Those jumbo jets, once full of Frisbees and bubble gum, will take our mail to Bubustan where tireless, efficient workers will sort it into the new 11-digit zip codes and load it into containers for redelivery to post offices all across America. We use containerization for ships. Why not for mail?

The Postal Authority will save billions, delivery time will be cut by several days and riots will be prevented in Bubustan. Out-of-work American postal sorters can be employed as fruit and egg sorters, an advantage to the public since illiteracy is not such a handicap in these professions.

I have written the President about my idea and I'm sure it will be implemented immediately. That is, if he gets my letter.

QUESTIONS

1. The problem is ————————————————————

2. The effect(s) ————————————————————

3. The cause(s) ————————————————————

4. The solution(s) ————————————————————

Answers on page 77.

WHAT TO DO

Set yourself up to look only for the problem, effects, causes, and solutions, merely glancing at details, reassured that they are there. You will be depriving yourself of familiar comfort in exchange for the excitement of finding what you are looking for fast. What a good trade-off! Time yourself. Go.

READ:

OUR SHOCKING ILLITERACY IN FOREIGN LANGUAGES

by Nick Thimmesch

Tongue-tied Americans are paying a heavy price, both diplomatically and commercially, for our inability to communicate

When Deng Xiaoping, the senior vice premier of the People's Republic of China, visited the White House for sensitive talks in January 1979, to communicate with him President Carter had to rely on one of Deng's own interpreters. The U.S. State Department did not have a single fully competent Chinese translator of its own.

Because of un-idiomatic translations, General Motors' "Body by Fisher" came out "Corpse by Fisher" in Puerto Rico, and Chevrolet's "Nova" did not sell well until its name was changed to "Caribe." In Spanish, *"no va"* means "it doesn't go"!

While an estimated 10,000 English-speaking Japanese businessmen are hard at work in the United States capturing markets here, fewer than 900 of the U.S. businessmen in Japan can speak Japanese. Last year this imbalance was one factor helping to push Japan's

"Our Shocking Illiteracy in Foreign Languages" is reprinted from the February 1981 Reader's Digest. *Copyright © 1981 by Nicholas Thimmesch.*

trade surplus vis-a-vis the United States to $6 million.

Cases like these, repeated countless times throughout the world, underscore the staggering consequences of America's virtual illiteracy in foreign languages. The days when American might and unchallenged product superiority spoke for themselves have long since ended. Today U.S. businessmen, who rarely master foreign languages, must compete in overseas markets with European and Japanese entrepreneurs who speak a multitude of tongues. In this competition the United States is, too often, literally tongue-tied. Reports a Presidential Commission on Foreign Language and International Studies: "Americans' incompetence in foreign languages is nothing short of scandalous."

Rep. Paul Simon (D., Ill.), who first proposed creating the Commission, had this fact brought home to him in 1977 when he was embarrassingly late for an appointment with Egypt's President Anwar el-Sadat. It happened because not one of the four U.S.-embassy staffers escorting him could speak Arabic to their Egyptian drivers.

Simon was so disturbed that when he returned home he began investigating the state of language study in the United States. He was shocked to learn that the State Department does not require knowledge of a foreign language for its incoming Foreign Service officer candidates. Digging further, Simon found that

only 8 percent of U.S. colleges and universities require a foreign language for admission (it was 34 percent in 1966), and that most universities do not require students to take a foreign language in order to graduate.

Americans have not always been so woefully deficient. As recently as 1965, 24 percent of America's high school students took foreign languages. Today the figure is 15 percent—and dropping. In the elementary-school grades—where foreign languages can be learned most easily—only one percent of our children study them.

What happened? During the late 1960s and early '70s, the President's Commission found, colleges revised their curricula under pressure from student activists who disapproved of traditional disciplines and demanded relevance—courses in ethnic history, contemporary problems and social reform. In rationalizing the de-emphasis of language study and such other disciplines as science and mathematics, administrators invoked the euphemism "individualized curricula."

The results were predictable in government agencies whose employees should be proficient in languages. A CIA survey of recruits hired between 1975 and 1978 showed that only 18 percent demonstrated "minimum professional proficiency" in a foreign language. Only one in five candidates accepted into the Foreign Service today meets

State Department language-competency standards.

Occasionally, the results are comic. An Agency for International Development officer tried to apologize to Peruvian leaders for his poor Spanish and, bumbling his idioms, announced that he was pregnant.

Some repercussions are tragic. Critics claim that the life of Adolph Dubs, the U.S. ambassador in Afghanistan, could have been saved had more embassy staffers trying to negotiate with his kidnappers been fluent in Dari, the official Afghan language. And who can forget President Carter in Warsaw telling the Poles—through a State Department contract interpreter who spoke with a Ukrainian accent—how he "lusted" for them—when he meant that he desired better relations?

Provincial notions about foreign languages have harmed U.S. business as well as government. At a time when one of every eight American manufacturing jobs depends on world trade, U.S. exports stagnate, and large import surpluses drag down the dollar. Meanwhile, West Germany's exports rose from one-sixth the U.S. figure in 1949 to near equality now. Japan, too, is close on our heels.

To be sure, European and other foreign competitors have improved their technology in recent decades—but their traditional language skills also give them an edge, often providing the nuances that can clinch a sale. And their sales representatives typically know the culture of countries where they work. By contrast, the complacent corporate attitude in America has been: "Why learn a foreign language when you can hire someone who speaks English?" Even businesses that want to hire bilingual employees have trouble finding them. Pan American World Airways, for instance, had to interview 16,000 Americans to fill 400 jobs calling for minimal, conversational foreign-language skills.

To improve American language skills and understanding, the President's Commission made 130 recommendations. Among them:

- Language requirements should be reinstituted for both college admission and graduation.
- Federal and foundation money should be used to upgrade skills of foreign-language teachers, through summer and overseas study and international exchanges.
- Up to 60 language and international-studies high schools should be set up in major cities. Business schools should require language courses.

The Commission put a $178-million price tag on its recommendations. But much can be accomplished without federal funding. Some colleges have kept or resumed strong language requirements. Georgetown University in Washington, D.C., for one, requires 90 percent of its students to take a foreign language. Harvard University's Arts and Sciences faculty recently voted to return to a required "core curriculum," including foreign languages.

Meanwhile, sheer good teaching at a number of institutions has sustained language excellence. Dartmouth College's Prof. John Rassias, for example, has a record of student performance far exceeding national norms. To bring his French and advanced literature courses alive, he acts out phrases, throws chairs, falls to his knees to beg hesitant students for a word, plants kisses on foreheads—and generally leaves students both exhausted and enthusiastic about the adventure of speaking a foreign tongue. As a result, enrollments in all languages taught at Dartmouth have doubled and tripled. Many Dartmouth students also spend a term overseas for credit, living with families in provincial European towns and keeping away from other Americans.

Perhaps the nation's most remarkable language training occurs at Vermont's Middlebury College. Every summer some 1,200 students attend seven language schools there, each with its own dorms, classes and recreations. For six to nine weeks they study, play, dine and *live* totally immersed in a foreign language: All sign the "Middlebury Pledge" not to speak English in or out of the classroom, not even at the lake.

"It's an emotional strain at first," said one young American who had to speak Russian all day. But many find it soon becomes fun. Since 1915, when Middlebury's first language school was opened, 15,000 students have completed the tough summer program, among them future ambassadors and leaders of industry. In recent years Middlebury has added Japanese and Chinese to its traditional European-language programs.

Languages are most easily learned in childhood, and there are hopeful indications in some public-school systems. In 1974, Cincinnati's school board established eight special elementary schools. In three, for a portion of each day, classes are taught in French; in the others, in Spanish and German. A visitor to a biology class marvels as fourth-graders listen raptly to a teacher describing, in German, how birds nest. All eight schools have waiting lists. In Chicago, the LaSalle Language Academy, a public school, teaches one of four foreign languages to 500 children from kindergarten through eighth grade. Parents move into the school's neighborhood so that their children can take advantage of LaSalle.

These creative programs show what can be done, but still more is required. Decisions must be made to impose language requirements again at key stages of our educational and occupational pyramids. Rep. Leon Panetta (D., Calif.), a member of the Presidential Commission, drafted one such step when he wrote an amendment to the International

Development Cooperation Act. It requires that henceforth key U.S. foreign-post positions be filled only by persons knowing the language and culture of an assigned country.

"We've been guilty of laziness," Panetta says. "We've assumed that the rest of the world would speak English for us. Well, it won't." It's time for America to grow up, and learn again the languages of this increasingly competitive world.

Write down your reading time in the blanks below. Then answer the questions and determine your comprehension level from your score, as calculated on page 77. Length of article: 1,406 words.

Mins._____ Secs._____Words per minute_____ Comprehension_____%

QUESTIONS

1. Check the major PROBLEM described in the article.
   a. Assistance for non-English-speaking refugees who enter the U.S. is inadequate.
   b. Too many Americans cannot speak a foreign language.
   c. American students are not entering the diplomatic service.
   d. Too many restaurants print their menus in foreign languages.
2. THREE of the main EFFECTS are:
   a. Local governments must pay for educational services to immigrants.
   b. Disastrous political misunderstandings with foreign governments
   c. Restaurant patrons don't get the food they think they ordered and are charged high prices for common dishes.
   d. Loss of trade with foreign countries
   e. Lack of qualified bilingual employees in government and business
   f. Higher taxes
   g. Refugees have tried to eat oven cleaner and furniture polish because they couldn't read labels.
   h. The "mystique" of menus in foreign languages is actually lowering the quality of the food served.
   i. Some key diplomatic posts are going unfilled for the lack of qualified personnel.
   j. There are not enough UHF TV channels to carry needed foreign-language programming.
3. THREE of the CAUSES are:
   a. Television is adversely affecting our young people.

b. Only 15% of local governments have applied for federal aid to educate refugees in English.
c. Only 15% of U.S. elementary schools offer foreign languages.
d. Manufacturers refuse to print product labels in several languages, as is common in the rest of the world.
e. Restaurant inspectors are allied with owners rather than with consumer groups.
f. Student disapproval of traditional disciplines
g. Drug use among students is increasing.
h. Only 8% of U.S. colleges require language courses for either admission or graduation.
i. The high unemployment rate
j. Snobbism among food editors and restaurant reviewers

4. FOUR suggested SOLUTIONS are:
a. More active consumer groups
b. Insistence by major corporations that their overseas employees know the language and culture of the country
c. Creation of more student programs such as college credit for a year abroad
d. A major federally funded advertising campaign to attract more college students to government jobs
e. Abolishing Civil Service
f. Higher pay for diplomats
g. Federal grants to upgrade the skills of foreign-language teachers
h. Church-sponsored schools for refugees
i. Foreign-language requirements for college admission and graduation
j. Local legislation requiring all menus to contain English translations

5. Check whether the following statements are True, False, or IRrelevant to this article.

T F IR   a. The LaSalle Language Academy in Chicago is a public school that offers four different foreign languages to its 500 pupils from kindergarten through eighth grade.

T F IR   b. More than 10,000 English-speaking Japanese businesspeople work in the U.S., but fewer than 900 Japanese-speaking Americans work in Japan.

T F IR   c. One woman in a Japanese restaurant assumed that teriyaki contained yak meat.

T F IR   d. The Middlebury Pledge is taken by all people entering the diplomatic service.

T F IR   e. The State Department does not require a knowledge of a foreign language for its incoming Foreign Service officer candidates.

Answers on page 77.

Optional Challenge

Write an outline of "Our Shocking Illiteracy in Foreign Languages" using the words *Problem, Effects, Causes,* and *Solutions* as headings. Check your version with the model on pages 77–78.

THE INSTRUCTION PATTERN: To Instruct

MATERIALS (optional)
STEP 1
STEP 2
STEP 3

Anything that starts with "How to" is probably an example of the instruction pattern. Instructions can tell us how to do anything from electrical wiring to world travel. Look for numbered steps, or words like "first," "second," "then," and "next."

Manufacturers and government agencies spend millions of dollars on instructions, yet some people can't program their VCRs or fill out the "easy" tax forms. Whose fault is it? Often the instructions aren't written clearly, but sometimes, even before they start, readers have already convinced themselves that they will not be able to understand. They run their eyes quickly down the page and just as quickly give up.

Instructions *can* be intimidating. Many have to be read slowly and carefully, one step at a time. If they are poorly written, you may have to rewrite them in your mind to make them comprehensible. Most of us will put extra effort into understanding and remembering instructions for something we find pleasurable, while we resist those that seem irrelevant or threatening. This is a conscious choice. Just remember that *not* reading instructions for things like medications, electrical appliances, or payment schedules can cost time, money, maybe even your life.

READ:

BULB INFORMATION

These bulbs are designed for use in 30 to 50-socket GE Merry Midget Series Light Sets, or can be converted to fit any other 'light set with 30 to 50 sockets. Each bulb has an internal shunt designed to keep your set lighted if a bulb burns out. Replace burnouts promptly to prolong the life of remaining bulbs.

CAUTION — BE SURE TO USE THE RIGHT BULB TO AVOID OVER-HEATING OR EARLY BURNOUTS

If this bulb does **not** fit your old 30-50 socket light set, you may convert it to fit by following directions below.

1. Make sure set is unplugged.

2. Remove base or reflector of burned-out bulb **by** straightening wires and gently pulling bulb out.

3. Remove base of GE Merry Midget bulb as in step 2.

4. Thread wires of GE bulb through holes in old base with one wire in each hole.

5. After bulb is fully inserted into base, bend wires up, one on each side, like other bulbs in your set.

6. CAUTION — TO AVOID ELECTRICAL SHOCK Before inserting bulb assembly into socket, trim off any excess wire which may extend above point A. When bulb is properly inserted into socket, all bare wire should be covered. Do not insert bulb when set is plugged in.

Made in Korea expressly for the General Electric Co., Nela Park, Cleveland, Ohio 44112

GENERAL ⊛ ELECTRIC

Do you know how to do it now? Certainly not! Many instructions have to be read slowly and carefully, one step at a time, or you may end up wasting time and money or even endangering your life.

Study and practice are a major part of mastering skills, so take your time when you need to.

Studying

There is a huge difference between reading and studying. You need different strategies. Studying usually implies locating specific information and either perceiving its pattern of organization or creating a structure within which to store it for easy retrieval. Then a reader needs to rehearse the information to become fluent. When the information is instruction, successful studying is frequently tested by performance.

WHAT TO DO

Tackle this excerpt from "The *Look* 20-Day Course in Quick Reading" without timing yourself. First read the questions on pages 69–70; then read the article to find the answers, filling in the blanks on page 69–70 as you go.

Do not be concerned about speed yet, but only on finding what you are looking for.

READ:

THE LOOK·20-DAY COURSE IN QUICK READING

Prof. James I. Brown, Ph.D.

The Speed-Up

Take that most precious of commodities—time. As one busy man put it: "If you know where I can buy a time-stretcher, I will give you a million dollars for it!" This series on reading should provide exactly that—an invaluable time-stretcher.

Here is how it works: Suppose you now read at 250 wpm. If you read an hour a day, on the average, doubling your rate means you have, in a sense, made yourself seven extra hours a week. You can now do 14 hours of reading in only seven hours' time. To put it another way, you will have stretched your customary seven hours of reading a week into 14 hours. Over the long pull, that means an extra 365 hours a year. Furthermore, you should work toward tripling or quadrupling your rate, not merely doubling it. In short, invest 15 minutes a day—make up to 21 extra hours a week.

This series should, in fact, serve three functions, not one—acting as time-stretcher, problem-solver and experience-extender. Carlyle catches this broad perspective so well when he says, "All that mankind has done, thought, gained, or been; it is lying as in magic preservation in the pages of books."

Now, how can this be done? By taking off the brakes! You would not think of driving your car with both foot and hand brake on. Yet as a reader, you probably have several brakes slowing you down.

Regressing

One brake is regressing—looking back every now and then at something already read. It is like stepping backward every few yards as you walk—hardly the way to move ahead in a hurry. Regression may be pure habit, a lack of confidence, a vocabulary deficiency or actual missing of a word or phrase. See what it does to a complex sentence complex sentence like this, which seems even more tangled than tangled than usual as the eyes frequently regress regress. Obviously this all-too-common habit plays havoc with reading speed, comprehension and efficiency.

Eye movement photographs of some 12,000 readers show that college students regress an average of 15 times in reading only 100 words. To be sure, they perform better than the average ninth grader, who regresses 20 times. In short, regressions consume one-sixth or more of your precious reading time, making them a major retarding factor. Release this brake and enjoy an immediate spurt in reading speed, perhaps over 100 wpm. Class results show that awareness of the problem, which you now have, plus application of the suggestions to follow, should bring an 80 percent decrease in regressions.

Vocalizing

A second brake is vocalizing or pronouncing words to yourself as you read. As beginning readers, we were all taught to pronounce words, syllables and even letters. No wonder traces of this habit persist, interfering later on whith general reading efficiency. To see how vocalizing slows reading speed, read these words s l o w l y, s o u n d i n g t h e syl la bles and l e t t e r s.

At the lip level, vocalizing pulls reading down to the speed of speech, probably below 200 wpm. To diagnose, put a finger over your lips as you read silently. Do you feel any movement? To get rid of that habit, keep a memory-jogging finger on your lips as you read.

Vocalizing at the voice-box level is far more common and much less obvious. If your top reading rate was close to 300 wpm, you have reason to suspect this kind of vocalizing. Check further by placing your thumb and forefinger lightly on each side of your voice box. If, as you read silently, you feel faint movements, you know your problem, an important step toward its solution.

Word-by-Word Reading

The third major brake is word-by-word reading. To move 200 books, you would certainly not make 200 trips, one book a trip. Ten trips, 20 books a trip, would be more likely. As a reader, keep that same principle in mind.

Eye-movement photographs reveal that in reading, the eyes move jerkily along a line of print, making a series of short stops to permit reading a portion of print. Research indicates that even college students are, without special training, word-by-word readers, taking in only 1.1 words per fixation or look. Obviously one way to double or triple your rate is by learning to take in two or three words at a glance instead of the usual one.

There they are—three major causes of reading inefficiency, three brakes that hold your reading to a snail's pace. Release them and enjoy immediate returns. Fortunately, one single key principle, properly applied, will do the job.

The Solution

Every successful reading-improvement course relies heavily on the key principle of faster-than-comfortable reading, whether it be the least or most publicized, whether it costs $30 or $175. This principle automatically reduces regressions. You push ahead too fast to look back. Furthermore, you have less time to vocalize, so that bad habit begins to disappear. Finally, the added speed actually forces you to deal with word groups, not single words.

Put this principle to immediate use with the following 20-day plan. For this, select a light, interesting book, and for 15 minutes every day, without fail, read it at a faster-than-comfortable speed, not worrying about comprehension. That will come later, as you gain added experience and skill at the new speeds.

Toward the end of each 15-minute session, have someone time you for exactly two minutes, to get an accurate rate figure. To determine rate, count the number of words in a representative passage of 20 consecutive lines. Divide that figure by 20 to get the average number of words per line. Then for the two-minute timing session, divide the number of lines read by two and multiply by the average number of words per line to get your wpm rate.

If these faster-than-comfortable sessions are not tiring, push to even faster speeds, sacrificing even more comprehension for the time being. Ten days of this regimen should reflect desired changes in speed of comprehension. At times, your rate may slow down or even drop back. But if it should level off or drop back for more than two days, you are not forcing yourself enough—not practicing the speeds you want to become skilled at.

Data from classes at Minnesota suggest

About 72 percent double their reading rates in 20 days

that the 20-day plan should permit about 72 percent to double their rate, 20 percent to triple it and eight percent to quadruple it. If you are still short of your objective, merely extend the plan.

Reading at Super-Speeds

The knowledge explosion being what it is, doubling or tripling your reading rate is but a good beginning. You must now learn to make quantum-like jumps to cover 20 to 30 times more print without increasing your rate—to read faster, in short, without reading faster. To understand that paradox, you must tap the full potential of three special techniques—surveying, skimming and scanning. They will put you not where the action is but where the essence is.

Surveying

Surveying is a special shortcut, designed to provide the best possible overview in the shortest possible reading time. With it, you make a gigantic leap in coverage, for you can survey 20 to 30 articles in the time normally taken to read one. This special technique is derived from certain common characteristics of written communication.

For example, with most articles or reports, the title usually provides the best concise indication of content. The first paragraph goes on to furnish the most complete orientation and foreshadowing of what is coming. From that point on, major subdivisions are likely to be marked with headings, other important parts emphasized by italics, heavy type, graphs or tables. More often than not, the final paragraph summarizes or suggests pertinent implications or applications.

Translate those characteristics into action and you know exactly how to survey an article. You read the title, first and last pararaphs, and all headings, italicized words, graphs and tables in between. In a sense, a survey is like a reader-made abstract, a distilling of the essence of meaning into neat capsule form.

Surveying also works with books. Here you read the title, table of contents, preface or foreword. Then you survey each chapter as you would a magazine article—title, first paragraph, headings, italicized words, graphs, tables and last paragraph.

Stop here, go back and survey that portion of the article from Reading at Super-Speeds to the end before reading on. The parts printed in bold type are the only parts you are to read for the survey. Read them, then return to this spot and continue reading.

Skimming

The second super-speed technique to add to your repertoire is skimming—a careful reading of selected parts. It, too, is solidly grounded on certain basic characteristics of written expression.

Skimming is built around common characteristics of paragraph structure. For example, the **bulk** of our reading, an estimated 55 to 85 percent, is of **expository paragraphs,** where the main idea is usually expressed in a topic sentence. In 60 to 90 percent of such paragraphs, the **topic sentence** comes **first.** The next most likely spot is the end of the paragraph. When the topic sentence leads off, the **last** sentence usually reiterates or **summarizes** the topic idea. In addition, certain **key words** through the paragraph **supply** further **detail** and support to the idea being developed. In short, as in this paragraph, reading one-fourth of the words still

gives you the substance. **Skimming capitalizes on awareness of structure.**

You superimpose skimming on the survey technique, with its reading of title, first and last paragraphs, subheads, italicized words, graphs and tables. All other paragraphs are skimmed. This means reading the first sentence in each one, shifting into high gear to pick key words, then reading the last sentence. The preceding paragraph illustrates the technique. Go back and read only those words printed in heavier type. See for yourself how the essentials stand out.

Skimming is often three or four times faster than reading, depending upon style and average paragraph length. Furthermore, a skilled skimmer often gets more comprehension than an average reader. Develop more skimming skill by consciously skimming at least one article every day.

To stop here, however, is to miss the important role of skimming as a reading accelerator. As you follow the 20-day plan, you practice fast reading 15 minutes daily, but you probably read slowly several hours a day. How can you expect progress when you practice slow reading more than fast?

It might look equally impossible for a 200-lb. father to teeter-totter with his 20-lb. son. But the solution is simple. He merely sits closer to the fulcrum and strikes a perfect balance. In the same way, skimming can be used to counteract and balance the slowing pull of normal reading.

For example, instead of reading an important 3,000-word article at 200 wpm, at 15-minute task, skim it at 1,500 wpm, then read it once at 250 wpm. This skimming-reading combination not only takes less time but usually means better comprehension and a distinct boost toward higher reading speeds.

Scanning

Scanning, the third-super-speed technique, also serves two functions. It lets you spot certain desired information as well as accelerate rate.

Scanning is a technique for finding a specific bit of information within a large body of printed matter—the proverbial needle in the haystack. This is the highest gear of all. Here you start with such specific questions as Who won? When? Where? In my university reading classes, students scan initially, without special training or practice, at about 1,300 wpm. One intensive scanning session is enough to shoot the average up to about 14,000 wpm, without loss of accuracy. Some students even passed the 25,000 mark.

1) Visualize the detail. Everyone has noticed how, in looking at a page of print, his own name jumps into sight. This psychological fact suggests one way to insure greater accuracy. If scanning for a date, for

Zigzagging down the page can help you find the facts you need

example, visualize exactly how it will look. Put a strong mind-set to work. For another example, compare the figures below, How many are identical?

The word "figures" was used to establish the wrong mind-set, one to hinder you from seeing the word in the illustration. Now let that new mind-set make the word TIE pop out.

2) Use all available clues. If scanning for a proper name, focus on the capital letter. Synonyms, hyphens, italics or quotation marks are other possible clues.

3) Use structural tips. If you want news about stock performance, let the phrase "Dow Jones average" pull you up short at the desired spot.

4) Use systematic scanning pattern. Zigzag down the column or middle of the page, as illustrated by the printed scanning pattern. Notice that if you look directly at the first and last words in the lines of print, you leave untapped the full perceptual span at your command. Looking as far in as the second or third word from each end should still let you see the words that came before and after. With a very narrow column, run your eyes straight down the middle.

Scanning is particularly useful after reading an article, when you want to fix pertinent details in mind. Increased skill will come by doing two or three scanning problems a day, in reading newspapers or magazines.

You are now ready to push ahead on your 20-day reading-improvement plan, as augmented by three super-speed techniques for extending coverage and accelerating progress. When fully developed and exploited, the approaches should provide the potential for handling the knowledge explosion with enviable facility.

With exponential change the very essence of life today, a company can be prospering one day and facing ruin the next. This means that the individual who concentrates on the present is actually jeopardizing his future. Balancing today's demands with tomorrow's needs is a key problem reading can help solve with particular effectiveness.

Expediters for Efficient Reading

To be most effective, the 20-day reading plan presented in the last issue should focus on both sides of the reading coin—

speed and comprehension, not speed alone. What you need next to give your efforts additional thrust are boosters in both areas. The following formulas, principles, insights and skills should provide exactly that.

Formulas to Expedite Progress

Today, there are formulas for everything—for getting men to the moon, for success, for millions of manufactured products. We would be remiss not to make intelligent use of formulas to improve reading efficiency.

The SD4 formula

This helps you organize the flow of reading matter coming your way with maximum effectiveness. A year after completing my reading course, a former student, a top Government official, said, "For me, the SD4 formula alone was worth ten times the price of the course." The formula focuses on a problem dating back to the sixteenth century, when Sir Francis Bacon said, "Some books are to be tasted, others to be swallowed, and some few to be chewed and digested: that is, some books are to be read only in parts, others to be read, but not curiously, and some few to be read wholly, and with diligence and attention."

Unfortunately, Bacon leaves the heart of the problem untouched. Only one person can decide intelligently exactly how you should read something—and you are that person. You alone know your own background, interests, problems and goals. Yet how can you decide before reading something whether it should be tasted, swallowed, or chewed and digested? That is the problem the SD4 formula is designed to meet.

The S stands for Survey, a technique you know from the earlier article in this series. You survey the material to Decide on one of 4 choices—to skip, skim, read or study it. If the initial survey uncovers little of personal relevance, you have already given the material all the attention it deserves. Skip it. If it has moderate pertinence, skim

it. This takes much less time than reading but still gives you what you want. If it is more relevant, apply the third choice—read it. Finally, if it is quite important, study it.

The beauty of this formula is that it lets you apportion to each article or book precisely the attention it deserves, no more, no less. Furthermore, that decision is intelligently made, in a minimum of time.

The SQ3R Formula

This one has a totally different purpose—to provide maximum comprehension and retention. Most readers, wanting to understand an article thoroughly, resort to rereading. Yet even two rereadings add only about eight percent more comprehension, hardly an effective use of time. Incorporating pertinent research, Dr. Francis P. Robinson, Ohio State psychologist, devised the SQ3R formula to supply a much improved approach.

Here also the first step is to Survey, to get a broad overview. Next, raise some Questions to be answered in the reading to follow. These tend to heighten interest and stimulate more active involvement. Next comes the Reading, with Reviewing and Reciting as final steps. Review the article, checking vague details. Finally, recite. Repeat the material to yourself or, better yet, to someone else. Reading something and repeating it soon afterward will help you remember it much longer. Start putting this formula to immediate use whenever you want improved comprehension and retention.

The VIP formula

The third and last formula, the VIP formula, expedites all kinds of reading through Visual Improvement Practice. Proper seeing, like playing golf or the piano, is a learned skill, with the average individual perceiving at about 20 percent efficiency. Since we read with our eyes, what helps us see better should also help us read better. Perceptual training, while usually accomplished with a tachistoscope, can also be done with the hand or, better yet, with an ordinary 3 x 5 card.

To check your present phrase-reading habits and see how to improve them, cover the lines below, where you see the black dots, leaving only the dots visible. Now, as quickly as possible, jerk your hand down and back to make a split-second exposure of the words below the first dot. Could you read them all? If not, expose them again. Continue until you have tried all the marked phrases below.

.

Work toward developing

.

sufficient span

.

to permit taking in

.

half a line at a glance

.

or from two to six words.

A 3 x 5 card works much better and lets you use this practice procedure with almost any printed material. You merely expose print, line by line, as quickly as possible, until you develop enough skill to get up to six words at a glance. Limit this drill to only five minutes a day, however. Faster-than-comfortable reading deserves most of your time. Each of these three formulas makes a distinctly different contribution to your reading efficiency. Fit each into its proper place in your 20-day plan, then consider the two key principles discussed next.

Principles to Expedite Progress

Pacing
With most people, the basic faster-than-comfortable principle usually breaks down somewhere along the way. You find yourself saying, "I just can't force myself any faster!"

At this point, a new principle is needed. Most of us have powers hidden in the unconscious mind, available for emergency use. Pacing provides the key to unlock those resources and to urge you on at ac-

celerated speeds. In some courses, pacing is done by mechanical accelerators, films, a stopwatch or the hand, with the newest and perhaps most versatile pacer of all being the cassette.

Why is pacing so common? It works! I remember one student plodding along at 80 wpm while the rest of the class patiently waited for him to finish reading. After class, I asked him to cancel, saying he was holding the others up. He begged to stay, saying, "I need this more than anyone! Don't wait for me: just let me get what I can." I finally consented.

A few weeks brought an amazing change. The class progressed nicely from 254 to 480 wpm, but the plodder had shot up from 80 to 460 wpm. What had he been doing? He had wired his electric clock to the radio so that when the sweep-second hand passed 12, the radio came on briefly to let him know a minute had passed.

Fifteen minutes every night, without fail, he used that as his pacer, reading a popular magazine with about 500 words per page. At first, he tried reading half a page a minute. When he could manage that, he then tried a full page—500 wpm. Enjoy those results yourself. Make pacing an integral part of your 20-day plan. All you need is someone to signal the minutes!

Swing two bats
Now you should start tapping the potential of still another new principle—swing two bats. Watch a batter swing two bats, drop one and step up to the plate. The remaining bat feels much lighter and easier to swing. The same psychology applies to reading. A jump from 250 to 400 wpm, then a drop back to 325 makes that speed seem much more comfortable and manageable than a corresponding jump from 250 to 325 wpm. In short, your top speed will always seem uncomfortable—unless you practice some at higher speeds. So— swing two bats. If your goal is 750 wpm, practice enough at 900 to make 750 feel relatively slow and easy.

Insights to expedite progress

Certain insights, as well as formulas and principles, contribute much to your development as a reader. Insight into the speed-comprehension relationship, for example, should eliminate one quite common barrier to progress.

Speed-comprehension relationship

Slow work usually suggests care and accuracy; speed suggests careless, shoddy work. Unless we realize the danger, this general frame of reference can be carried over into reading to create a major psychological barrier.

I remember one student who, after two weeks of classwork, had never read faster than 190 wpm, 170 wpm being his beginning speed. Comprehension was abysmally low—only 30 to 40 percent. When I suggested he try 250 wpm, he looked incredulous. "I don't get much at slower speeds," he explained, "I wouldn't get anything if I read faster." I told him that in reading, the faster one reads—within limits—the better his comprehension. Reluctantly, he tried a 260-wpm rate, for him a breakneck speed. To his surprise and pleasure, comprehension soared to 70 percent—his all-time high.

To understand why this is so, compare reading with driving. Driving along a quiet country road at 20 miles an hour actually invites wandering attention. But turn onto a freeway and accelerate. See how that top freeway speed pushes distractions aside and forces improved concentration on the road. So it is with reading. Slow reading invites loss of concentration. Fast reading eliminates distractions and improves concentration. No wonder, the faster the better—within limits.

This is so for still another reason. Fast reading forces you out of word-by-word habits into more desirable phrase-reading patterns. By analogy, a 20-piece jigsaw puzzle is much easier than the same puzzle with 80 smaller pieces. In the same way, fitting 20 phrases together is much easier than fitting 80 separate words together.

Now comes the tricky part. What, for you, are those limits? For most adults, increases of from 50 to 125 wpm over their normal rate will still mean improved concentration. Fortunately, added experience at higher speeds will extend those limits dramatically. No wonder the insights you now bring to the speed-comprehension relationship are so important to progress. No wonder it pays you, the reader, to "know thyself," as the Greeks so concisely put it.

Making purpose prevail

Another insight essential to progress concerns the purpose-comprehension relationship. A good hunter, for example, does not rush into the woods and start shooting blindly, expecting to hit something by chance. No. If he is hunting ducks, that purpose dominates all his plans, preparations and actions. So it is with reading. If the purpose is not clear, comprehension inevitably suffers. The sharper and clearer the target, the better the results.

For that reason, sharpening your awareness of five target areas should pay dividends in improved comprehension. First comes information, perhaps the prime purpose for most readers, with understanding a close second, a move into depth. Information supplies the raw material for thought. Just as Sherlock Holmes noted facts and built them into case-solving hypotheses, so we need information plus understanding. A third purpose is entertainment. We read some things because we have to, others because we want to—because they are so exciting, moving or funny that they refresh and entertain us in a special way—reason enough, surely. A fourth purpose is stimulation. Just as a catalyst sparks a chemical reaction, so reading often sparks invention and insight. Finally, there is inspiration, found so often in what we read.

Overlooking any one of these general purposes can make life less satisfying, as Darwin's *Journal* so eloquently testifies.

After losing his taste for poetry, pictures and music, he wrote pathetically, "If I had to live my life again, I would have made a rule to read some poetry and listen to some music at least once every week: for perhaps the parts of my brain now atrophied would thus have been kept alive through use. The loss of these tastes is a loss of happiness, and may possibly be injurious to the intellect, and more probably to the moral character, by enfeebling the emotional part of our nature."

While no one can live his life again, fortunately we can, through reading, profit from the experience of others, which amounts to almost the same thing. In short, purpose contributes much to comprehension as well as to life itself.

Receptive vs. reflective comprehension

Comprehension divides itself broadly into two categories: receptive and reflective. Receptive comprehension refers to factual information such as figures, names, dates, formulas, places, rules or specific statements. Reflective comprehension refers to the reader's ability to fit such details into main ideas, draw reasonable inferences and conclusions, note relationships, weigh evidence or judge intent.

What are your habits? Some readers cannot see the forest for the trees; they get the details but miss the larger picture. Others get the main ideas but remain vague and inaccurate about details. They see the forest, not the trees. Of course, the ideal reader is one who gets both details and main ideas. Actually, main ideas deserve slightly more attention, since it is somewhat easier to infer details from main ideas, than main ideas from details.

You can check and improve your comprehension in this way. Read a full page, say, from LOOK. When you have finished, list all the specific information you can—names, dates, figures, exact statements. Then formulate the main ideas or major points. After you have taken both steps,

check back to see how accurately you performed. For additional practice, cover all but the first sentence in a paragraph, read it, and infer what probably follows in the paragraph. Or reverse the procedure. Read all the paragraph but the first sentence, then infer what it probably says. Check the accuracy of your inferences.

Road signs for readers

One last factor contributing to comprehension lies in sharpening your awareness and insight into certain words with a strong directional function. In driving, we must note road signs if we are not to lose our way. Similarly, in reading, we must take full advantage of all directional cues if we are to follow the writer's train of thought. This means we should recognize and deal effectively with each of three kinds of paragraphs and the words most frequently used to indicate their function.

Introductory paragraphs normally have two functions: to arouse interest and to suggest content. In a sense, the writer shines a flashlight in your face to get attention, then turns the beam down a path to give you a quick glimpse of the direction to be followed. A rhetorical question is sometimes used—the question arousing interest, the answer focusing on content.

Transitional paragraphs, usually short, help the reader follow the writer even when he makes an abrupt change in his train of thought. Phrases such as *Still another aspect, Turning now to,* and *A second method* are typical indicators.

Concluding paragraphs are often introduced by such road signs as *In conclusion, Finally, In closing, To summarize,* and *In essence.* These paragraphs are likely to be particularly important in getting the main idea and reinforcing the chief points covered.

Of course, most paragraphs in an article explain and develop ideas in a wide variety of ways. Sometimes the explanation involves enumeration or restatement; sometimes analysis, comparison or contrast;

sometimes definition or example. Here, too, key words and phrases help catch direction. *For example* lets you know that a point is to be developed by a specific instance or example. *By comparison* or *By contrast* are also phrases that make the road of print easier to travel.

To sharpen your awareness of such words and phrases, circle all of them you can find on a page of print, noting exactly how they function to keep you on the track.

Skills to Expedite Progress

At this point, have all major components of a truly successful reading-improvement program been covered? No. One last consideration remains.

We must check what factors actually contribute most to improved reading speed and comprehension. How important, for example, is perceptual skill? After all, we do read with our eyes. But we also read with our mind, which shifts the emphasis to intelligence. Yet two equally intelligent readers often differ markedly in the general background and experience they bring to print. How important are those factors? Furthermore, what do we read with our eyes, mind, background and experience? Why words, of course! Does that mean word power deserves top consideration? In short, what are the most important factors?

Fortunately, Dr. Jack Holmes and Dr. Harry Singer of the University of California have given this question major research attention, analyzing 37 possible factors. They isolated the seven that contribute most to reading performance, uncovering a veritable galaxy of word-power skills, as suggested in the charts below.

Factors contributing to reading speed

Word sense	23%
Word discrimination	28%
Span of recognition	5%
Not accounted for	44%

Factors contributing to comprehension

Perception of verbal relations	8%
Intelligence	27%
Vocabulary in context	39%
Fixations	4%
Not accounted for	22%

Word discrimination and word sense contribute most to reading speed. Vocabulary in context, intelligence and perception of verbal relations contribute most to comprehension. Such evidence indicates that vocabulary deserves major emphasis in all reading-improvement programs. In fact, attention to vocabulary may well be the hallmark of an up-to-date program. Obviously it must be included here. Now check your vocabulary. How do you deal with words? Try the following difficult five-item test:

effete	a) strong, b) hard, c) shut in, d) worn out, e) young ____
ebracteate	a) with bracts, b) without bracts, c) rounded bracts, d) stunted bracts, e) thin bracts ____
expunge	a) dive in, b) soak, c) erase, d) swim, e) rest ____
ebullition	a) blackness, b) boiling out, c) moving on, d) repair, e) warmth ____
exostosis	a) outgrowth, b) leg bone, c) paralysis, d) bruise, e) stone ____

14 words offer keys to over 14,000 meanings

At age 25, the average person's vocabulary development becomes almost moribund. It is 95 percent complete, with only five percent more to be added from that time on—unless interest is regenerated or a new approach adopted.

At the University of Minnesota, efforts to revitalize interest in vocabulary focus on 14 words that make all the difference. They deserve that label because they contain the most important prefix and root elements in the English language—elements found in over 14,000 words from a desk dictionary or an estimated 100,000 from the big unabridged dictionary—an amazingly useful shortcut to word meanings. Here they are:

The Fourteen Words

Keys to the meanings of over 14,000 words

Words	Prefix	Common meaning	Roots	Common meaning
1. Precept	*pre-*	(before)	*capere*	(take, seize)
2. Detain	*de-*	(away, down)	*tenere*	(hold, have)
3. Intermittent	*inter-*	(between, among)	*mittere*	(send)
4. Offer	*ob-*	(against)	*ferre*	(bear, carry)
5. Insist	*in-*	(into)	*stare*	(stand)
6. Monograph	*mono-*	(alone, one)	*graphein*	(write)
7. Epilogue	*epi-*	(upon)	*logos*	(speech, study of)
8. Aspect	*ad-*	(to, toward)	*specere*	(see)
9. Uncomplicated	*un-* *com-*	(not) (together, with)	*plicare*	(fold)
10. Nonextended	*non-* *ex-*	(not) (out, beyond)	*tendere*	(stretch)
11. Reproduction	*re-* *pro-*	(back, again) (forward, for)	*ducere*	(lead)
12. Indisposed	*in-* *dis-*	(not) (apart, not)	*ponere*	(put, place)
13. Oversufficient	*over-* *sub-*	(above) (under)	*facere*	(make, do)
14. Mistranscribe	*mis-* *trans-*	(wrong) (across, beyond)	*scribere*	(write)

For a dramatic proof of their usefulness, turn to any page in LOOK. You should find at least one of those elements in almost every 50 words. They are identified for you in the next paragraph, prefixes in bold face, roots in italics.

To **compre**hend this **ap**proach, **re**turn to the five-item test you just **com**pleted. Did you **con**sciously think of the **com**mon **prefix ex-**, or the **rela**ted Greek **prefix exo-**, meaning "out"? With that meaning uppermost, **re**take the test. Careful **app**lication of **pre**fix meaning should **per**mit you to **cor**rect any earlier mistakes. Do that now before checking the answers that follow. See for yourself how **pre**fix meaning **im**proves **ac**curacy.

Now for the answers. Effete means "worn out," ebracteate means "without bracts," expunge means "erase" (or "rub out"), ebullition means "boiling out," and exostosis means "outgrowth." If you did not think of prefix meaning when you first took the test, you now know that this approach is, for you, a revitalized way of dealing with words.

Working with these elements as directed, you will gradually develop an awareness of certain basic principles that apply to all prefix and root elements. A special text, *Programed Vocabulary*, developed with 3M and IBM personnel, spotlights these principles. Their potential is suggested by results from a class of 28 executives who took the educational TV course, *Success Through Word Power.* The 14 who read 114 or more pages of the 128-page text improved 89 percent; those reading 101 pages or fewer improved 53 percent.

Put those 14 words to work for yourself. Look each one up in the dictionary, noting the meaning of prefix and root. Then look up the prefix; most dictionaries will indicate variant forms. Note other words containing the prefix. Next, look up a word beginning with the first few letters of the root. To get the meaning of capere, for example, look up capable and note derivation. Gradually, you will develop the insights and skills needed for effective use of such elements.

When you bring to bear on the knowledge explosion all the component elements in these articles, you have, in a sense, created a personal reading explosion that should let you face the print-filled world with new assurance. The dynamic management of time, perhaps more than anything else, determines your success or failure.

The book, Programmed Vocabulary, *3rd edition, by James I. Brown, published by Prentice-Hall, Inc., provides a complete in-depth coverage built around this shortcut. It includes a diagnostic check which lets you know what you should emphasize to insure maximum vocabulary.*

QUESTIONS

1. Name three "brakes" that slow down your reading.

    a. _____

    b. _____

    c. _____

2. Name three speed techniques and describe them.

    a. _____

    _____

    b. _____

    _____

    c. _____

    _____

3. Using the SD4 formula (Survey, Decide, 4 choices), what are your four choices?

    a. _____

    b. _____

    c. _____

    d. _____

4. What is the purpose of the SQ3R formula (Survey, Question, Read, Review, Recite)?

    _____

    _____

5. Describe the technique used in VIP (Visual Improvement Practice).

    _____

    _____

6. What is the purpose of pacing?

    _____

    _____

7. What two things improve comprehension?

    a. _____

    b. _____

Answers on page 79.

WHAT TO DO

Here are novel instructions with a twist. Read the following article as if you are preparing to teach the author's approach to organization, and her instructions, to a colleague. As you read, imagine you are storing its main points on a computer screen. Break down the subject into three sections. When you're finished reading, review what you've been retaining.

READ:

NINE STEPS TO ORGANIZATION

by Anacaria Myrrha

There are nine steps you can take to move you along the path of being organized. The first four are internal attitudes and have to do with willingness on your part to make the necessary commitments. The next four steps are external components: a format for systems to help you get organized. The last, but not the least, is where you can go for help.

ATTITUDES

You Must Be Willing to:

(1) Commit the necessary time and attention to set up the systems. This investment will save you hundreds of hours in the future. The initial systems can be set up in anywhere from a week to a month, depending on the volume of your task and the number of hours you can devote on any given day. After getting everything in place, use the next three to six months to refine and modify your systems. At the end of the year, evaluate, update, clean up and clear out.

(2) Make the necessary decisions to set up the initial systems. Don't get stuck in the fear of doing it wrong. A wrong decision is better than no decision because it will keep you moving through the process. If a decision is wrong you will know it soon enough and you can correct it.

(3) Develop new habits and embrace new habits. If you find yourself saying "That's the way I've always done it," or "I've always been disorganized, unfocused, late . . ." try a new approach. Begin to say, "I used to be disorganized, unfocused and late, but now I'm organized, focused, and on time." Positive speaking, like positive thinking, is a very powerful tool. Use it to your advantage.

(4) Commit regular time to maintain your systems. Remember, being organized is a process and not a static condition. These days, there is a constant flow of paperwork, information and ideas in our lives. Our projects, personal needs and goals change and progress as time passes. Therefore, you must schedule regular time to plan, file, clean out and update your systems.

COMPONENTS OF ORGANIZATION

(5) Container
One of the reasons things become disorganized is the lack of boundaries. Paper piles spill onto other paper piles. Pens and pencils, rubber bands and paper clips become a jumble in desk drawers. Children's toys, kitchen utensils, tools and hardware all mixed together are time consuming and annoying to retrieve.

A container is the first step in the solution. A container sets limits on the space the item inhabits and keeps it in its place. Some examples of containers are: file folders and cabinets, horizontal and vertical files, racks, drawer organizers, planning notebooks, and even increments of time. A task scheduled from 1:00 to 3:00 can then be put out of your mind until it is time to do it.

(6) Label
The right label on a container tells you (and others) what belongs in the container. Even more important, it tells you (and others) what does *not* belong in the container. For instance, once you have gone through your in-basket, items should be sorted into ACTION files by task: To Do, To Pay, To Delegate, To File, To Copy, etc. They should not be put back into your in-basket.

(7) Procedure
A procedure should be thought out for getting things into and out of each container. If it has several steps, it can be written down on a card and posted on the container. For instance, the steps in filing health insurance claims.

(8) Location
If you have old IRS records in your desk drawer and your current bank account files in a cabinet in the closet, your system will not work with ease. Arrange your files, tools and materials according to where and how often you must use them.

THE PROFESSIONAL ORGANIZER

(9) Help
Most of us have mechanics to doctor our cars, accountants to prepare our tax returns, lawyers to negotiate our contracts, and housekeepers to tidy our nests. However, it is often difficult for us to ask for help with a task we feel out of control and embarrassed about, and that we feel we ought to be able to do ourselves.

What's true is, first, being organized is not a moral issue. And, second, no one has taught us how to do it. In the past, our parents were not faced with the onslaught of the information age, and schools did not include it in their curriculum. Even now, with all the excellent organizing books available, the task of getting organized may still overwhelm us.

The good news is help is available. You can now hire a Professional Organizer to help you with the task. A Professional Organizer can offer you creative problem solving and an objective view, provide you with practical solutions custom-made for you, and support you and keep you on track during the process of change.

QUESTIONS

The three divisions of the article are:

1. _____

2. _____

3. _____

The nine steps to organization are:

1. _____

2. _____

3. _____

4. _____

5. _____

6. _____

7. _____

8. _____

9. _____

Answers on pages 79–80.

WHAT TO DO

Instruction articles are not so obvious in their arrangement of steps as you found in "Nine Steps to Organization." In the next article, "Summer's Last Stand," the author creates background in which to think about late-summer vegetables. Straightforward instructions can be seemingly camouflaged while enveloped in a larger context. Underline each place where the author instructs the reader on how to prepare vegetables. Here you can push for speed as you focus only on the preparation aspects described.

READ:

Summer's Last Stand

by Molly O'Neill

*In the race against
ripeness, all you need
is a little technique*

Like many a last stand, summer's is a rococo barrage, a swollen and smug onslaught with no apparent end. Farm stands sag under the weight of green beans, lima beans, corn, tomatoes, zucchini, eggplant, mountains of cauliflower and early autumn squash. The diversity is at first exhilarating and then a little embarrassing. These are the vulgar days of plenty: plenty of food, plenty of heat and, as summer's lethargic sunsets continue to creep into evening, plenty of time.

The glib salads and quick meals of early summer begin to seem silly and insubstantial. Summer's end seems to ask for deeper, huskier flavors, the kind that come from roasting, toasting, slow simmering and baking. Tiny new potatoes, thumb-size zucchini and slender green beans need be nothing but their youthful selves in June and July. But come September, when they are heftier and more mature, they are more to contend with.

Eggplant, for example, grows bitter and needs to be either seeded or cut in half, salted for an hour and rinsed before cooking. Bat-sized zucchini need to be cooked in a slower way than a quick toss on the grill, to balance their nascent bitterness and complement the spicy girth they acquire in maturity.

Likewise, the season's heftier green beans lend themselves to a more leisurely treatment. This is the time to simmer them Southern-style with fatback, to serve them soft-boiled or in a vinaigrette that partially pickles their woodsy facade and softens their edges.

Late-summer tomatoes are bloated and ask not to bask on the window sill. Rather, they require immediate attention. Oven-drying is one quick way of preserving them, while allowing their sugar to caramelize into the sort of husky, pungent flavor that late summer requires. The tomatoes can then be covered with oil and refrigerated in a glass container for up to two weeks, to be used on pasta or pizza, baked with chicken, fish or pork or turned into a soup with a touch of curry to accentuate their roasted flavor.

Elephantine sweet peppers become sweeter and more distilled when roasted or grilled. Once peeled, peppers can be layered with oil and stored for up to a week in the refrigerator. They can then be served as an appetizer with cheese, used to garnish grilled food or lend color and smoky sweetness to a late-summer vegetable pie.

Like tomatoes and peppers, September's corn is swollen—its kernels grow milkier as they stretch against their jackets and their flavor becomes less concentrated. Grilling the ears gives the kernels a smoky nuance that becomes more apparent when sauteed with chicken, mushrooms or chilies. Grilled corn also adds variety to succotash and, combined with minced cilantro, makes an alluring chutney or salsa for garnishing grilled fish or pork.

Grilling and oven-drying are segues to autumn. Both techniques soften the thick skin of late-harvested vegetables, turning the almost bitter to butter. And both techniques enable you to cope with the bounty of late summer, while suggesting the flavor and chewier texture of the season to come.

It is probably no coincidence that one lowers cooking temperatures and begins to reach for dried grains and beans during summer's last stand. The old and the young, after all, mirror the uneasy cusp between summer and fall.

The New York Times

Answers on pages 80–81.

DAY 2 ANSWERS

THIS BUTTON SURVIVES THE LAUNDRY

Problem————————Buttons are the bane of the $2.5 billion men's shirt business. Never mind fine fabrics, microscopic stitching and exquisite tailoring: If *Effects* shirt buttons crack under pressure or the heat of commercial laundering, that is what customers will remember.

"The No. 1 complaint we get from customers is that the buttons on *Causes* their shirts break when they have them laundered," said Jack Irving, executive vice president for Nordstrom's men's division.

Solution Enter Coors Ceramicon Designs Ltd., which makes components for cars, computers, radios and bulletproof vests. Joe Coors Jr., president of Ceramicon's parent company, asked Ceramicon to join the quest.

The result was the Diamond button, which made its debut on Nordstrom shirts and shirts manufactured by men's designer Ike Behar. Made of sand transformed into zirconia and fired at 3,200 degrees, the buttons have more than twice the flexible strength of steel and resist cracking.

There is a drawback to the Diamond Z buttons. They cost 8 cents to 10 cents each for a shirt maker to buy, compared with roughly a penny for buttons made from ground shells and epoxy, or less than a penny for plastic buttons.

IF YOU DON'T HAVE ENOUGH WOES

Problem:
There are fewer bees.
Effect:
Crop yields are lower.
Causes:
Pesticides, fewer feeding areas, reduced economic incentive to beekeepers
Solutions:
Increased honey prices, protecting colonies from poisons, perhaps learning to talk to bees

SPEEDING THE MAILS

Problem:
   Slow mail delivery and surcharges for handling oversize envelopes
Effects:
   Return of important papers and missing a big game because tickets
      were delayed
Causes:
   Postal regulations and illiteracy of employees
Solution:
   Export our mail to Bubustan for more efficient processing.

OUR SHOCKING ILLITERACY

1. b (Score 25 points)
2. b–d–e (Score 5 points each)
3. c–f–h (Score 5 points each)
4. b–c–g–i (Score 5 points each)
5. (Score 5 points each)
   a. T
   b. T
   c. IR
   d. F
   e. T

   100 points equals 100%.

Problem:
   Too few Americans speak any language other than English.

Effects:
   Disastrous political misunderstandings
   Difficult business negotiations
   U.S. trade is comparatively low.
   Businesses have trouble finding qualified bilingual applicants.

Causes:
   Relating to politics:
   People in foreign service are not required to know a foreign language.

Relating to education:
Only 15% of elementary schools offer language courses.
Only 8% of U.S. colleges require language courses for either admission or graduation.
Students disapprove of traditional disciplines and demand more "relevant" requirements.

Solutions:
Relating to business:
Employ sales representatives who know foreign culture and language.
Relating to education:
Reinstitute language requirements for college admission and graduation.
Make federal grants available to upgrade skills of language teachers.
Create more programs such as college credit for term abroad.

COMPUTE YOUR RATE FOR "OUR SHOCKING ILLITERACY"
(Approximate number of words: 1,406)

Time	Wpm	Time	Wpm
1 min.	1406	5 min.	281
1 min. 15 sec.	1125	5 min. 15 sec.	268
1 min. 30 sec.	937	5 min. 30 sec.	256
1 min. 45 sec.	803	5 min. 45 sec.	245
2 min.	703	6 min.	234
2 min. 15 sec.	625	6 min. 15 sec.	225
2 min. 30 sec.	562	6 min. 30 sec.	216
2 min. 45 sec.	511	6 min. 45 sec.	208
3 min.	469	7 min.	201
3 min. 15 sec.	433	7 min. 15 sec.	194
3 min. 30 sec.	402	7 min. 30 sec.	188
3 min. 45 sec.	375	7 min. 45 sec.	182
4 min.	352	8 min.	176
4 min. 15 sec.	331	8 min. 15 sec.	170
4 min. 30 sec.	312	8 min. 30 sec.	165
4 min. 45 sec.	296	8 min. 45 sec.	161

Your rate is ＿＿＿＿＿＿ wpm.
(Record this on page 224.)

LOOK 20-DAY COURSE IN QUICK READING

1. Regressing, vocalizing and word-by-word reading.
2. *Surveying* read title for indication of content
   read first paragraph for orientation
   read main points indicated by:
   headings
   bold faces
   italics
   charts
   read final paragraph for summary
   Skimming for topic sentences, usually first or last in paragraph.
   Scanning for key word. Visualize word or focus on key characteristic such as a capital letter, synonym, hyphen, italics or quote marks.
3. Four choices are: Skip, skim, read, study.
4. Purpose of SQ3R Formula is to provide maximum comprehension and retention.
5. Visual Improvement Practice consists of flashing (quickly exposing and covering) ever-larger groups of words until you are able to read long phrases in a split second.
6. Pacing should force you to read at an uncomfortably fast speed so that when you drop back slightly, it becomes "comfortable."
7. The two things that improve comprehension are speed and purpose.

NINE STEPS TO ORGANIZATION

The three divisions of the article are:

1. Attitudes
2. Components of organization
3. The professional organizer

The nine steps to organization are:

1. Commit the necessary time and attention to set up the systems.
2. Make the necessary decisions to set up the initial systems.
3. Develop new habits and embrace new habits.
4. Commit regular time to maintain your systems.
5. Container
6. Label
7. Procedure
8. Location
9. Help

SUMMER'S LAST STAND

Like many a last stand, summer's is a rococo barrage, a swollen and smug onslaught with no apparent end. Farm stands sag under the weight of green beans, lima beans, corn, tomatoes, zucchini, eggplant, mountains of cauliflower and early autumn squash. The diversity is at first exhilarating and then a little embarrassing. These are the vulgar days of plenty: plenty of food, plenty of heat and, as summer's lethargic sunsets continue to creep into evening, plenty of time.

The glib salads and quick meals of early summer begin to seem silly and insubstantial. Summer's end seems to ask for deeper, huskier flavors, the kind that comes from roasting, toasting, slow simmering and baking. Tiny new potatoes, thumb-size zucchini and slender green beans need be nothing but their youthful selves in June and July. But come September, when they are heftier and more mature, they are more to contend with.

Eggplant, for example, grows bitter and needs to be either seeded or cut in half, salted for an hour and rinsed before cooking. Bat-sized zucchini need to be cooked in a slower way than a quick toss on the grill, to balance their nascent bitterness and complement the spicy girth they acquire in maturity.

Likewise, the season's heftier green beans lend themselves to a more leisurely treatment. This is the time to simmer them Southern-style with fatback, to serve them soft-boiled or in a vinaigrette that partially pickles their woodsy facade and softens their edges.

Late-summer tomatoes are bloated and ask not to bask on the window sill. Rather, they require immediate attention. Oven-drying is one quick way of preserving them, while allowing their sugar to caramelize into the sort of husky, pungent flavor that late summer requires. The tomatoes can then be covered with oil and refrigerated in a glass container for up to two weeks, to be used on pasta or pizza, baked with chicken, fish or pork or turned into a soup with a touch of curry to accentuate their roasted flavor.

Elephantine sweet peppers become sweeter and more distilled when roasted or grilled. Once peeled, peppers can be layered with oil and stored for up to a week in the refrigerator. They can then be served as an appetizer with cheese, used to garnish grilled food or lend color and smoky sweetness to a late-summer vegetable pie.

Like tomatoes and peppers, September's corn is swollen—its kernels grow milkier as they stretch against their jackets and their flavor becomes less concentrated. Grilling the ears gives the kernels a smoky nuance that becomes more apparent when sauteed with chicken, mushrooms or chilies. Grilled corn also adds variety to succotash and, combined with minced cilantro, makes an alluring chutney or salsa for garnishing grilled fish or pork.

Grilling and oven-drying are segues to autumn. Both techniques soften the thick skin of late-harvested vegetables, turning the almost bitter to butter. And both techniques enable you to cope with the bounty of late summer, while suggesting the flavor and chewier texture of the season to come.

It is probably no coincidence that one lowers cooking temperatures and begins to reach for dried grains and beans during summer's last stand. The old and the young, after all, mirror the uneasy cusp between summer and fall.

DAY 3

The Information Pattern
Previewing

THE INFORMATION PATTERN: To Share Information

FACET 1
FACET 2
FACET 3

The Information Pattern consists of lots of facts about something. While the author may be enthusiastic about the subject (have an opinion about it) and may even describe some problems related to it, the primary purpose of the piece is to tell you lots of different facts.

The trick to structuring and storing great quantities of facts and figures is to divide the material into topical sections as you read. Each section represents a different facet of the main subject. Sometimes the author has already arranged the facets in a structure—by time, by location, by category. Even better, each category has a headline identifying the facet. But sometimes you have to do the work, sorting facets yourself.

MIT professor Marvin Minsky describes the heart of the MIT structural approach to information:

> . . . if we ask . . . about the common everyday structures—that which a person needs to have ordinary common sense—we will find first a collection of indispensable categories, each rather complex: geometrical and mechanical properties of things and of space; uses and properties of

a few thousand objects; hundreds of "facts" about hundreds of people, thousands of facts about tens of people, tens of facts about thousands of people; hundreds of facts about hundreds of organizations. As one tries to classify all his knowledge, the categories grow rapidly at first, but after a while, one encounters more and more difficulty. . . .

Suddenly there are too many categories, some overlapping each other, and some sort of simplification is essential. Just as new technologies are generally enormously complex at first and then are simplified, so our information systems first grow more and more intricate and then more and more simple, depending on our need to distinguish. For example, rats, termites, and wasps are quite different, but for the purpose of inspiring a call to the exterminator they all assume the common group status of "pests."

WHAT TO DO

The following article has already been divided. See how quickly you can decide what facet of the platypus is covered in each section. Don't read it. Just glance at each section, allowing key words to seemingly rise off the page. You are only scooping up the fewest words that tell you just enough to predict the appropriate heading. In the blanks provided write headings as you go.

READ:

THE SHY MONSTER: AN EVOLUTIONARY ENIGMA

Is it a mammal? Or a reptile? Scientists ponder the mysteries of the elusive platypus, an animal so unique that it shares its order with only one other creature.

I

[   ]

When the first dried specimens of the mysterious creature appeared in England in 1800, they were greeted with shouts of derision. Just a few months earlier, imported mermaids had been an expensive and popular fad until it was discovered that they were actually fish with monkeys' heads cleverly stitched on.

Now people refused to believe that this biological crazy quilt from Australia was a real animal. It was obviously a beaver with ducks' feet and bill attached.

What sophisticated Londoners failed to realize was that they were looking at a creature fully as wonderful as a mermaid, an actual present-day missing link. Not a link between man and monkey but the link between man and reptiles. The furry little monster was a platypus.

II

[   ]

Platypuses (or platypi, if you prefer) are an amazing hodge-podge of animal parts. Like mammals, they are warm-blooded, have fur and nurse their young. Like reptiles they lay leathery eggs, have a single combined outlet for eliminating body wastes and laying eggs, and have a distinctive reptilian walk because their limbs extend laterally. The hairs on their rubbery duck-like bills are arranged in a pattern similar to the scales of a lizard. They use these highly sensitive beaks to locate and strain food from the river bottom as they cruise along, eyes and ears tightly shut against the mud and sand. The males can measure up to two feet long and weigh as much as 4.5 pounds. The female is smaller, seldom more than 18 inches and 2.5 pounds. Both have thick brown fur.

III

[   ]

For a long time no one was sure how platypuses reproduced. They are shy little creatures who only come out at dawn and dusk and stay in relatively secluded locations. Then in 1884, a Cambridge zoologist, W. H. Caldwell, spent a year in Australia and sent back the now famous telegram:

"Monotremes   oviparous,   ovum meroblastic."

This means that platypuses lay eggs with a yolk that acts like that of birds and reptiles during embryonic development. Recently scientists have learned that the platypus egg is unique among eggs in that it grows after formation, continuing to get nourishment from the mother as it passes down the egg canal just as mammal fetuses get nourishment from the placenta.

These eggs begin their journey the size of a pea and are then fed by the "corpus luteum," a distinctly mammalian structure that gives off hormones to develop the egg until it reaches the size of a sparrow's egg. Like birds, the female platypus has a single ovary on one side.

Male platypuses have sperm that is unlike any mammal sperm. Instead of the usual "tadpoles" of mammals, they have tiny thread-like sperm similar to reptiles and birds. They have undescended testes like reptiles and these organs have a rich blood supply provided through long, coiling arteries as in mammals. They also possess exotic poisonous spurs on their hind legs which may be used to ward off other males during mating.

The female's milk flows from glands under her skin and dribbles down onto her fur where the babies suck it up with their tiny bills. It is probable that the more elaborate and efficient mammary equipment of later mammals evolved from some now-extinct reptile-mammal similar

to the platypus. "The platypus," says Frank Carrick, a field biologist at the University of Queensland, "is a pivotal creature for understanding the evolution of live birth."

IV

[   ]

Platypuses eat up to half their weight each day, mostly fresh worms, insects, shellfish and small frogs. One captive nursing platypus ate 400 earthworms, 338 ground grubs and 38 crayfish in one sitting, 1.75 pounds of food, equal to her own body weight. She would have required half a day of foraging to feed herself that much food in the wild. Oddly, the captive platypuses' favorite diet is insect larvae while the platypus in nature seems to eat much less of this food.

V

[   ]

When the platypus was first discovered in 1797 along the Hawkesbury River in Eastern Australia it was called a water mole. The first English scientist to confirm its authenticity called it a *Platypous anatinua,* "flat-footed animal like a duck." A German scientist also obtained a specimen of the little creature and dubbed it *Ornithorhynchus paradoxus,* "bird's beak animal, a paradox." Eventually zoologists compromised on *Ornithorhynchus anatinus* because "platypus" was already the name of a genus of beetle. However the popular name "platypus" stuck.

The platypus shares its order, Monotremata, with only one other animal, the spiny anteater or echidna of New Guinea, who lays its eggs and places them in an open stomach pouch like a marsupial.

VI

[   ]

Many of the platypus's secrets remain uncovered. Once hunted almost to extinction for their soft, brown fur, platypuses have been protected by Australian law since 1906. But it is only recently that scientists have renewed their studies of this shy elusive beast. They are difficult to observe in nature and harder still to trap and keep in a laboratory setting. There are still many unanswered questions about their behavior, their physiology and most important, their position in the evolutionary cycle from reptiles to mammals. Of course, the platypus knows all the answers. But he's not talking.

QUESTIONS

What are the facets of the platypus article?

I. _____

II. _____

III. _____

IV. _____

V. _____

VI. _____

Answers on page 120.

WHAT TO DO

The next reading exercise is to create headings for each of the facets considered in "Scruffy Desert Plant." A line has been drawn below each section. Write below each section what you think the section is about. Answers are on page 120.

READ:

SCRUFFY DESERT PLANT, ONCE VITAL TO U.S., IS BOUNCING BACK

by William E. Blundell

Staff Reporter of The Wall Street Journal

Guayule, a Wartime Source of Rubber, Has a Revival; It Packs Its Own Power

CASA GRANDE, Ariz.—Bill Klink surveys cultivated rows where seedlings peep at the desert sun from between clods of earth. "You're looking at a new industry—maybe," he says.

Mr. Klink is a partner in Agri-Business Research Corp., a Scottsdale, Ariz., company that specializes in growing experimental crops on arid lands. His 30-acre planting here is guayule (pronounced why-oo-lee), a scruffy, three-foot desert shrub with spiky, blue-gray leaves, a long and checkered history, and increasing economic importance.

Some big companies are getting interested in guayule. So are whole tribes of Indians. A federal agency is aching to spend money on it. Its seeds sell for up to $1,000 a pound. Some nations view it nervously, others hopefully.

Guayule, native to northern Mexico and southwest Texas, is generating all this interest because it is 10% to 20% rubber by weight. Nobody needs natural rubber more than the auto-crazy U.S., which grows none

of its own and imports a quarter of the total world supply—almost $1 billion worth a year, making natural rubber the nation's most expensive resource import after oil. The tire industry also uses a lot of synthetic rubber, which is generally produced from oil and therefore is becoming increasingly expensive.

_____ A

PRIMARY SOURCES

Most of the nation's natural rubber supply comes from rubber cartel nations in politically unstable Southeast Asia, and rubber companies in the U.S. are edgy about that. A couple of coups or an invasion, says an official of one tire maker, and the already-unhealthy U.S. industry could be in even worse trouble. Finally, even without coups and invasions, there soon won't be enough hevea, or tree rubber, to go around.

_____ B

Demand is outstripping supply, and the long growing cycle of the rubber tree makes it impossible to increase production quickly. Goodyear Tire & Rubber Co., the biggest rubber importer and main partner in the guayule venture here, sees a worldwide shortage of more than 500,000 tons of hevea within 10 years.

_____ C

Enter guayule—again. Getting rubber from the innocuous little shrub may be the oldest new idea around. The Aztecs chewed the plant and made rubber balls out of it, and a group led by financier Bernard Baruch and including such fat cats as John D. Rockefeller and Daniel Guggenheim used it to produce half the nation's modest rubber requirements in 1910.

——————————————— D

But, eclipsed by cheaper and more abundant tree rubber, the industry soon died. In 1930 an Army major named Dwight Eisenhower urged its revival, but his advice was ignored until World War II, when the Japanese cut off hevea from Southeast Asia, and the U.S. had to launch a crash guayule program. After the war, however, all 32,000 acres were burned or plowed under.

——————————————— E

Now, with shortages looming and rubber prices more than tripling in the past decade, the "orphan of the desert," as it has been called, may yield a permanent industry at last. Hardy, requiring little water, amenable to genetic improvement and harvestable two or three years after planting, it could grow on up to five million desert acres in the Southwest. Eventually it could fill all U.S. natural-rubber needs and form a living stockpile as well. Almost a third of its rubber is in the roots, which

survive to send up new shoots after the bush is lopped off.

But the guayule industry, such as it is today, is still a sleeping beauty waiting for the kiss of the prince.

There are a lot of reasons. Tire firms know how to extract rubber from the bush with hexane. Firestone Tire & Rubber Co. has a laboratory-scale processing unit going, and Mexico is operating a pilot plant in Saltillo extracting rubber from wild shrubs. But the economics of a commercial-scale plant are still murky.

Then there is what one Goodyear executive calls "the chicken or egg problem." Big companies don't want to build multimillion-dollar plants to process guayule unless they are assured of sizable crops nearby. But harvested guayule won't keep for long, and farmers don't want to risk planting thousands of acres without assurance that a processing plant will be there to buy the stuff. Apparently no one wants to chance a farm-to-market venture alone.

"No clear leadership is evolving in the commercialization of guayule, and this is a real constraint," says Kennith Foster, associate director of the Office of Arid Lands Studies at the University of Arizona.

He and others believe the investment would be more than repaid in the benefits to the balance of payments and in the creation of new jobs. They also note that just such aid created the synthetic rubber industry from scratch in World War II.

——————————————— F

But a peacetime government has been divided within itself over funding guayule. The Interior Department has pushed for a program because it wants to ease poverty and unemployment on Southwestern Indian lands. The National Academy of Sciences strongly recommended a federal role in a 1977 report, and the next year Congress authorized spending of $30 million on the bush.

But no new funds were appropriated, and the Agriculture and Commerce Departments, charged with running the program, have chosen to lavish their budgets on other things.

So attention now has shifted to the Federal Emergency Management Agency, keeper of the nation's strategic stockpiles. The FEMA has only 119,000 tons of natural rubber in its larder, far below the 850,000 tons it needs, and it can't buy any more without seriously disrupting a world market already affected by tight supplies and high prices.

With congressional approval, the FEMA can also provide money for domestic ventures to produce needed materials. Last year, it proposed a 10-year, $200 million guayule project, including a commercial-scale plant to process 25,000 acres of the shrub, but the Office of Management and Budget shot down the idea. Since then, however, congressional concern over supplies of strategic materials has been mounting, and President Reagan just announced the first purchases for the strategic stockpile in 20 years. He also said other measures to expand domestic supplies were being considered. The FEMA, heartened by the change in attitude, is expected to resubmit its proposal for guayule.

Even if the plan is rejected again, and government support never exceeds present levels, development probably will only be slowed, rather than killed. "It isn't a matter of *if* guayule is commercialized, it's a matter of when," says Mr. Foster of the University of Arizona.

Most analysts believe that the price of natural rubber can only go up, adding to guayule's appeal. Because synthetic rubbers, which account for 70% of the world rubber use, are made from oil, their prices have climbed steeply, and they couldn't fill much of the looming rubber-supply gap anyway. The natural product has heat resistance and other qualities that synthetics lack, and natural rubber is still indispensable in tire making.

Some products, including aircraft and heavy-equipment tires, must be made almost entirely of natural rubber. And radial passenger-car tires currently taking over the market require more natural rubber than standard types. "We could easily use more natural rubber in products, but it would be difficult to go the other way and use more synthetic without a decline in quality and performance in critical uses," says John Lawrence, Goodyear's manager.

_____ G

WHAT TO DO

In "Make Way for Microwave Cooking" draw a line between paragraphs every time the author switches to a new facet of microwave cooking, and then write captions for the facets of this article.

READ:

MAKE WAY FOR MICROWAVE COOKING

by Jack Denton Scott

A space-age oven has arrived: it's incredibly speedy, and it's easy on electricity

One afternoon in 1945, Percy L. Spencer laid a chocolate bar beside a radar vacuum tube he was testing at Raytheon Company's laboratory in Waltham, Mass. Moments later, the candy bar was a gooey mess.

Spencer's mind made a large leap. He sent out for a bag of popcorn kernels and a raw egg. He put the corn in front of a small radar horn antenna. The kernels danced into fluffy white popcorn. Next, he placed the egg near the horn. It exploded.

The scientist had just discovered an astounding fact: he could cook with radio waves. With microwaves.

Today, many of the two million people using microwave cookery consider it the greatest discovery since fire. And some believe that the

waves may eventually make electric and gas ovens as obsolete as the wood-burning stove.

In *one* minute, those invisible microwaves cook a slice of bacon (on a paper towel without burning it!) to crisp perfection. A potato that takes an hour to bake in an ordinary oven is whipped out in *four minutes*. Microwaves also defrost frozen foods faster and more efficiently than any other medium. A one-pound steak, frozen solid, is ready to cook in three to five minutes.

The microwave oven, which looks much like a television set, has other assets besides speed. It does not heat up the kitchen; it can greatly reduce dishwashing; and it saves on energy.

The first oven was manufactured by Raytheon in 1947. Trademarked the Radarange, it cost about $3000 and was offered only to hotels and restaurants. In 1965, Raytheon acquired Amana Refrigeration, and in 1967 Amana came out with the first U.S. microwave oven to use standard household circuits. By the 1970s, Litton Industries, Tappan, General Electric, Thermador, Magic Chef, Roper and others—among them several Japanese firms—were in the portable-oven market, but in the United States Amana's and Litton's products soon reached the forefront, where they remain.

I've been cooking with microwaves for more than six years. My initial contact was while watching a professional demonstrator in a department store. When asked by a viewer what made the microwaves cook food so quickly, she told the man to rub the palms of his hands together rapidly. He did, and she asked the result. Heat, the man said. That, she explained, is exactly how the microwaves work on food.

When microwaves enter food, they cause the liquid or moisture molecules to vibrate 2450 million times a second. The resulting friction causes the food to heat.

Microwaves do not use the direct application of heat, as all other cooking mediums do. Electromagnetic waves from the magnetron power source (or tube, not unlike the one in your TV set) are instantly absorbed *into* the food, becoming heat. These microwaves are waves of energy (with short wavelengths—from approximately one-tenth inch to 40 inches; and high frequencies—300 million to 100 billion cycles per second) similar to those sent out by television and radio stations.

Another microwave surprise: Not only can cooking be done on paper, plastic, glass, china and ceramics, but these materials, not having the moisture molecules of food, transmit the waves without absorbing them. Thus, dishwashing time is reduced, as food does not stick to the materials used, and paper plates may simply be thrown away.

Cleaning the oven is easy. Just wipe with a damp cloth, since the food does not bake onto the oven walls.

Microwave cooking can enhance the flavor of food because it is fast and can cook with little or no water. The natural color is also preserved. Leftovers can be brought back to original fresh-cooked flavor in a matter of minutes. Many precooked frozen foods can be on the table piping hot in six minutes.

Is there anything the microwave oven can't do? The use of metal utensils is limited. It isn't effective in baking bread, and it will not brown small pieces of meat such as hamburgers and steaks, or put a flaky crust on a pie. Food must be cooked longer than 15 minutes to brown in a microwave oven.

But the manufacturers claim to have beaten the browning bugaboo with the invention of special micro-plates (browning skillets) now on the market. The micro-plate, which is glass-ceramic but looks like china, has a special coating that absorbs the waves, and it will brown, sear and grill. For a brown, juicy four-ounce hamburger, for example, insert the micro-plate and pre-heat it for six to seven minutes; then grill the meat on it for about 1.5 minutes on each side. (The times vary according to the make of the oven and how you like your hamburger.)

For the tabletop model of the microwave oven, prices today range from less than $200 to $600. Units combined with an electric oven cost more. While other cooking-appliance sales plummeted 35 to 40 percent in the past two years, microwave-oven sales have spiraled upward more than 50 percent. Sales in 1974 were 725,000 units, with a retail value of $300 million—up 65 percent over 1973. The forecast for sales in 1976 is 1.3 million units.

The energy crisis is one reason for the microwave-oven success; it cooks many foods in about one-fourth the time required by the ordinary range. There is practically no waste heat; almost all microwave energy goes directly into the food. According to an industry study, the microwave oven, compared with the ordinary oven, saves a median 62 percent in kilowatt-hours. On the national average, a microwave oven can save between $25 and $60 a year, depending on the kilowatt-hour rate in your area.

Answers on page 120.

WHAT TO DO

Often you will be looking for information from only one or two parts of an article, so your ability to organize and classify the material this way is very useful in finding information quickly and easily.

Preview "Erik Erikson's Eight Ages of Man" looking for headings to give you a general idea of what territory the author has bitten off.

After Previewing

You've already noticed that the center section has headings that correspond with Erikson's descriptions of the "Eight Ages of Man." Convert each heading like "Trust vs. Mistrust" to a question: "What are the characteristics of the Trust vs. Mistrust Age?" We are only practicing how to recognize the point at which the author switches to a new facet of his subject. In this section we are practicing reading questions rather than answering them.

WHAT TO DO

What about information that has no headings? That's where the fun begins. Imagine yourself a textbook editor whose job is to cook up headings. Now read the first part of the article. As you go, draw a line every time the author moves to a new facet, then write your own headings and turn them into questions. When you finish, turn to page 121 and compare your questions with those listed.

ERIK ERIKSON'S EIGHT AGES OF MAN

One man in his time plays many psychosocial parts

by David Elkind

His descriptions of the stages of the life cycle have advanced psycho-analytic theory to a new level of understanding.

At a recent faculty reception I happened to join a small group in which a young mother was talking about her "identity crisis." She and her husband, she said, had decided not to have any more children and she was depressed at the thought of being past the childbearing stage. It was as if, she continued, she had been robbed of some part of herself and now needed to find a new function to replace the old one.

When I remarked that her story sounded like a case history from a book by Erik Erikson, she replied, "Who's Erik Erikson?" It is a reflection on the intellectual modesty and literary decorum of Erik H. Erikson, psychoanalyst and professor of developmental psychology at Harvard, that so few of the many people who today talk about the "identity crisis" know anything of the man who pointed out its pervasiveness as a problem in contemporary society two decades ago.

Erikson has, however, contributed more to social science than his delineation of identity problems in modern man. His descriptions of the stages of the life cycle, for example, have advanced psychoanalytic theory to the point where it can now describe the development of the healthy personality on its own terms and not merely as the opposite of a sick one. Likewise, Erikson's emphasis upon the problems unique to adolescents and adults living in today's society has helped to rectify the one-sided emphasis on childhood as the beginning and end of personality development.

Finally, in his biographical studies, such as *Young Man Luther* and *Gandhi's Truth* (which has just won a National Book Award in philosophy and religion), Erikson emphasizes the inherent strengths of the human personality by showing how individuals can use their neurotic symptoms and conflicts for creative and constructive social purposes while healing themselves in the process.

It is important to emphasize that Erikson's contributions are genuine advances in psychoanalysis in the sense that Erikson accepts and builds upon many of the basic tenets of Freudian theory. In this regard, Erikson differs from Freud's early co-workers such as Jung and Adler who, when they broke with Freud, rejected his theories and substituted their own.

Likewise, Erikson also differs from the so-called neo-Freudians such as Horney, Kardiner and Sullivan who (mistakenly, as it turned out) assumed that Freudian theory had nothing to say about man's relation to reality and to his culture. While it is true that Freud emphasized, even mythologized, sexuality, he did so to counteract the rigid sexual taboos of his time, which, at that point in history, were frequently the cause of neuroses. In his later writings, however, Freud began to concern himself with the executive agency of the personality, namely the ego, which is also the repository of the individual's attitudes and concepts about himself and his world.

It is with the psychosocial development of the ego that Erikson's observations and theoretical constructions are primarily concerned. Erikson has thus been able to introduce innovations into psychoanalytic theory without either rejecting or ignoring Freud's monumental contribution.

The man who has accomplished this notable feat is a handsome Dane, whose white hair, mustache, resonant accent and gentle manner are reminiscent of actors like Jean Hersholt and Paul Muni. Although he is warm and outgoing with friends, Erikson is a rather shy man who is uncomfortable in the spotlight of public recognition. This trait, together with his ethical reservations about making public even disguised case material, may help to account for Erikson's reluctance to publish his observations and conceptions (his first book appeared in 1950, when he was 48).

In recent years this reluctance to publish has diminished and he has been appearing in print at an increasing pace. Since 1960 he has published three books, *Insight and Responsibility, Identity: Youth and Crisis* and *Gandhi's Truth*, as well as editing a fourth, *Youth: Change and Challenge*. Despite the accolades and recognition these books have won for him, both in America and abroad, Erikson is still surprised at the popular interest they have generated and is a little troubled about the possibility of being misunderstood and misinterpreted. While he would prefer that his books spoke for themselves and that he was left out of the picture, he has had to accede to popular demand for more information about himself and his work.

The course of Erikson's professional career has been as diverse as it has been unconventional. He was born in Frankfurt, Germany, in 1902 of Danish parents. Not long after his birth his father died, and his mother later married the pediatrician who had cured her son of a childhood illness. Erikson's stepfather urged him to become a physician, but the boy declined and became an artist instead—an artist who did portraits of children. Erikson says of his post-adolescent years, "I was an artist then, which in Europe is a euphemism for a young man with some talent and nowhere to go." During this period he settled in Vienna and worked as a tutor in a family friendly with Freud's. He met Freud on informal occasions when the families went on outings together.

These encounters may have been the impetus to accept a teaching appointment at an American school in Vienna founded by Dorothy Burlingham and directed by Peter Blos (both now well known on the American psychiatric scene). During these years (the late 1920s) he also undertook and completed psychoanalytic training with Anna Freud and August Aichhorn. Even at the outset of his career, Erikson gave evidence of the breadth of his interests and activities by being trained and certified as a Montessori teacher. Not surprisingly, in view of that training, Erikson's first articles dealt with psychoanalysis and education.

It was while in Vienna that Erikson met and married Joan Mowat Serson, an American artist of Canadian descent. They came to America in 1933, when Erikson was invited to practice and teach in Boston. Erikson was, in fact, one of the first if not the first child-analyst in the Boston area. During the next two decades he held clinical and academic appointments at Harvard, Yale and Berkeley. In 1951 he joined a group of psychiatrists and psychologists who moved to Stockbridge, Mass., to start a new program at the Austen Riggs Center, a private residential treatment center for disturbed young people. Erikson remained at Riggs until 1961, when he was appointed professor of human development and lecturer on psychiatry at Harvard. Throughout his career he has always held two or three appointments simultaneously and has traveled extensively.

Perhaps because he had been an artist first, Erikson has never been a conventional psychoanalyst. When he was treating children, for example, he always insisted on visiting his young patients' homes and on having dinner with the families. Likewise, in the 1930s, when anthropological investigation was described to him by his friends Scudder McKeel, Alfred Kroeber and Margaret Mead, he decided to do field work on an Indian reservation. "When I realized that Sioux is the name which we [in Europe] pronounced 'See ux' and which for us was *the* American Indian, I could not resist." Erikson thus antedated the anthropologists who swept over the Indian reservations in the post-Depression years. (So numerous were the field workers at that time that the stock joke was that an Indian family could be defined as a mother, a father, children and an anthropologist.)

Erikson did field work not only with the Oglala Sioux of Pine Ridge, S.D. (the tribe that slew Custer and was in turn slaughtered at the Battle of Wounded Knee), but also with the salmon-fishing Yurok of Northern California. His reports on these experiences revealed his special gift for sensing and entering into the world views and modes of thinking of cultures other than his own.

It was while he was working with the Indians that Erikson began to note syndromes which he could not explain within the confines of traditional psychoanalytic theory. Central to many an adult Indian's emotional problems seemed to be his sense of uprootedness and lack of continuity between his present life-style and that portrayed in tribal history. Not only did the Indian sense a break with the past, but he could not identify with a future requiring assimilation of the white culture's values. The problems faced by such men, Erikson recognized, had to do with the ego and with culture and only incidentally with sexual drives.

The impressions Erikson gained on the reservations were reinforced during World War II when he worked at a veterans' rehabilitation center at Mount Zion Hospital in San Francisco. Many of the soldiers he and his colleagues saw seemed not to fit the traditional "shell shock" or "malingerer" cases of World War I. Rather, it seemed to Erikson that many of these men had lost the sense of who and what they were. They were having trouble reconciling their activities, attitudes and feelings as soldiers with the activities, attitudes and feelings they had known before the war. Accordingly, while these men may well have had difficulties with repressed or conflicted drives, their main problem seemed to be, as Erikson came to speak of it at the time, "identity confusion."

It was almost a decade before Erikson set forth the implications of his clinical observations in *Childhood and Society*. In that book, the summation and integration of 15 years of research, he made three major contributions to the study of the human ego. He posited (1) that, side by side with the stages of psychosexual development described by Freud (the oral, anal, phallic, genital, Oedipal and pubertal), were psychosocial stages of ego development, in which the individual had to establish new basic orientations to himself and his social world; (2) that personality development continued throughout the whole life cycle; and (3) that each stage had a positive *as well as* a negative component.

Much about these contributions—and about Erikson's way of thinking—can be understood by looking at his scheme of life stages. Erikson identifies eight stages in the human life cycle, in each of which a new dimension of "social interaction" becomes possible—that is, a new dimension in a person's interaction with himself, and with his social environment.

TRUST VS. MISTRUST

The first stage corresponds to the oral stage in classical psychoanalytic theory and usually extends through the first year of life. In Erikson's view, the new dimension of social interaction that emerges during this period involves basic *trust* at the one extreme, and *mistrust* at the other. The degree to which the child comes to trust the world, other people and himself depends to a considerable extent upon the quality of the care that he receives. The infant whose needs are met when they arise, whose discomforts are quickly removed, who is cuddled, fondled, played with and talked to, develops a sense of the world as a safe place to be and of people as helpful and dependable. When, however, the care is inconsistent, inadequate and rejecting, it fosters a basic mistrust, an attitude of fear and suspicion on the part of the infant toward the world in general and people in particular that will carry through to later stages of development.

It should be said at this point that the problem of basic trust-versus-mistrust (as is true for all the later dimensions) is not resolved once and for all during the first year of life; it arises again at each successive stage of development. There is both hope and danger in this. The child who enters school with a sense of mistrust may come to trust a particular teacher who has taken the trouble to make herself trustworthy; with this second chance, he overcomes his early mistrust. On the other hand, the child who comes through infancy with a vital sense of trust can still have his sense of mistrust activated at a later stage, if, say, his parents are divorced and separated under acrimonious circumstances.

This point was brought home to me in a very direct way by a 4-year-old patient I saw in a court clinic. He was being seen at the court clinic because his adoptive parents, who had had him for six months, now wanted to give him back to the agency. They claimed that he was cold and unloving, took things and could not be trusted. He was indeed a cold and apathetic boy, but with good reason. About a year after his illegitimate birth, he was taken away from his mother, who had a drinking problem, and was shunted back and forth among several foster homes. Initially he had tried to relate to the persons in the foster homes, but the relationships never had a chance to develop because he was moved at just the wrong times. In the end he gave up trying to reach out to others, because the inevitable separations hurt too much.

Like the burned child who dreads the flame, this emotionally burned child shunned the pain of emotional involvement. He had trusted his mother, but now he trusted no one. Only years of devoted care and patience could now undo the damage that had been done to this child's sense of trust.

AUTONOMY VS. DOUBT

Stage Two spans the second and third years of life, the period which Freudian theory calls the anal stage. Erikson sees here the emergence of *autonomy*. This autonomy dimension builds upon the child's new motor and mental abilities. At this stage the child can not only walk but also climb, open and close, drop, push and pull, hold and let go. The child takes pride in these new accomplishments and wants to do everything himself, whether it be pulling the wrapper off a piece of candy, selecting the vitamin out of the bottle or flushing the toilet. If parents recognize the young child's need to do what he is capable of doing at his own pace and in his own time, then he develops a sense that he is able to control his muscles, his impulses, himself and, not insignificantly, his environment—the sense of autonomy.

When, however, his caretakers are impatient and do for him what he is capable of doing himself, they reinforce a sense of shame and doubt. To be sure, every parent has rushed a child at times and children are hardy enough to endure such lapses. It is only when caretaking is consistently over-protective and criticism of "accidents" (whether these be wetting, soiling, spilling or breaking things) is harsh and unthinking that the child develops an excessive sense of shame with respect to other people and an excessive sense of doubt about his own abilities to control his world and himself.

If the child leaves this stage with less autonomy than shame or doubt, he will be handicapped in his attempts to achieve autonomy in adolescence and adulthood. Contrariwise, the child who moves through this stage with his sense of autonomy buoyantly outbalancing his feelings of shame and doubt is well prepared to be autonomous at later phases in the life cycle. Again, however, the balance of autonomy to shame and doubt set up during this period can be changed in either positive or negative directions by later events.

It might be well to note, in addition, that too much autonomy can be as harmful as too little. I have in mind a patient of 7 who had a heart condition. He had learned very quickly how terrified his parents were of any signs in him of cardiac difficulty. With the psychological acuity given to children, he soon ruled the household. The family could not go shopping, or for a drive, or on a holiday if he did not approve. On those rare occasions when the parents had had enough and defied him, he would get angry and his purple hue and gagging would frighten them into submission.

Actually, this boy was frightened of this power (as all children would be) and was really eager to give it up. When the parents and the boy came to realize this, and to recognize that a little shame and doubt were a worthy counterpoise to an inflated sense of autonomy, the three of them could once again assume their normal roles.

INITIATIVE VS. GUILT

In this stage (the genital stage of classical psychoanalysis) the child, age 4 to 5, is pretty much master of his body and can ride a tricycle, run, cut and hit. He can thus initiate motor activities of various sorts on his own and no longer merely responds to or imitates the actions of other children. The same holds true for his language and fantasy activities. Accordingly, Erikson argues that the social dimension that appears at this stage has *initiative* at one of its poles and *guilt* at the other.

Whether the child will leave this stage with his sense of initiative far outbalancing his sense of guilt depends to a considerable extent upon how parents respond to his self-initiated activities. Children who are given much freedom and opportunity to initiate motor play such as running, bike riding, sliding, skating, tussling and wrestling have their sense of initiative reinforced. Initiative is also reinforced when parents answer their children's questions (intellectual initiative) and do not deride or inhibit fantasy or play activity. On the other hand, if the child is made to feel that his motor activity is bad, that his questions are a nuisance and that his play is silly and stupid, then he may develop a sense of guilt over self-initiated activities in general that will persist through later life stages.

INDUSTRY VS. INFERIORITY

Stage Four is the age period from 6 to 11, the elementary school years (described by classical psychoanalysis as the *latency phase*). It is a time during which the child's love for the parent of the opposite sex and rivalry with the same sexed parent (elements in the so-called family romance) are quiescent. It is also a period during which the child becomes capable of deductive reasoning, and of playing and learning by rules. It is not until this period, for example, that children can really play marbles, checkers and other "take turn" games that require obedience to rules. Erikson argues that the psychosocial dimension that emerges during this period has a sense of *industry* at one extreme and a sense of *inferiority* at the other.

The term *industry* nicely captures a dominant theme of this period during which the concern with how things are made, how they work and what they do predominates. It is the Robinson Crusoe age in the sense that the enthusiasm and minute detail with which Crusoe describes his activities appeals to the child's own budding sense of industry. When children are encouraged in their efforts to make, do, or build practical things (whether it be to construct creepy crawlers, tree houses, or airplane models—or to cook, bake or sew), are allowed to finish their products, and are praised and rewarded for the results, then the sense of industry is enhanced. But parents who see their children's efforts at making and doing as "mischief," and as simply "making a mess," help to encourage in children a sense of inferiority.

During these elementary-school years, however, the child's world includes more than the home. Now social institutions other than the family come to play a central role in the developmental crisis of the individual. (Here Erikson introduced still another advance in psychoanalytic theory, which heretofore concerned itself only with the effects of the parents' behavior upon the child's development.)

A child's school experiences affect his industry-inferiority balance. The child, for example, with an I.Q. of 80 to 90 has a particularly traumatic school experience, even when his sense of industry is rewarded and encouraged at home. He is "too bright" to be in special classes, but "too slow" to compete with children of average ability. Consequently he experiences constant failures in his academic efforts that reinforce a sense of inferiority.

On the other hand, the child who had his sense of industry derogated at home can have it revitalized at school through the offices of a sensitive and committed teacher. Whether the child develops a sense of industry or inferiority, therefore, no longer depends solely on the caretaking efforts of the parents but on the actions and offices of other adults as well.

IDENTITY VS. ROLE CONFUSION

When the child moves into adolescence (Stage Five—roughly the ages 12–18), he encounters, according to traditional psychoanalytic theory, a reawakening of the family-romance problem of early childhood. His means of resolving the problem is to seek and find a romantic partner of his own generation. While Erikson does not deny this aspect of adolescence, he points out that there are other problems as well. The adolescent matures mentally as well as physiologically and, in addition to the new feelings, sensations and desires he experiences as a result of changes in his body, he develops a multitude of new ways of looking at and thinking about the world. Among other things, those in adolescence can now think about other people's thinking and wonder about what other people think of them. They can also conceive of ideal families, religions and societies which they then compare with the imperfect families, religions and societies of their own experience. Finally, adolescents become capable of constructing theories and philosophies designed to bring all the varied and conflicting aspects of society into a working, harmonious and peaceful whole. The adolescent, in a word, is an impatient idealist who believes that it is as easy to realize an ideal as it is to imagine it.

In his approach to his work, Erikson appears neither drawn nor driven, but rather to be following an inner schedule as natural as the life cycle.

Erikson believes that the new interpersonal dimension which emerges during this period has to do with a sense of *ego identity* at the positive end and a sense of *role confusion* at the negative end. That is to say, given the adolescent's newfound integrative abilities, his task is to bring together all of the things he has learned about himself as a son, student, athlete, friend, Scout, newspaper boy, and so on, and integrate these different images of himself into a whole that makes sense and that shows continuity with the past while preparing for the future. To the extent that the young person succeeds in this endeavor, he arrives at a sense of psychosocial identity, a sense of who he is, where he has been and where he is going.

In contrast to the earlier stages, where parents play a more or less direct role in the determination of the result of the developmental crises, the influence of parents during this stage is much more indirect. If the young person reaches adolescence with, thanks to his parents, a vital sense of trust, autonomy, initiative and industry, then his chances of arriving at a meaningful sense of ego identity are much enhanced. The reverse, of course, holds true for the young person who enters adolescence with considerable mistrust, shame, doubt, guilt and inferiority. Preparation for a successful adolescence, and the attainment of an integrated psychosocial identity must, therefore, begin in the cradle.

Erikson has offered hope for all of us by showing that each phase of growth has its strengths as well as its weaknesses and that failures at one stage can be rectified by successes at later stages.

Over and above what the individual brings with him from his childhood, the attainment of a sense of personal identity depends upon the social milieu in which he or she grows up. For example, in a society where women are to some extent second-class citizens, it may be harder for females to arrive at a sense of psychosocial identity. Likewise at times, such as the present, when rapid social and technological change breaks down many traditional values, it may be more difficult for young people to find continuity between what they learned and experienced as children and what they learn and experience as adolescents. At such times young people often seek causes that give their lives meaning and direction. The activism of the current generation of young people may well stem, in part at least, from this search.

When the young person cannot attain a sense of personal identity, either because of an unfortunate childhood or difficult social circumstances, he shows a certain amount of *role confusion*—a sense of not knowing what he is, where he belongs or whom he belongs to. Such confusion is a frequent symptom in delinquent young people. Promiscuous adolescent girls, for example, often seem to have a fragmented sense of ego identity. Some young people seek a "negative identity," an identity opposite to the one prescribed for them by their family and friends. Having an identity as a "delinquent," or as a "hippie," or even as an "acid head," may sometimes be preferable to having no identity at all.

In some cases young people do not seek a negative identity so much as they have it thrust upon them. I remember another court case in which the defendant was an attractive 16-year-old girl who had been found "tricking it" in a trailer located just outside the grounds of an Air Force base. From about the age of 12, her mother had encouraged her to dress seductively and to go out with boys. When she returned from dates, her sexually frustrated mother demanded a kiss-by-kiss, caress-by-caress description of the evening's activities. After the mother had vicariously satisfied her sexual needs, she proceeded to call her daughter a "whore" and a "dirty tramp." As the girl told me, "Hell, I have the name, so I might as well play the role."

Failure to establish a clear sense of personal identity at adolescence does not guarantee perpetual failure. And the person who attains a working sense of ego identity in adolescence will of necessity encounter

challenges and threats to that identity as he moves through life. Erikson, perhaps more than any other personality theorist, has emphasized that life is constant change and that confronting problems at one stage in life is not a guarantee against the reappearance of these problems at later stages, or against the finding of new solutions to them.

INTIMACY VS. ISOLATION

Stage Six in the life cycle is young adulthood; roughly the period of courtship and early family life that extends from late adolescence till early middle age. For this stage, and the stages described hereafter, classical psychoanalysis has nothing new or major to say. For Erikson, however, the previous attainment of a sense of personal identity and the engagement in productive work that marks this period gives rise to a new interpersonal dimension of *intimacy* at the one extreme and *isolation* at the other.

When Erikson speaks of intimacy he means much more than lovemaking alone; he means the ability to share with and care about another person without fear of losing oneself in the process. In the case of intimacy, as in the case of identity, success or failure no longer depends directly upon the parents but only indirectly as they have contributed to the individual's success or failure at the earlier stages. Here, too, as in the case of identity, social conditions may help or hinder the establishment of a sense of intimacy. Likewise, intimacy need not involve sexuality; it includes the relationship between friends. Soldiers who have served together under the most dangerous circumstances often develop a sense of commitment to one another that exemplifies intimacy in its broadest sense. If a sense of intimacy is not established with friends, or a marriage partner, the result, in Erikson's view, is a sense of isolation—of being alone without anyone to share with or care for.

GENERATIVITY VS. SELF-ABSORPTION

This stage—middle age—brings with it what Erikson speaks of as either *generativity* or *self-absorption*, and stagnation. What Erikson means by generativity is that the person begins to be concerned with others beyond his immediate family, with future generations and the nature of the society and the world in which those generations will live. Generativity does not reside only in parents; it can be found in any individual who actively concerns himself with the welfare of young people and with making the world a better place for them to live and to work.

Those who fail to establish a sense of generativity fall into a state of self-absorption in which their personal needs and comforts are of predominant concern. A fictional case of self-absorption is Dickens' Scrooge in *A Christmas Carol*. In his one-sided concern with money and in his disre-

gard for the interests and welfare of his young employee, Bob Cratchit, Scrooge exemplifies the self-absorbed, embittered (the two often go together) old man. Dickens also illustrated, however, what Erikson points out: namely, that unhappy solutions to life's crises are not irreversible. Scrooge, at the end of the tale, manifested both a sense of generativity and of intimacy which he had not experienced before.

INTEGRITY VS. DESPAIR

Stage Eight in the Eriksonian scheme corresponds roughly to the period when the individual's major efforts are nearing completion and when there is time for reflection—and for the enjoyment of grandchildren, if any. The psychosocial dimension that comes into prominence now has *integrity* on one hand and *despair* on the other.

The sense of integrity arises from the individual's ability to look back on his life with satisfaction. At the other extreme is the individual who looks back upon his life as a series of missed opportunities and missed directions; now in the twilight years he realizes that it is too late to start again. For such a person the inevitable result is a sense of despair at what might have been.

These, then, are the major stages in the life cycle as described by Erikson. Their presentation, for one thing, frees the clinician to treat adult emotional problems as failures (in part at least) to solve genuinely adult personality crises and not, as heretofore, as mere residuals of infantile frustrations and conflicts. This view of personality growth, moreover, takes some of the onus off parents and takes account of the role which society and the person himself play in the formation of an individual personality. Finally, Erikson has offered hope for us all by demonstrating that each phase of growth has its strengths as well as its weaknesses and that failures at one stage of development can be rectified by successes at later stages.

The reason that these ideas, which sound so agreeable to "common sense," are in fact so revolutionary has a lot to do with the state of psychoanalysis in America. As formulated by Freud, psychoanalysis encompassed a theory of personality development, a method of studying the human mind and, finally, procedures for treating troubled and unhappy people. Freud viewed this system as a scientific one, open to revision as new facts and observations accumulated.

The system was, however, so vehemently attacked that Freud's followers were constantly in the position of having to defend Freud's views. Perhaps because of this situation, Freud's system became, in the hands of some of his followers and defenders, a dogma upon which all theoretical innovation, clinical observation and therapeutic practice had to be grounded. That this attitude persists is evidenced in the recent remark by a psychoanalyst that he believed psychotic patients could not be treated by psychoanalysis because "Freud said so." Such attitudes, in which Freud's authority rather than observation and data is the basis of deciding what is true and what is false, has contributed to the disrepute in which psychoanalysis is widely held today.

Erik Erikson has broken out of this scholasticism and has had the courage to say that Freud's discoveries and practices were the start and not the end of the study and treatment of the human personality. In addition to advocating the modifications of psychoanalytic theory outlined above, Erikson has also suggested modifications in therapeutic practice, particularly in the treatment of young patients. "Young people in severe trouble are not fit for the couch," he writes. "They want to face you, and they want you to face them, not as a facsimile of a parent, or wearing the mask of a professional helper, but as a kind of over-all individual a young person can live with or despair of."

Erikson has had the boldness to remark on some of the negative effects that distorted notions of psychoanalysis have had on society at large. Psychoanalysis, he says, has contributed to a widespread fatalism—"even as we were trying to devise, with scientific determinism, a therapy for the few, we were led to promote an ethical disease among the many."

Perhaps Erikson's innovations in psychoanalytic theory are best exemplified in his psycho-historical writings, in which he combines psychoanalytic insight with a true historical imagination. After the publication of *Childhood and Society,* Erikson undertook the application of his scheme of the human life cycle to the study of historical persons. He wrote a series of brilliant essays on men as varied as Maxim Gorky, George Bernard Shaw and Freud himself. These studies were not narrow case histories but rather reflected Erikson's remarkable grasp of Europe's social and political history, as well as of its literature. (His mastery of American folklore, history and literature is equally remarkable.)

While Erikson's major biographical studies were yet to come, these early essays already revealed his unique psycho-history method. For one thing, Erikson always chose men whose lives fascinated him in one way or another, perhaps because of some conscious or unconscious affinity with them. Erikson thus had a sense of community with his subjects which he adroitly used (he calls it *disciplined subjectivity*) to take his subject's point of view and to experience the world as that person might.

Secondly, Erikson chose to elaborate a particular crisis or episode in the individual's life which seemed to crystallize a life-theme that united the activities of his past and gave direction to his activities for the future. Then, much as an artist might, Erikson proceeded to fill in the background of the episode and add social and historical perspective. In a very real sense Erikson's biographical sketches are like paintings which direct the viewer's gaze from a focal point of attention to background and back again, so that one's appreciation of the focal area is enriched by having pursued the picture in its entirety.

This method was given its first major test in Erikson's study of *Young Man Luther*. Originally, Erikson planned only a brief study of Luther, but "Luther proved too bulky a man to be merely a chapter in a book." Erikson's involvement with Luther dated from his youth, when, as a wandering artist, he happened to hear the Lord's Prayer in Luther's German. "Never knowingly having heard it, I had the experience, as seldom before or after, of a wholeness captured in a few simple words, of poetry fusing the aesthetic and the moral; those who have suddenly 'heard' the Gettysburg Address will know what I mean."

Erikson's interest in Luther may have had other roots as well. In some ways, Luther's unhappiness with papal intermediaries of Christianity resembled on a grand scale Erikson's own dissatisfaction with the intermediaries of Freud's system. In both cases some of the intermediaries had so distorted the original teachings that what was being preached in the name of the master came close to being the opposite of what he had himself proclaimed. While it is not possible to describe Erikson's treatment of Luther here, one can get some feeling for Erikson's brand of historical analysis from his sketch of Luther:

"Luther was a very troubled and a very gifted young man who had to create his own cause on which to focus his fidelity in the Roman Catholic world as it was then. . . . He first became a monk and tried to solve his scruples by being an exceptionally good monk. But even his superiors thought that he tried much too hard. He felt himself to be such a sinner that he began to lose faith in the charity of God and his superiors told him, 'Look, God doesn't hate you, you hate God or else you would trust Him to accept your prayers.' But I would like to make clear that someone like Luther becomes a historical person only because he also has an acute understanding of historical actuality and knows how to 'speak to the condition' of his times. Only then do inner struggles become representative of those of a large number of vigorous and sincere young people—and begin to interest some troublemakers and hangers-on."

After Erikson's study of *Young Man Luther* (1958), he turned his attention to "middle-aged" Gandhi. As did Luther, Gandhi evoked for Erikson childhood memories. Gandhi led his first nonviolent protest in India in 1918 on behalf of some mill workers, and Erikson, then a young man of 16, had read glowing accounts of the event. Almost a half a century later Erikson was invited to Ahmedabad, an industrial city in western India, to give a seminar on the human life cycle. Erikson discovered that Ahmedabad was the city in which Gandhi had led the demonstration about which Erikson had read as a youth. Indeed, Erikson's host was none other than Ambalal Sarabahai, the benevolent industrialist who had been Gandhi's host—as well as antagonist—in the 1918 wage dispute. Throughout his stay in Ahmedabad, Erikson continued to encounter people and places that were related to Gandhi's initial experiments with nonviolent techniques.

The more Erikson learned about the event at Ahmedabad, the more intrigued he became with its pivotal importance in Gandhi's career. It seemed to be the historical moment upon which all the earlier events of Gandhi's life converged and from which diverged all of his later endeavors. So captured was Erikson by the event at Ahmedabad, that he returned the following year to research a book on Gandhi in which the event would serve as a fulcrum.

       *   *   *

At least part of Erikson's interest in Gandhi may have stemmed from certain parallels in their lives. The 1918 event marked Gandhi's emergence as a national political leader. He was 48 at the time, and had become involved reluctantly, not so much out of a need for power or fame as out of a genuine conviction that something had to be done about the disintegration of Indian culture. Coincidentally, Erikson's book, *Childhood and Society,* appeared in 1950 when Erikson was 48, and it is that book which brought him national prominence in the mental health field. Like Gandhi, too, Erikson reluctantly did what he felt he had to do (namely, publish his observations and conclusions) for the benefit of his ailing profession and for the patients treated by its practitioners. So while Erikson's affinity with Luther seemed to derive from comparable professional identity crises, his affinity for Gandhi appears to derive from a parallel crisis of generativity. A passage from *Gandhi's Truth* (from a chapter wherein Erikson addresses himself directly to his subject) helps to convey Erikson's feeling for his subject.

"So far, I have followed you through the loneliness of your childhood and through the experiments and the scruples of your youth. I have affirmed my belief in your ceaseless endeavor to perfect yourself as a man who came to feel that he was the only one available to re-verse India's fate. You experimented with what to you were debilitating temptations and you did gain vigor and agility from your victories over yourself. Your identity could be no less than that of universal man, although you had to become an Indian—and one close to the masses—first."

The following passage speaks to Erikson's belief in the general significance of Gandhi's efforts:

"We have seen in Gandhi's development the strong attraction of one of those more inclusive identities: that of an enlightened citizen of the British Empire. In proving himself willing neither to abandon vital ties to his native tradition nor to sacrifice lightly a Western education which eventually contributed to his ability to help defeat British hegemony— in all of these seeming contradictions Gandhi showed himself on intimate terms with the actualities of his era. For in all parts of the world, the struggle now is for the *anticipatory development of more inclusive identities* . . . I submit then, that Gandhi, in his immense intuition for historical actuality and his capacity to assume leadership in 'truth in action,' may have created a ritualization through which men, equipped with both realism and strength, can face each other with mutual confidence."

There is now more and more teaching of Erikson's concepts in psychiatry, psychology, education and social work in America and in other parts of the world. His description of the stages of the life cycle are summarized in major textbooks in all of these fields and clinicians are increasingly looking at their cases in Eriksonian terms.

Research investigators have, however, found Erikson's formulations somewhat difficult to test. This is not surprising, inasmuch as Erikson's conceptions, like Freud's, take into account the infinite complexity of the human personality. Current research methodologies are, by and large, still not able to deal with these complexities at their own level, and distortions are inevitable when such concepts as "identity" come to be defined in terms of responses to a questionnaire.

Likewise, although Erikson's life-stages have an intuitive "rightness' about them, not everyone agrees with his formulations. Douvan and Adelson in their book, *The Adolescent Experience,* argue that while his identity theory may hold true for boys, it doesn't for girls. This argument is based on findings which suggest that girls postpone identity consolidation until after marriage (and intimacy) have been established. Such postponement occurs, say Douvan and Adelson, because a woman's identity is partially defined by the identity of the man whom she marries. This view does not really contradict Erikson's, since he recognizes that later events, such as marriage, can help to resolve both current and past developmental crises. For the woman, but not for the man, the problems of identity and intimacy may be solved concurrently.

Objections to Erikson's formulations have come from other directions as well. Robert W. White, Erikson's good friend and colleague at Harvard, has a long standing (and warm-hearted) debate with Erikson over his life-stages. White believes that his own theory of "competence motivation," a theory which has received wide recognition, can account for the phenomena of ego development much more economically than can Erikson's stages. Erikson has, however, little interest in debating the validity of the stages he has described. As an artist he recognizes that there are many different ways to view one and the same phenomenon and that a perspective that is congenial to one person will be repugnant to another. He offers his stage-wise description of the life cycle for those who find such perspectives congenial and not as a world view that everyone should adopt.

It is this lack of dogmatism and sensitivity to the diversity and complexity of the human personality which helps to account for the growing recognition of Erikson's contribution within as well as without the helping professions. Indeed, his psycho-historical investigations have originated a whole new field of study which has caught the interest of historians and political scientists alike. (It has also intrigued his wife, Joan, who has published pieces on Eleanor Roosevelt and who has a book on Saint Francis in press.) A recent issue of *Daedalus*, the journal for the American Academy of Arts and Sciences, was entirely devoted to psycho-historical and psychopolitical investigations of creative leaders by authors from diverse disciplines who have been stimulated by Erikson's work.

Now in his 68th year, Erikson maintains the pattern of multiple activities and appointments which has characterized his entire career. He spends the fall in Cambridge, Mass., where he teaches a large course on "the human life cycle" for Harvard seniors. The spring semester is spent at his home in Stockbridge, Mass., where he participates in case conferences and staff seminars at the Austen Riggs Center. His summers are spent on Cape Cod. Although Erikson's major commitment these days is to his psycho-historical investigation, he is embarking on a study of pre-school children's play constructions in different settings and countries, a follow-up of some research he conducted with pre-adolescents more than a quarter-century ago. He is also planning to review other early

observations in the light of contemporary change. In his approach to his work, Erikson appears neither drawn nor driven, but rather to be following an inner schedule as natural as the life cycle itself.

Although Erikson, during his decade of college teaching, has not seen any patients or taught at psychoanalytic institutes, he maintains his dedication to psychoanalysis and views his psycho-historical investigations as an applied branch of that discipline. While some older analysts continue to ignore Erikson's work, there is increasing evidence (including a recent poll of psychiatrists and psychoanalysts) that he is having a rejuvenating influence upon a discipline which many regard as dead or dying. Young analysts are today proclaiming a "new freedom" to see Freud in historical perspective—which reflects the Eriksonian view that one can recognize Freud's greatness without bowing to conceptual precedent.

Accordingly, the reports of the demise of psychoanalysis may have been somewhat premature. In the work of Erik Erikson, at any rate, psychoanalysis lives and continues to beget life.

The New York Times

PREVIEWING

The Most Efficient Reading Strategies

There are two extraordinarily simple strategies that can double your "reading comprehension" without effort. In fact, both are things you already do naturally, unless your teachers succeeded in curbing such "misbehavior." They are:

1. Read at a variable speed.
2. Preview.

Reading studies in 1987 reported by Richard Wagner and Robert J. Sternberg found that highly efficient readers don't read faster or with greater effort than ordinary readers, but they "have the intelligence to know what to read and how to read it. [He or she is] a master of time allocation and wastes no time responding inappropriately."

Perhaps your grade school teachers, coping with students at different reading levels, struggled valiantly to keep you all on the same page. Reading at a consistent speed and "knowing the place" became more important than letting your curiosity push you ahead to find out more. Happily, you can now find your own place.

You absorb information most efficiently when you give yourself permission to read at different speeds. Start by flying high over what you already know. Whenever something stands out that is different, swoop down and examine it. This lets you use the structure of what you already know to notice and file new information.

Another childhood injunction to discard is "Don't look ahead." There you were, eager to flip through the entire book, but that was often discouraged. Your new instruction is to preview long articles and books before you start. Previewing gives you a lot back for a very little energy.

Anytime you set out on a trip, a map helps you to get an idea of the distances and terrain. Previewing is like scanning a map. You look over the territory to see how long the journey will be, how simple or complicated.

By "pre-viewing" reading material, you may find signposts in the form of headings and chapter names. The lengths of the paragraphs will provide clues on how thickly packed the ideas are. Lots of short paragraphs usually mean lots of different ideas but fewer supporting details. Long paragraphs hint at fewer ideas but lots of supporting data.

There are two big advantages to previewing material:

1. Familiarizing yourself with the material before reading makes it possible to read it faster later. When you absorb even a little of it, going through it again is easier because you are more secure with "familiar" material. The recognizable landmarks increase your motivation, and your mind is less likely to wander.
2. You may learn all you need to know from the headings, pictures, and charts *or* decide you don't need to read it after all. Previewing gives you a lot back for a little energy.

WHAT TO DO

Preview the following material, reading *only* the headings, and then take the quiz that follows.

OVERLAND JOURNEY TO THE PACIFIC

by K. Peletz

During the 1850's, there was a mass migration to the Pacific which exploded with the opening of the Oregon territory in 1846 and the Gold Rush of 1848. It is estimated that from the 1840's to the 1870's, as many as 250,000 to half a million people journeyed to the Pacific Coast and other parts of the West. This was one of the best documented movements in American history.

The overland journey to the Pacific in the 1850's presented a variety of experiences to the emigrants. There were enjoyable times and difficult times, hardships and dangers. The journey was long and tiresome. The chances of encountering unfriendly Indians, disease or raging rivers were high. Almost everyone was faced with the reality and closeness of death as they fought to survive the long journey across the country.

PIONEERS KEPT DIARIES

Because the experience was so different from everyday life, many chose to write about it. Although each writer had his own style, each followed a similar pattern: preparation, sadness at departure, the excitement of the start. Most tell of the "firsts" and new things they came across. Most comment on scenic wonders and most describe the same places: Courthouse Rock, Chimney Rock, Ash Hollow, Independence Rock, Devil's Gate and the City of Rocks. Much of the scenery was flat and dreary and anything interesting gave journalists something to write about. All document something of the pleasures and hardships of the trip. Most expressed concerns about the practical aspects of the trip and the health and safety of the traveling party.

Emigrants left many diaries, letters and written recollections. The quality of writing varies, but all contain a lot of information about individuals, travel and the attitudes and beliefs of the time. Each writer had different experiences and observed different things, although there is a pattern to all of them.

WOMEN AND MEN HAD DIFFERENT PERSPECTIVES

It can be seen that the style of men's and women's diaries differs greatly. The women usually wrote in the first person and shared much more of what they were feeling. This is apparent from the following entry of Mary Powers:

Oh, how I have felt to see how they would whip those poor oxen. The sides of some of them would be all covered with great gashes and the blood would be dripping from their bellies.

Men rarely expressed themselves in the first person and tended to use "we," although this only referred to the men in the group. Rarely did men show any feelings or emotions and they tended to just record the events of the journey. This can be seen in the following passage written by a man:

September 23, 1843. We went up the ford and fastened our wagons together as we did at the upper crossing and drove about 8 or 10 inches deeper than the upper one. Then we went strate a craws, and camped on the bank. Grazing indifferent.

EMIGRANTS WERE A DIVERSE GROUP

The emigrants represented almost every state of European society. There were those from the country and those from the city, those who were educated and those who were barely literate, those who were young and those who were old, and, to an extent, there were those who were rich and those who were poor.

Basically, the emigrants were middle class. Guides estimated that the cost of animals, tools and provisions for one wagon was between $600 and $700. The very poor could not afford the initial outfitting cost plus other expenses of the journey, such as tools, repairs, additional clothing and food. The very rich had little reason to migrate to the Pacific.

SEEKING THE BETTER LIFE

They came for many reasons. The winters in the West were milder, the climate healthier and there was the promise of free land and changed circumstances. Farmers wanted to claim new and better farmland. Clarence Danhof wrote:

> The impulse toward removal to the West did not arise from a desire to recreate the pattern of Eastern farms left behind, but came from a vision of a rich soil, producing an abundant surplus of products, readily salable for cash upon markets which, if not immediately available, would certainly develop and could somehow be reached.

According to Phoebe Judson who traveled in 1853:

> The motive that induced us to part with the pleasant associations and the dear friends of our childhood days was to obtain from the government of the U.S. a grant of land that 'Uncle Sam' had promised to give the head of a family who settled in this new country.

PREPARING FOR A SIX-MONTH JOURNEY

There were many preparations that had to be made before departure. The trip took from four to six months of slow travel, covering about ten to twenty miles a day by wagon. The essentials had to be gathered. These included a wagon, a team, food, utensils and firearms. This was also difficult because of the weight limitations. Some families took extra wagons and had no need to worry about space and weight, while others were forced to economize. A family of four could just fit into one wagon, although a majority of families chose to take more than one.

Families needed to take all clothing, medicine, firearms and bullets, tools, domestic animals and utensils they would need on the journey plus most of the food. Often they had to choose between taking extra food or extra bullets to hunt on the way, between extra supplies for a longer journey or extra oxen that might shorten the time on the road.

SORROWS AND EXCITEMENT OF DEPARTURE

Departure was a sad time as the emigrants left home and friends to set off for new country 2000 miles away, knowing they might never return. Robert Milton wrote:

> As we drove off, very solemn feelings prevailed among all the company. As for my part, I do confess that I never felt more solemn in all my life before to think of the great journey which was before us and that I was in all probability going never to return again to my parents and friends to enjoy their smiling embraces, but the journey was commenced and now was no time to back out.

Upon starting out in 1857, Helen Carpenter wrote:

Ho, for California. At last we are on the way—only seven miles from home (which is to be home no longer), yet we have really started, and with good luck may some day reach the 'promised land.' The trip has been so long talked of, and the preparations have gone under so many disadvantages, that to be ready to start is something of an event.

TWO TRAILS WEST FROM THE MISSOURI

Families usually drove to the Missouri in small groups and then joined other groups to Oregon and California for support and protection. The most popular of the overland routes followed the Platte River to Fort Bridger, then turned northward toward the Columbia River and the Cascade Range or southward to the Humboldt River and the Sierra Nevada toward California.

There was another land route that began near Tucson and joined the trail along the Gila River to Yuma, turned south into Mexico and went northwest across the Forty Mile Desert to the southern California slopes.

A TYPICAL PIONEER DAY

Each day brought new vistas and challenges, but some things were routine. Helen Carpenter wrote:

From the time we get up in the morning until we are on the road it is necessary to hurry-scurry to get breakfast and put away the things that necessarily had to be pulled out last night. While under way, there is no room in the wagon for a visitor. Nooning is barely long enough to eat a cold bite and at night all the cooking utensils and provisions are to be gotten about the camp fire and cooking enough done to last until the next night. Although there is not much to cook, the difficulty and inconvenience in doing it amounts to a great deal. So, by the time one has squatted around the fire and cooked bread and bacon, made several trips to and from the wagon, washed the dishes (with no place to dry them) and gotten things ready for an early breakfast, some of the others have already gotten their nightcaps on. At any rate, it is time to bed.

NEW FRIENDSHIPS AND NEW SIGHTS

There were enjoyable times. Mary Bailey wrote of being "camped with our friends, the McGrews, or very near them. We received calls from all. It seems like seeing old friends to meet them." She wrote of pleasant times: "very pleasant weather, but dry and dusty. Nothing of importance has occurred. We see our friends that travel near us every day." And again: "We enjoy ourselves better as we get used to this way of traveling & living out of doors. We have good appetites and plenty to eat although we sit down and eat like Indians."

On her first view of Scott Bluffs, she called it "Most romantic scenery I ever saw. It would not require much imagination, however, to think it some ancient city with high walls, great towers and every prerequisite to it. Why, I could not compare it to anything else. Would like to have spent days there."

LOST, TIRED AND SICK

Travelers were sometimes disoriented. Robert Milton Wilson wrote:

Turned around north down a small creek. Traveled 20 miles and encamped. No person knew where they were or where they were going.

Helen Carpenter told of a dangerous river crossing: "Sitting in the wagon under such circumstances is not only very unpleasant, but dangerously near frightful, yet it is the only thing to do since these places must be crossed," and Mary Bailey described a 15-hour passage through a desert: "did not see anything but bones and dead animals."

The need for rest increased as the pressures of time became greater. Mary Bailey wrote: "How I wish we could have a day of rest. My eyes are getting very weak. Our faces and hands are chapped & sore."

Conditions of the trail were harsh, water quality often poor and the diet unbalanced: "About the only change we have from bread and bacon is bacon and bread."

Children and adults frequently fell from wagons, horses and cattle stampeded and short tempers produced gun fights. Merril Mattes noted that the most common accidents "in descending order of magnitude" were shootings, drownings, wagon mishaps and "injuries resulting from handling domestic animals."

Cholera, small pox, intestinal disorders and scurvy were common. Helen Carpenter wrote:

Consequently many have died at this point and their bodies lie in the stream and there is no other drinking water. It has come to be the rule that such conditions prevail. We are reminded of the old adage that 'one can get used to anything' and again of the calf that died 'just as it got used to doing without eating.' Are we to share its fate? It is getting very cold.

On one occasion the exhausted travelers built their campfire and discovered the next morning that it was situated on a grave. In their growing indifference to death, they joked about it and did not move it.

INDIANS FRIENDLY AT FIRST

Experiences with Indians varied depending on which tribe the travelers encountered and when they crossed the country. In the 1840's and early 1850's Indians were not a serious danger and didn't direct war parties at the emigrants.

Some Indians helped travelers by ferrying wagons, guiding lost parties and sharing food and drink. Often Indians visited the trains and swapped goods. Lavinia Porter wrote: "It truly seemed to us in our long journey traveling alone that the Indians watched over us. In our ignorant fearlessness, we came through the many hostile tribes unmolested and unhurt." On another occasion: "We received a visit from an Indian early in the morning. He brought a paper stating that the tribe were in a very destitute condition. This one was nearly naked. At night two others came and slept under the wagons."

Helen Carpenter wrote of friendly Indians visiting her camp:

A lot of company tonight . . . they call themselves the 'Piutahs.' We got some small fish from them which are very good. They also brought a few wild ducks . . . Thoe most of them can speak a little English. It was a great novelty to see them dance, which they did very energetically.

In the late 1850's and 1860's most people got through with little or no difficulty. Occasionally small parties were massacred, but travelers were more likely to encounter begging, thievery and horse stealing. The emigrants probably killed and injured more Indians than Indians did emigrants, stimulating the massive Indian resistance of the last quarter of the 18th century.

To warn each other of danger, travelers would leave messages beside the road, sometimes penciled on dried animal bones. Helen Carpenter told of finding such a note amidst a pile of feathers. The following day, her group encountered another who had found nine bodies at that site plus an injured woman, scalped and left for dead by marauding Indians.

LABOR DIVIDED BY SEXES

Men and women performed very different work. The women did the cooking, washing and caring for the children and were responsible for health and sanitation. Men tended the stock and wagons, selecting the roads and camp grounds and taking responsibility for the safety of the wagon train. Social life was basically masculine, for the women were always doing chores after the men's work was done. The men were free to socialize while the women cooked and washed.

Women did acquire new skills on the march, though. Mary Powers was very proud of her new abilities as a teamster. But most activities were still dictated by sex. Children played at catching fish and then the boys would pretend to clean them and the girls would pretend to cook them, set the table and serve them.

SOME SORRY THEY MADE THE JOURNEY

The first relief at reaching the Pacific Coast, leaving their cramped life in the wagons and eating a more varied diet sometimes gave way to depression when the realities of the new life became apparent.

Lucy Ide wrote: "Well, this is not so romantic; thoughts stray back (in spite of our attempts to the contrary) to the comfortable homes we left and the question arises in my mind—is this a good move—but echo answers back not a word."

Mary Powers expressed a stronger view:

If anyone should ask my advice about coming to this country in that way, I should say 'Take a good dose of arsenic one week before you think of starting. Your death would be speedier and easier and your friends would have more comfort in knowing where your bones were reposing.'

And Mary Bailey wrote:

It really seems as though it was not right for us to come to California & lost so much. I do not think that we shall be as well off as at home.

Californians seemed "A very delicate people, as their complexions contrast so strongly with those of the sun-burned travelers" according to Eliza Ann Egbert, but she noted that "one enthusiastic miner declared he would give an ounce of gold dust for the sight of (one of our) sunbonnets."

Yet, fortunately for the settlement of the United States, enough people were optimists who believed the unknown was better than the known and set out to better their place in life. They took their lives in their hands as they traveled 2000 miles across the plains to the new territory, participating in the largest voluntary mass movement in American history.

QUESTIONS

1. The story is about _____

2. The information came from _____

3. Men and women had _____ view of the experience.

4. _____ kinds of people made the journey.

5. They went looking for _____

6. The journey took _____

7. Departure was filled with _____ and _____

8. There were _____ trails from the Missouri.

9. Some of the pleasures of the journey were _____

   _____

10. Some of the hardships of the journey were _____

    _____

11. Indians were _____

12. When it came to labor on the trail, men and women _____

    _____

13. Some of the travelers were _____ they had made the journey.

Now check your answers against the article.
Number correct _____

WHAT TO DO

Read the foregoing article, "Overland Journey to the Pacific," quickly. What piques your interest? Notice what you want to gain from the article. As you read, make predictions about what's ahead.

Use your desire to know what happened to spur you on at a faster speed than you are accustomed to so far. Push against your old speed boundaries, temporarily tolerating the discomfort of going faster than your old, slower reading habit.

Set your timer. When you finish reading the article, but before you answer the questions, write down your completion time to compute your words per minute later.

Write down your reading time in the blanks below. Then answer the questions and determine your comprehension level from your score, as calculated on p. 121.

Length of article: 3,276 words.

Mins. _____ Secs. _____ Words per minute _____

Comprehension _____%

QUESTIONS

Check the appropriate answer.

1. The mass migration across America to the Pacific occurred in the (a) 1600s, (b) 1700s, (c) 1800s, (d) 1900s.
2. Pioneers kept diaries (a) for publication, (b) to record their adventure, (c) as tax records, (d) because there was nothing else to do on the journey.
3. Very few rich people made the journey because (a) they could afford to go by sea around the cape, (b) they wanted to wait until the roads were better, (c) they were happy staying right where they were, (d) Uncle Sam would only give free land to the poor.
4. The journey took four to six months, and the wagons traveled (a) two to three miles a day, (b) ten to twenty miles a day, (c) about thirty miles a day, (d) fifty to sixty miles a day.
5. One of the two routes to the Pacific took the travelers through (a) Kentucky, (b) Canada, (c) Mexico, (d) Chicago.
6. The principal diet was (a) buffalo and corn, (b) beans and rice, (c) bread and bacon, (d) beef and wild deer.
7. The diseases that most plagued the emigrants were (a) diphtheria, typhoid, and measles, (b) tetanus and yellow fever, (c) whooping cough and anthrax, (d) smallpox, cholera, and scurvy.
8. Indians were (a) a major threat to the early settlers, (b) friendly at first, (c) rarely seen, (d) the reason so many children contracted whooping cough.
9. On the journey, women (a) were restricted to "women's work," (b) occasionally did "men's work," (c) shared all tasks with men equally, (d) were not required to work.
10. When they reached the Pacific, some of the emigrants (a) continued sleeping in their wagons, (b) were sorry they came, (c) sold their clothes to the natives, (d) had a big party.

Answers on page 121.

DAY 3 ANSWERS

THE SHY MONSTER

    I. Introduction/significance
   II. Description
  III. Reproduction
  IV. Diet
   V. History and name
  VI. Study of platypus

SCRUFFY DESERT PLANT

Compare your headings with those below. Of course, you won't have exactly the same words, but are the meanings similar?

  A. New source of rubber
  B. U.S. sources of natural rubber
  C. Potential shortages
  D. Guayule worked in the past; let's try it again
  E. Potential rubber yield of guayule
  F. Investors needed
  G. Importance of development

MAKE WAY FOR MICROWAVE COOKING

Compare your headings with those below. Of course, you won't have exactly the same words, but are the meanings similar?

Through paragraph 3—Discovery
Through paragraph 6—Significance
Through paragraph 7—History of oven manufacture
Through paragraph 13—What oven can do
Through paragraph 14—What oven can't do
Through paragraph 15—Solving these problems
Through paragraph 16—Cost and sales
Through paragraph 17—Energy effectiveness

ERIK ERIKSON'S EIGHT AGES OF MAN

Some Questions
 1. Who is Erikson?
 2. What does he emphasize in his biographical studies?
 3. How does he differ from Freud, Jung, Adler, Horney, Kardner, and Sullivan?
 4. What developments did Erikson concern himself with?
 5. What are the author's impressions of Erikson?
 6. What has Erikson written since 1960?
 7. What is the focus of these books?
 8. What is Erikson's background?
 9. How was Erikson different from conventional analysts?
10. What special groups did Erikson work with?
11. What were his three major contributions to the study of the human ego?

OVERLAND JOURNEY TO THE PACIFIC

1–c   2–b   3–c   4–b   5–c
6–c   7–d   8–b   9–b   10–b

Score 10% for each correct answer.
Words per minute _____ Comprehension _____%

COMPUTE YOUR RATE FOR "OVERLAND JOURNEY"
(Approximate number of words: 3,276)

Time	Wpm	Time	Wpm
1 min.	3276	5 min.	655
1 min. 15 sec.	2621	5 min. 15 sec.	624
1 min. 30 sec.	2184	5 min. 30 sec.	596
1 min. 45 sec.	1872	5 min. 45 sec.	570
2 min.	1638	6 min.	546
2 min. 15 sec.	1456	6 min. 15 sec.	524
2 min. 30 sec.	1310	6 min. 30 sec.	504
2 min. 45 sec.	1191	6 min. 45 sec.	485
3 min.	1092	7 min.	468
3 min. 15 sec.	1008	7 min. 15 sec.	452
3 min. 30 sec.	936	7 min. 30 sec.	437
3 min. 45 sec.	874	7 min. 45 sec.	423
4 min.	819	8 min.	410
4 min. 15 sec.	771	8 min. 15 sec.	397
4 min. 30 sec.	762	8 min. 30 sec.	385
4 min. 45 sec.	690	8 min. 45 sec.	374

Your rate is _____ wpm.
(Record this on page 224.)

DAY 4

The Opinion Pattern
The Thesis Pattern

THE OPINION PATTERN: To Persuade

OPINION
REASONS
SIGNIFICANCE

In the first few paragraphs or pages, the Opinion Pattern is sometimes hard to distinguish from the Problem Pattern or Thesis Pattern. Any writers offering a Problem Pattern or Thesis Pattern piece are automatically expressing an opinion. In their opinions, there is a problem or an important new way to evaluate something. You can identify an Opinion Pattern piece more by what is missing than by what is present. The pure Opinion Pattern offers *no* proposed solutions (essential for the Problem Pattern) and *no* originality of opinion supported by scientific proofs (both essential for the Thesis Pattern).

Why is it so important to recognize an Opinion Pattern when you see it? Because when you do, you won't read an opinion piece as if it were fact or "hard news." Editorial bias can be present in the most innocent piece as if it were fact or "hard news." Editorial bias can be present in the most innocent phrasing or juxtaposition of articles on a newspaper page. Be an informed consumer of print! Don't be tricked by patterns in disguise. Most newspapers and journals contain both news stories and commentary, and it is all too easy to accept an opinion as something it isn't. Here are your danger signals.

Opinion Masquerading as Information

1. The information is obviously incomplete and/or open to other inter-
   pretations.
2. The author's observations are very personal and subjective.

Opinion Masquerading as Problem

1. The author offers an observation rather than a solution.
2. The reasons for the opinion don't represent causes or effects of a
   problem.

Opinion Masquerading as Thesis

1. The writer states a proposition but supports it with opinions instead of
   facts.
2. The supports cannot be confined. (For example, the data is anecdotal
   or cannot be duplicated; or the sources of the quotes or figures are
   unknown; or the supports are incomplete.)

How else is the Opinion Pattern different from the others? Well,
for one thing, it may not be about a problem or a new idea. It can be
frivolous or serious, and the supporting reasons are more likely to express
the author's personal point of view rather than presenting any verifiable
data.

Essays are a classic form of the Opinion Pattern. Most bylined newspaper columns represent the opinions of the author. We even get "commentary" on the evening TV news and the editorial page—a newsman's
way of pointing out what is important in the jumble of facts that comes at
us every day.

As you read "Books Are Not Fast Food," set yourself up to ask, What
are the author's opinion, reasons, and significance? (Significance is always the answer to "So what, who cares?")

READ:

BOOKS ARE NOT FAST FOOD

by Bob Greene

Radio programming changes; fads come and go, and last year's album-oriented-rock is replaced by this year's all-news-and-talk, which will be replaced by next year's new-age-top-40.

One thing never changes, however: the endless commercials for speed-reading courses. It seems they have been a part of America's background noise for 20 years or more. The other day—as I was listening to yet another pitch for a free, introductory speed-reading seminar—I wondered why it was that I had never even considered giving the concept a try.

The answer was a simple one. Speed-reading is not a good thing. It was never meant to be. It deserves not to be learned.

Reading is one of life's great pleasures. Reading should be savored; words should be chewed like the most expensive fine food, should be lingered over, should be cherished.

Speed-reading promises to do away with all that. The commercials and advertisements say that, if only we will all learn to speed-read, we will be able to devour phenomenal amounts of words in mere minutes.

Well . . . if that's what happens, I'd rather not know how. The greatest pieces of literature known to man—elegant novels, love letters, room-service menus—were not meant to be gobbled. Everything else in this world has been speeded up, but reading should be left the way it always was.

In this electronic age, information is fed to us instantaneously, we get our news from television as fast as the ear can hear and the eye can see. I am typing this column on a computer device that, with the pressing of a button, can transfer it to the type you see on your newspaper page. All communications technology in the last three or four decades has been devoted to making us garner our information faster.

So reading should be left alone. If it takes you three weeks to get through a good, thick novel . . . fine. Who is better served if you learn to read that novel in an hour-and-a-half? Those three weeks are not wasted time; if the novel pulls you into it, if it makes you believe you know its characters and care about their lives, then you probably would like the three weeks to go on longer, not to be shortened.

Many authors work years on books. Is it necessary for us to learn to read those books in a day? The reason a book can take so long to write is that conscientious authors labor to find just the right phrase, to set just the right tone. They are doing it for us, the readers; they want us to become part of the world they are creating.

Is it a good idea, then, to master a

technique in which our eyes can zap in a scanning pattern over a page? The radio commercials for speed-reading say that, even at the free introductory lesson, you can learn to read 100 percent faster. Undoubtedly, the commercials are true.

I must confess that I do not wish to read 100 percent faster. I am a fairly slow reader, and I like that about myself. Often, when I read a paragraph that pleases me, I will go over it a few times. This gives me pleasure. If I really like it, I will call a friend and read it aloud. There is a certain magic to the way the best writers put together words; I do not think I want to know how to avoid that magic.

The speed-reading proponents promise that comprehension is improved, too, when one masters their technique. I'm not sure how something called "comprehension" is measured; if it means that when you've finished reading something you can recall what the piece was about, then I'm sure they have a point.

But there are certain bits of writing that are so beautiful I cherish them, and I refuse to believe that I would even have noticed them if I had known how to speed-read. Here is something from John Barth:

"She paused amid the kitchen to drink a glass of water; at that instant, losing a grip of 50 years, the next-room ceiling plaster crashed. Or he merely sat in an empty study, in March-day glare, listening to the shelf let go. For ages the fault creeps secret through the rock; in a second, ledge and railings, tourists and turbines all thunder over Niagara. Which snowflake triggers the avalanche? A house explodes; a star. In your spouse, so apparently resigned, murder twitches like a fetus at some trifling new assessment, all the colonies rebel."

If you knew how to speed-read, you would have passed over that in a tenth of a second—maybe even faster. But would you have been any richer for it? Would there have been a relationship between you and the author?

There are many arguments to be made for the streamlining of our society. It is cost-efficient to make certain things less complex, more easy to absorb.

But as we become a nation governed by computer chips and video screens, it seems to be that the process of reading should be left as is. For a civilization to remain a civilization, there must be time left for thought and reflection. For a people to remain a people, there must be honor left in that thought and reflection.

I have no doubt that—in countless Holiday Inn ballrooms around the country—speed-reading teachers have the ability to make us know the mastery of their craft. But it seems like a craft not worth knowing; reading is magic, and to reduce it to a sprint for the eyes serves only to diminish the magic, and in the end render it meaningless.

QUESTIONS

1. The author's opinion is _____

   _____

2. Reason(s) _____

   _____

3. The significance is _____

   _____

Answers on page 160.

WHAT TO DO

Sometimes an author expresses more than one opinion. In the following article, "A Chink in the Wall," look for three opinions and five reasons, checking them off as you read. When you finish, write what you think the significance is. Remember, the significance is always the answer to "So what? Who cares?"

READ:

A CHINK IN THE WALL

A Medical Student's Glimpse Across the Divide of Race and Class

by Kyra Minninger

Two years ago, as a second-year medical student, I was assigned to a "patient-based" program. I was given the file of an unmarried Black nineteen-year-old named Darling, who was pregnant with her first child, and was told I would be largely in charge of her care over the next two years.

The prospect thrilled me. A photo of a young student doctor holding up a smiling toddler had set off fantasies in my mind. "My" mother, her baby and I would share an intense and very special experience.

My first meeting with Darling shattered this delightful image. Alone together in a small room, it was as if a huge wall stood between us. I asked what seemed the obvious and essential questions. *How did she feel about the pregnancy? How was it affecting her life? What was her present relationship with the father of her child?* These were hardly questions that could be answered with a *yes* or *no*, but those words were the only words Darling seemed willing to grant me. Her stolidness was frustrating. I so wanted to be her friend and guide. Instead, I felt like an intruder. I blamed her attitude on my being white and therefore alien. Naturally, she was suspicious of me. What else could she be? No doubt she saw me as trying to control her, or attempting to force her to expose more than she wanted to expose.

It was my job, I decided, to break down the wall and win her trust, so that she would let me help her. The problem was, I had no idea how to begin.

Our lectures in school had taught us all about how to hold a child during breast-feeding and the importance of the car seat. Not a word of this was relevant to Darling, who would not hear of breast-feeding and who owned no car. Darling was in the process of becoming a welfare mother, and the father of her child beat her regularly. On two occasions, in fact, he had caused enough damage to land her in the emergency room. Yet lectures on the welfare system and domestic abuse formed no part of our curriculum.

To me, Darling's attitude seemed baffling and even irresponsible. How could a woman associate with a man who kept sending her to the hospital? How could she cover up for him, and tell me she got her bruises in a fall? How could she speak so casually of naming her unborn child for such a man? How, in fact, could she think of exposing that child to his violence?

I yearned to convince her that better alternatives existed, yet I did not want her to think I was judging or patronizing her. This was quite a dilemma, and I had no way to resolve it. The best I could do was give her the name and number of a shelter and begin educating myself on the nature of abusive relationships.

Her way of life was almost unimaginable to me. She seemed to drift freely between her mother's place, her cousin's apartment and wherever her boyfriend was living at the moment, whether with his father or with his mother and sister.

I had assumed that all expectant mothers were intensely interested in pregnancy and labor. Darling was not. I tried offering her books on fetal development and parenting. She showed no interest. Guessing that her reading skills might be poor, I took time to explain as much as I could, but the details did not engage her.

In a way, she seemed like the least trusting of persons. Yet, in another way she was totally trusting. She blandly assumed that there was nothing to worry about, that the pregnancy would go well, that the birth would be uneventful, that her baby would be healthy, and that she would always know just what to do when the time came.

In fact, her pregnancy did not go well. She failed to gain weight and had some disquieting tests. The ultra-sound showed decreased amniotic fluid and, in her thirty-sixth week, she was transferred to the high-risk clinic. I was frightened for her. I worried that some emergency would arise and she would not respond to it, or that she would panic during her delivery.

A few weeks before she was due, the father of her baby was shot in the neck by a policeman. He went through hours of brain surgery, and it remained unclear how much permanent damage he had sustained. While he was still recovering at one hospital, Darling labored at another. I tried to imagine myself in her situation, and suddenly found myself awed by how much better she was coping than I ever could have done.

Rather to my surprise, Darling had an uncomplicated labor and gave birth to a healthy son. Seconds later, she held him to her chest and cut the cord herself. She handled the slippery child with confidence and really did seem to know just what to do. Through all the medical scares, she had held firm to her conviction that everything would be fine, and now her faith had been justified.

Little Jonathan's birth created a kind of chink in the wall between us. Now I could look through and at least glimpse what lay on the other side. I could see, for example, why my initial questions had held so little meaning for Darling. My notions of pregnancy were typical of my class and background, which bore little resemblance to hers. Pregnancy, to me, was a life-changing event, an immense and serious responsibility, preferably undertaken by a conscious decision. Under the right conditions, it was a great—if solemn—joy. Under the wrong conditions, it was at best a problem, at worst a very serious misfortune.

For Darling, pregnancy was none of these things. She had made no decision to become pregnant. It had simply happened. She had greeted the event as neither a joy nor a misfortune. I am still not entirely sure how she did perceive it, but it was obviously not as a burden or a problem. She did not take it solemnly or see it as something that would drastically and forever change her life.

Darling had professed to have no worries about the responsibility she was taking on. I had attributed this to unthinking youth, ignorance, or denial of her fears. Now it dawned on me that having a child need not be so monumental an event as I had assumed. Darling had failed to respond because she saw me as blowing things out of proportion. Embarrassing as it was to admit, I must have struck her as silly.

As of this writing, Darling's son is thirteen months old. Yet Darling has experienced none of the isolation and exhaustion typical of first-time middle-class mothers. From the start, she found child-care natural and familiar, having looked after her sister's four-year-old. Living on close terms with an extended family, she got ample help from her mother and her older cousin, who pitched in with the feedings and diaper-changes. She never felt trapped, but always had someone to leave him with when she went out and did not feel like taking him along. She has never been torn between a family and a career. Her world is all a piece—in an environment that offers easy-going acceptance, helping hands and support.

Darling herself shows a daily strength and resilience, of a kind unfamiliar to me. Comparing myself to her, I discovered how habitual it was with me to anticipate the worst, and how seldom reality lived up to my fears. Darling takes life as it comes. She does not borrow trouble as I do, but she copes with it calmly when it does appear.

All through her pregnancy, I had worried about her baby's future safety. At one point, the father had threatened Darling's mother with a gun. How would such an abusive and violent man treat a helpless child?

As things turned out, I worried for nothing. The child's father is now in prison. The baby is tended by a houseful of affectionate women. He is following the growth curves beautifully. He is smiling and exploring his world. Darling, who had seemed so uninterested in her pregnancy, is a loving mother. She showers pride and attention on her "little man."

When the time comes for me to have children of my own, I intend to model myself, as best I can, on Darling. She has shown me that one can be comfortable about pregnancy and child-raising, and integrate them into one's life, rather than turning them into issues and approaching them with vast anxiety. I am also trying to apply some of her attitude to life in general, and quit borrowing trouble so much.

Obviously, I would not want to pattern myself on Darling entirely. She happened to luck out this time, but she had certainly been courting disaster. I would never wish to give up setting goals, using foresight and acting preventively. But there is no doubt that leavening my approach with hers has already made me more open and adaptable.

What I have learned is that Darling and I both need to learn from the other, that each needs more of what the other has in overabundance. Darling could use some of my awareness of choices and consequences. I could use some of her ability to take life as it comes without trying to control everything.

Above all, Darling has taught me to view my own wisdom with a comforting skepticism, and to approach my patients with a lot more respect.

QUESTIONS

1. Circle the THREE major OPINIONS the author gives in the article.
   a. The doctor wants to live her life with a "take it as it comes" attitude rather than worrying so much.
   b. Black teenagers get pregnant more easily than whites and see it as "no big deal."
   c. Welfare rules should be tightened so that girls like Darling can't get away with having illegitimate children.
   d. The birth of her baby changed Darling's life forever.
   e. An unplanned pregnancy for a poor, unmarried black teenager with family to help her is not necessarily the crisis it would be for a middle-class, single white professional woman.
   f. When the author decides to become pregnant, she will try to do it the way Darling did: comfortably and naturally.
   g. Doctors who are white and middle-class are not as qualified to treat poor black patients as black doctors are.
   h. Teenage pregnancy is not such a big social problem as many people think.
2. Circle FIVE of the REASONS the author gives to support her opinions.
   a. White people and black people see the world so differently they can hardly communicate with each other.
   b. Darling was comfortable as a mother because she learned child-care skills by taking care of other children in her family.
   c. The doctor's medical school training had not shown her how to develop rapport with poor people.
   d. Darling had faith that everything would work out okay for her and had confidence she would be a good mother.
   e. The doctor saw pregnancy and child care as big responsibilities that would change her life. To Darling, it had "simply happened" and was not a burden or problem.
   f. No black students were admitted to the doctor's medical school.
   g. If a social worker had monitored Darling, she would not have gotten pregnant.
   h. The doctor realized the things she worried about don't usually happen.
   i. Darling is a loving mother, showering pride and affection on her "little man."
   j. Medical schools don't teach enough about patients as people.

3. Circle the ONE letter that best describes the SIGNIFICANCE of the article.
   a. Middle-class whites have too many prejudices against poor blacks.
   b. Patients get better medical care from doctors of the same race and social class.
   c. Well-educated doctors can learn important lessons from poor, uneducated patients when something happens to open "a chink in the wall" that separates them.
   d. Overly anxious doctors should loosen up and be like regular people.

Answers on page 160.

WHAT TO DO

"The Search" on the following pages asks the question "Should adoptees be free to learn about their past?" Before you read it, predict some reasons the author may give both for and against such a search and write them below.

_____

_____

_____

_____

By noticing what you know on a subject before you read, you concentrate more easily. As you read, glance through the supporting details enough to know they are there. Then, as you read, focus totally on collecting the author's reasons. Move yourself more quickly through the reasons you predicted, pushing beyond your old comfort zone.

Now gear yourself up to swiftly move through "The Search" looking for the answers to: What's the problem? Effects? Causes? Solution? The answers to these questions are what you want to hear in your head. Move ninety miles an hour over the details! Time yourself. Go.

READ:

THE SEARCH

by Betty Jean Lifton

If the birth record of Baby Girl Foster refers to the record of birth for the person known as Susan Long, we cannot issue a copy of it. The original record of birth was, by law, impounded when the new record was prepared. A copy of the impounded record cannot now be issued without a court order.

> —*Department of Public Health State of Illinois, Sept. 30, 1975*

Susan Long, known as Baby Girl Foster when she was born, is an adoptee who recently went on a search for her lost past. The above is the rejection she received when she tried to obtain her original birth certificate with the hope that it would have her mother's full name. Since the 40's, such records have been sealed in all but three states. Only the new record with the adoptive family's name is available to an adoptee.

While it is estimated that there are as many as five million adoptees in this country, there are no statistics as to how many adult adoptees are involved, like Susan, in what has come to be known as The Search. Adoption workers put the number anywhere from 2,000 to 6,000, and the number of reunions as high as 2,000. Some, but not all, of these searchers are members of the various adoptee lib groups that have sprung up in the past few years.

Until recently, the need to search for one's biological origins was dismissed by society as an act of ingratitude and by psychiatric conventional wisdom as a neurotic quest or an unresolved Oedipal conflict. Some psychiatrists felt that this whole problem might be avoided by never telling children they were adopted. Fortunately, this way of thinking was discredited when it was realized that such secrets could not be kept: Children usually learned the truth from neighbors or playmates. Still, once told, adoptees were expected to suppress all curiosity about the past. Those who couldn't—or wouldn't— were considered emotionally unstable. No wonder most of them, like myself, were too intimidated by all the implicit taboos even to entertain the idea of trying to find their natural parents. Like Lot's wife, we might meet a disastrous end should we dare to look back.

However, psychological investigators are now beginning to explore The Search phenomenon sympathetically in the light of contemporary identity theory. A pioneering research team in California—psychiatrist Arthur Sirosky and social workers Annette Baran and Reuben Pannor—sees the adult adoptee as struggling to establish continuity between the past and present. They believe that by late adolescence and young adulthood virtually all adoptees feel a sense of "genealogical bewilderment," which means a psychological confusion about their genetic origins. The Search, then, reflects both a sociological and biological need, and not a rejection of the adoptive parents.

"Adoptive parents are understandably feeling threatened by their children's desire to search because of the previous pattern of anonymity and secrecy," says Mrs. Baran. "What is to be hoped is that they will come to understand that they are not being replaced—that part of parenting an adopted child is to free him to seek his origins and put together his special identity."

Should adoptees be free to learn about their past? "I thought everything would be clear when I found my natural mother," says one. "Now I know it's not that easy."

"The search is a symptom made necessary by law," says William Reynolds, a psychologist at Queens College, referring to the sealed records. The way the law stands now, the records cannot be opened unless a judge in the court where the adoption was finalized decides that "good cause" has been shown.

But what is good cause?

Adoptees like Susan Long believe that it is their constitutionally based civil right to know their heritage. But state judges, when they do open the records, tend to base their decisions on health reasons, property rights or possible inheritance, viewing the adoptee's intense need to know as mere curiosity.

Because going into the courts is an expensive, uncertain and humiliating experience, the majority of searchers such as Susan opt for underground sleuthing, which has its own hazards. I myself found it a time-consuming and emotionally draining experience that requires courage, cunning and persistence as well as the luck to encounter record clerks and social workers willing to ignore both the law and the adoption-agency policy of secrecy.

What drives the searchers on a search that is so stacked against them from the beginning? The California team believes the need becomes most intense for women, who are the majority of searchers, when they are about to become mothers themselves. It can also be triggered by the death of an adoptive parent or a medical necessity for genetic information. In my case, it happened at the age of 30, when I learned that the parents I had been told were dead might be very much alive.

However, it seems obvious that anyone would want to know the full story of his or her origins. "I always felt I was separate, even though I was adopted when I was six weeks old," says Susan, an attractive woman in her late 20's who is now training in family therapy. "One has to feel separate because it is such an unnatural way to go into a family."

While she was growing up, Susan's adoptive parents told her they knew nothing about her mother or father. They, like so many other adoptive couples, seemed to feel that their *not* knowing the full story effectively erased the reality of those other parents' existence. Instead, it sent Susan into her private self to brood about them alone. "I always lived in two different worlds, one the world around me, the other within," she says. "I felt older than my friends. I had a whole set of complicated things I had to deal with every day of my life, and it had a profound effect upon me."

Like so many adoptees, Susan made an unsuccessful stab at discovering her heritage when she was in her late teens. The hospital in which she was born informed her by mail that everything she wanted to know was on microfilm which she, being adopted, was not permitted to see. "After that letter, I was devastated, but I had to go on with my life," she recalls. "I had to close the issue to survive. I didn't pick it up again until years later, when things had calmed down."

Those who close the issue at this point, as Susan did, are considered "well-adjusted" by society. But the fact that Susan opened it again later brings us to the question of why some people search and others don't.

Dr. Reynolds has been investigating just this question. His prelimi-nary findings suggest that those who report an "unsatisfactory adoptive relationship" are more likely to search than those who consider their relationship "satisfactory." But a large number of those in the satisfactory group also search, while some of the unsatisfactory group refrain from searching because of what he calls "angry guilt" toward the adoptive parents. He is beginning to conclude that the intensity of curiosity about origins may not be so much a matter of adjustment or disturbance as of individual personality differences among adoptees.

Dr. Norman Paul, a Boston psychiatrist who is concerned with "intergenerational continuity" as a key to mental health, takes the view that those adoptees who claim no need to search are repressed. "Adoptive parents unwittingly extract a sense of loyalty that excludes the child's need to know the original family," he says. "Some adoptees I've seen are like mannequins. They have this need to please the adoptive parents. But at some point they crack."

During her teens and early 20's, Susan had what she describes as "self-destructive tendencies"—she was accident-prone and had a need to fail at whatever she showed talent in. Then she began traveling restlessly around the country, taking odd jobs to support herself—a kind of wandering that some psychiatrists view as a symbolic search for the natural parents. While taking some night courses in psychology at

Hunter College in New York, she went into psychotherapy, only to discover what the California researchers are also finding out—that, after one has worked through neurotic conflicts, there remains the need to know about one's hereditary background.

At that point, Susan heard of ALMA (the Adoptees' Liberty Movement Association) and went to a meeting. She was shaken when a genealogist who was helping other adoptees with their searches asked her: "Are you going to wait until your natural parents are dead to look for them?" When she got home, she knew that he had touched the nerve center of her need. The Search was the missing link in the integration of her personality.

The Search is not easy on any level. Susan had to confront her highly emotional adoptive parents with a request for their copy of her adoption decree, which turned out to be in the family's safe deposit box. She had to endure their accusations of disloyalty, their hurt remarks like "Your mother didn't want you." Then, armed with her mother's maiden name, she spent every free moment of the next year going through birth and death records, cemetery listings, old phone books. Finally, in a Midwest directory, she found the name of her mother's brother and, by posing as an old school friend of his sister, she managed to get the forbidden address and phone number.

Many adoptive parents seem to fear that, when such a moment arrives, their adoptee will move in with the natural mother and disappear from their lives forever. As one adoptive mother put it: "Why would you raise a child only to have him go off with strangers?"

But this is not what happens. Most adoptees do not find the ideal mother of their fantasies waiting to reclaim her long-lost darling babe. In Susan's case, her mother, a telephone operator on the West Coast, discouraged her from coming out because she was on crutches owing to a bad fall. Susan flew out anyway for four days, but admits she was actually relieved when it was time to return East. She found that, although her mother was divorced after a short marriage and had no other children, she was reluctant to enter into a relationship. She seemed to be experiencing a mixture of relief and pain at seeing her grown daughter, but needed time to absorb the experience.

Was Susan sorry she had searched? Is there such a thing as a successful or unsuccessful reunion? "I'm beginning to understand it doesn't matter what happens in the reunion," says Susan, who also managed to find her father, a company employee in the Midwest who is reluctant to introduce her to his wife and three children. "What's important is that I'm beginning to have roots growing out of my feet. I was just drifting before, but I've really planted myself here in New York now."

My own mother was filled with ambivalence at my reappearance in her life: On the one hand, she was overjoyed to see me; on the other hand, she was fearful her son would discover this shameful secret in her life. It took some time for me to get over my disappointment that she wasn't going to let me meet my half-brother. Many adoptees have felt closer to their half-siblings than to their natural parents.

Despite the difficulties, I wasn't sorry I had searched, nor was anyone I've spoken with. It is the truth of one's past one is searching for, not a relationship with another set of parents.

On investigating 150 cases of reunions between adoptees and birth mothers, the California team found that the majority of adoptees felt that they had personally benefited from the reunion, even though in many cases they were disappointed with the mothers—a disappointment that Dr. Paul feels is inevitable, given the intensity of the mystery and the search.

"An adoptee's ignorance of his true story can lead to crucial defects in his functioning."

Then what of that familiar refrain: Isn't it better not to know if what you find is painful? Rona Olsen, a young married woman who was bitterly dis-appointed to find her mother the proverbial "loose" woman who had put her other children in and out of foster care, told me she was still glad she had searched. "If you didn't find your natural parents, it would be worse," she said. "You'd spend your life wondering and regretting." She, like so many adoptees I've heard from, feels closer to her adoptive mother now that she's filled in her story.

Jane Thompson, now in her early 30's, became obsessed with learning about her biological background when she was pregnant for the first time. After years of searching, she found her mother, still unmarried, in a state hospital where she had been for the last 15 years with degenerative multiple sclerosis. While thrilled to learn what had happened to Jane, whom she gave up at birth, her mother was reluctant to keep in touch by phone or mail. A devout Catholic, she seemed to feel she had no right to the relationship, and had accepted her condition as punishment for her sin.

In spite of this new responsibility in her life, Jane says, "I feel a tremendous weight lifted. Even when I wasn't thinking about it, I was thinking about it. I'm much more at ease with myself now. If I find my father, it will be all over. It's like the other half." But she adds wistfully, "I thought everything would be clear when I found my mother. Now I know it is not that easy."

Although some adoptees have

been reunited with natural mothers who are happily married and/or professional women and were delighted to see them—sharing similar interests, even to liking the same food and making the same gestures—there are barriers that all are aware of, as if the conflicts and guilts from the past are still separating them. No matter whom they find, adoptees are coming to realize that they have a whole new set of complications to deal with. As one of them wrote to me: "We need so much more than help in searching. We need counseling in the emotional and psychological aspects of The Search—both before and after reunion. But who is available for counseling who really understands?"

Dr. Paul found himself doing such counseling when a fair number of adult adoptees came to him for help with other problems, such as marital or parent-child disorders. In his Boston office, he showed me a videotape he had made of the second meeting in a reunion between a 46-year-old chemist and his natural father of 81.

The patient, who had come to Dr. Paul with a dissolving marriage, low self-esteem, a history of alcoholism and suicidal gestures, had never confronted his adoptive status before. Dr. Paul believes that one reason so few men are searching is that boys are encouraged by society to deny hurt feelings. He helped his patient petition the court for his records on medical grounds and supported him in his search. His natural parents proved to have been married, his mother dying in childbirth and his father giving him up for adoption to acquaintances after trying to keep him for a year. Yet his adoptive parents had not told him he was adopted until he was 10, and had never revealed to him that they knew who his father was.

Dr. Paul encouraged both now. The son said: "Well, it gives me a sense of, you know, who I am in a strange way. The experience of living with an adoptive family is not really knowing where you came from except from the story that somebody told you—it's like you were born inside a book or something. And having a real person involved, who is, by God, my father, that gives me a sense of roots, a place in the world, if you like. Some sense of security, I guess. Identity or something. I can talk about it now and it's a nice thing. It's not that big a deal. I should have done it a long time ago."

The father, who had also suppressed his sense of loss, finally admitted to himself as well as to the camera that he had thought of his son over the years. "Oh, I'm tickled to death . . . anything we can share together," he said. "I haven't got far to go down the road, you know."

It was too late to save the marriage, but the patient, who sees his natural father about once a month, has stopped drinking and has begun to reconstruct his life.

Dr. Paul believes that one of the main values of a reunion is that it gives the adult adoptee a chance to forgive the parent who abandoned him, and to forgive himself for hating that parent. And it gives the natural parent a chance to overcome his or her guilt at relinquishing the child. "Whether or not the natural parents feel relieved to see their grown children depends on whether they were able to share the secret with their spouse and other offspring," he said. "Otherwise the reappearance of this child makes for an even greater secret." This was certainly true in my mother's case.

How long will it be before the state courts and private adoption agencies open their records to adult adoptees? No one I've spoken to can say for sure, although in some states, such as New York and California, newly formed commissions of legislators, attorneys and adoption workers are considering legislative changes while weighing the rights of all parties concerned.

In the meantime, the Child Welfare League of America, in trying to keep up with the times, has just prepared a new position paper advising its 400 member and associate agencies to tell everything now— everything that is but the *name*. It still sees itself as protecting the confidentiality of the natural mother it has not been in touch with for 20, 30 or 40 years. A very few agencies, like the New York Foundling Hospital, are getting around the no-name policy by searching for the natural parents themselves, when possible, and

acting as intermediaries in reunions. They, like the California researchers, are finding that few natural mothers are reluctant to meet their grown children, and most express a lifelong need to know what happened to them.

Adoptees view the policy of confidentiality as a euphemism for putting everyone's rights over their own, although as babies they had no say in the transaction. Dr. Reynolds, who is himself an adoptive father, agrees with them that the agencies and the law are really protecting the adoptive parents' need for exclusive possession of the child—the "our very own baby" syndrome. He believes in giving top priority to the child, while Dr. Paul states emphatically: "Kids—all kids—have an inalienable right to know their origins." However, there are still psychological authorities who hold to secrecy, claiming that a reunion can only intensify a natural mother's guilt and interrupt her present life, while resulting in added trauma for the adoptee.

At present, it is between confidentiality and the right to know that the battle lines are drawn. Some of the adoptee lib groups hope to test the constitutionality of the sealed record in the courts, and eventually take the issue to the Supreme Court. Yet some veteran searchers, like Jean Paton of Orphan Voyage in Colorado, are already saying that in the long run an enlightened social climate will prove more important to adoptees than any court ruling. "Legislation alone cannot change people's hearts," she warns, adding that society must be reeducated to understand the adoptees' need. Otherwise, guilt will overwhelm them when it comes time to search.

Dr. Paul is aware of this problem, too. "Parents must help their children to feel it is a legitimate request to see the records," he says. "They must realize that an adoptee's ignorance of his true story can lead to crucial defects in his capacity to function adequately as an adult and a parent."

According to Dr. Sirosky and his coworkers in California, adoptive parents are beginning to understand more about the true nature of their children's curiosity and to feel less threatened by it. One such mother wrote to me recently that her adoptive parents' association in Massachusetts is reading and discussing everything it can in an effort to remain open to all the implications of adoption. She pointed out that she and her husband would certainly support their daughter's desire to search and would actively help her if she wanted their help.

An adoptive father, trying to find a little humor in a subject that weighs heavily on everyone in the adoption triangle, posed this question: "Will I feel I am a failure if it turns out my son doesn't want to search?"

Betty Jean Lifton is an author whose latest book is Twice Born, Memoirs of an Adopted Daughter.

Write down your reading time in the blanks below. Then answer the questions and determine your comprehension level from your score, as calculated on p. 161.

Length of article: 3,325 words.

Mins. _____ Secs. _____ Words per minute _____

Comprehension _____%

QUESTIONS

1. Check the author's major OPINION in the article.
   a. Children who seek out their biological parents are either ungrateful or emotionally unstable.
   b. Parents shouldn't tell children they are adopted.
   c. Adoptees should have access to their adoption records.
   d. Adoptees should have access to their adoption records only when medically necessary.
   e. Parents who give up children for adoption need to be protected from harassment.

2. Check FIVE of the REASONS she gives to support her opinion.
   a. The mother may have later married a husband who does not know of the child's existence.
   b. Child might develop a mature, positive relationship with biological parents.
   c. Adoptive parents might be hurt.
   d. Adoptee may need medical treatment for hereditary disease.
   e. Dr. Norman Paul advocates "intergenerational continuity" as a key to mental health.
   f. Adoptee may be entitled to inheritance from biological parents.
   g. Adoptee experiences relief at discovering his or her "roots."
   h. Adoptees only reinforce infantile behavior patterns by searching for biological parents.
   i. Finding his or her biological parents solves all the adoptee's problems.
   j. Discovering one's biological parents may be too devastating.
3. Check those things the author regards as POSITIVE.
   a. The Adoptees' Liberty Movement Association
   b. Laws preventing children from finding out who their biological parents are
   c. Current laws on adoption records
   d. Children who seek out their biological parents
   e. Counseling for adoptees
   f. Waiting until biological parents are dead to look for them
   g. Wanting to know your origins
   h. Reunions with biological parents
   i. "It's better not to know."
   j. The position paper of the Child Welfare League of America

Answers on page 161.

THE THESIS PATTERN: To Prove Something

THESIS
PROOFS
IMPLICATIONS

Don't be intimidated by the word *thesis*. Whenever you see someone expressing an original, controversial, or unproven idea and supporting it with solid facts that can be verified, you are probably reading the Thesis

Pattern. If the writer offers a significant answer to the question "So what?" that implies a consequence or implication, you have a thesis.

A thesis can be profound or trivial, weighty or gossamer, valid or invalid. Most "important" nonfiction books, those landmark tomes that become classics, are theses. They offer exciting new ways to look at generally known facts, or they provide a newly discovered piece of information that completely changes the accepted picture of something.

$$OPINION + facts = THESIS$$
$$THESIS + solution = PROBLEM$$

When you make predictions about what is ahead and then actually find them, you'll be able to sail through these "familiar" sections at surprising speed.

WHAT TO DO

The title "We Can Teach Reading Better" suggests a "how to" or information article, but this is a thesis. Most workshop participants get bogged down in the specialized vocabulary the author uses to address the readers of *Today's Education,* a journal for teachers. Unfamiliar specialized vocabulary is a barrier to rapid reading.

At this point, preview the article. Read any headings. Get an overview of the territory so that you can make your private map of what you want to cover.

If you are interested in the Piaget material on how children's minds develop, ask yourself, "Is this a good place to learn it?" If your answer is yes, study that section. If it is no, don't abandon ship. Train yourself to ask, "What's left if I don't want to struggle with the unknown? Is it worth skipping over to anything else?"

Preview the whole article. While you are previewing, does your eye catch any visual cues, any words that say, "Pssst, over here"?

As you continue previewing, notice the headings that stand out:

Visual Independence
Meaning Construction
Receptive Discipline

Then make questions out of the above readings, underlining the answers in each section as you find them. When you finish, check your selections with those on pages 162–63.

WE CAN TEACH READING BETTER

by David Elkind

Professor of Psychology, Psychiatry, and Education, University of Rochester, New York.

Can we do a better job of teaching children to read? Yes, I believe we can if we take into consideration how their minds develop. To illustrate this point, I'd first like to discuss beginning reading and the child's concept of letters and then move on to how children who are more advanced readers use their accumulated storehouse of knowledge to give meaning to the printed word.

A basic error in much beginning reading instruction centers about the concept of the letter, which is, in many ways, the basic unit of reading. To the adult, the letter appears as a discrete object which is a conventional representation of one or more sounds. But the letter as adults see it is not the letter known to the beginning reader.

As Piaget points out, children and adults see the world in different ways. The well-known "conservation" experiments are a case in point. Most adults are amazed to discover that young children believe that changing the shape of a piece of clay will change the *amount*.

This amazement suggests that most adults assume that children see the world in much the same way

they do. They make this assumption because they are unable to recall or reconstruct the course of their own cognitive growth. This phenomenon, the loss of awareness of their own part in the construction of reality, is what Piaget means by *externalization*.

In general, externalization serves a useful adaptive purpose and allows the individual to operate more effectively in the environment. *Externalization* only becomes a problem when we try to teach the young, that is, when we try to present material that we have already mastered. In that case, we as adults, who have conceptualized and externalized many facets of the world, have trouble appreciating the difficulties children encounter in their attempts at making sense out of their world.

From the child's point of view, the concept of the letter poses many of the same problems as concepts of number, space, and time. Before the age of six or seven, most children lack a true unit or number concept because they cannot coordinate two dimensions or relationships simultaneously. Such coordinations are basic to the construction of a unit concept because a unit is, by definition, both like every other unit and different from it in its order of enumeration.

In many ways, children's problems in understanding the concept of a letter are even more difficult than those they encounter in constructing the concept of a number.

Like numbers, letters have an ordinal property, which is their position in the alphabet. And letters also have a cardinal property, which is their name (A, B, C, etc.) and which each letter shares with all other letters of the same name (all B's are B and so on).

Letters are even more complicated than numbers because, in addition to their ordinal and cardinal properties, they also have phonic, contextual properties. One letter can stand for one or more sounds and one sound can be represented by different letters. Hence, to understand phonics, a child must be able to perform logical operations on letters and sounds to understand all their possible combinations.

A rich background of early experience with spoken and written language is important for successful reading.

Many different kinds of evidence support this logical analysis of the difficulties in early reading. Written languages that are more regularly phonetic than English are apparently much easier to learn to read than is English. In these alphabets such as Japanese, the logical difficulties are removed because one and the same element always has one and the same sound regardless of its position or phonetic context.

In addition to this cultural evidence, various collaborators and I have published a body of research which also points to the logical difficulties inherent in beginning reading. We have shown that reading achievement and logical ability are highly correlated; that average readers are superior in logical ability to slow readers of comparable overall intelligence; and that training children in logical skills has a significant positive effect upon some aspects of reading achievement.

All these findings are consistent with the view that the letter is a complex logical construction that requires the ability to reason, which Piaget attributes to the appearance of *concrete operations* for its full elaboration. To test this hypothesis in still another way, we have begun in the last few years, to look at the cognitive competencies of children who read early, that is, children who read before they enter kindergarten. One of our hypotheses was that if reading involves concrete operations, which are usually attained at age six to seven, then early readers should show these abilities at an early age. In addition to assessing children's cognitive abilities, we were also interested in the personal-social characteristics of these children and in the educational-emotional climate that prevails in their homes.

We have now completed two studies of early readers, one with 16 early readers and another with 38. In both studies, the early readers were matched with a control group of non-early-reading children on such things as age, sex, IQ, and socio-economic status. All the children were given a large battery of achievement and intelligence tests as well as personality and creativity tests. In addition, their parents were interviewed. In both studies, we found that early-reading children were superior to non-early-reading children on Piagetian measures of conservation. They were also better on certain psycholinguistic measures, such as sound blending.

It is important to emphasize, however, that cognitive construction of a letter is only one of the requirements for successful early reading. Our parent interview data suggest that a rich background of early experience with spoken and written language provided by homes where books and magazines are plentiful and where parents frequently read to the children is also important for successful reading. In addition, social motivation to please significant adults appears to be a necessary, if not a sufficient, factor in giving zest to the dull and unrewarding process of learning to read.

In talking about cognitive development and early reading, it is therefore important to avoid the two extremes that are sometimes advocated when cognitive "readiness" is discussed. One extreme is the effort to train children of preschool age in cognitive abilities they have not yet attained. I have seen no evidence that such early intervention has any lasting effectiveness. But the alternative extreme, allowing children to learn in their own time and in their own way, is also unwarranted. Children need instruction in learning to read, but only after they have demonstrated the requisite cognitive abilities.

In summary, there appear to me to be at least four requirements for successful beginning reading: a language-rich environment, attachment to adults who model and reward reading behavior, attainment of concrete operations, and an instructional program. All other things being equal, namely, that the children in question are of at least average intellectual ability and are free of serious emotional or physical handicaps, the presence of these four characteristics should ensure that most children will learn to read with reasonable ease and considerable enjoyment.

Let us now turn to advanced reading and the construction of meaning. It has already been suggested that the intellectual processes involved in beginning reading are analogous to those involved in concept formulation. A child who is learning to read has to coordinate similarities and differences and construct concepts of letters which are both like every other letter in that they represent sounds but different in the specific sounds they stand for.

Concept formation also involves inferential processes, and these can be observed in beginning reading as well. Many errors in beginning reading, such as reading *where* for *when*, are inferential errors rather than discrimination errors. The child is inferring the whole from observing the part (the *wh*). Such inferential errors are high-level cognitive errors inasmuch as the child is doing what more advanced and accomplished readers do. These processes should be encouraged by temporarily sacrificing accuracy for fluency. Experience indicates that once children are fluent readers, they can always correct for accuracy, but an overconcern with accuracy can retard fluent reading.

When concept formation and inferential aspects of reading have become automatized and children can recognize printed words with ease and rapidity, they enter the phase of rapid silent reading. In silent reading, the major cognitive task is no longer concept formation and inference but rather interpretation, the construction of meaning. In constructing meanings, children have to relate representations—in this case, printed words—with their own concepts and ideas. Success in interpretation, or comprehension, depends upon a different set of characteristics than learning to read, and these are described below.

Visual Independence. Rapid silent reading and comprehension require, at the very outset, that the visual verbal system become independent of the sensory motor system. Rapid reading involves fewer motor fixations and wider visual segments of scanning, and this in turn means less motor involvement and more conceptual inferential activity. In effect, in rapid silent reading, the brain does more work and the eyes do less. We have some recent evidence that supports the importance of visual independence in advanced reading.

In one study we found that while tactile discrimination of sandpaper letters was positively related to reading achievement among beginning readers, it was negatively correlated with reading achievement among advanced readers. Apparently, motoric identification and discrimination of letters, as advocated by Fernald and Montessori, is beneficial in the beginning phases of learning to read, but the coordination of visual and motor processes has to be given up if more rapid reading is to develop.

Put more concretely, it is helpful for beginning readers to use their fingers as markers to direct attention and exploration of printed matter. But once they become advanced readers, using a finger as a marker would impede reading. Rapid reading requires a certain independence from the tactile motor system.

Some recent data on perceptual exploration and memory demonstrate this growth of visual independence in another way. Children at different age levels (from age four through age eight) were shown large cards upon which were pasted 16 pictures of familiar objects. On one card, the pictures were pasted in an upright position whereas on another, the same pictures were pasted at 180 degrees from their normal position.

At each age level, half the children viewed the cards with the pictures upright, while the other half viewed the cards with the pictures at 180 degrees to the upright. Each child had two tasks: to name each of the figures on the cards and then to recall as many of the figures as possible once the cards were turned over.

Among young children (age four to five), there was a significant difference in recall scores in favor of the figures rotated 180 degrees. This difference, however, diminishes as children grow older and disappears at about the age of eight or nine. A similar pattern appears to hold true for children with limited hearing, who use finger spelling and vocalization in communication. These data suggest that in young children the motoric system is still tied to the visual system. In identifying the 180-degree figures, these children may implicitly try to "right" the figures, which produces increased motoric involvement.

Our hypothesis is that the increased motoric involvement and attendant heightened attention account for the superior memory for upside-down figures in young children. Among older children, in whom identification can occur without implicit motoric "righting," this attentional advantage for upside-down figures is no longer present.

There is thus some direct as well as indirect evidence that rapid, silent reading involves the attainment of considerable visual independence from the tactile motor system. Apparently this occurs even among children with limited hearing who use finger spelling as well as vocalization to communicate. Indeed, among older deaf children, the rapidity with which they finger spell and read finger spelling is very much like rapid reading. Visual independence amounts to a kind of automatization of the visual aspect of reading in which the visual scanning process is relatively independent of tactile motor input.

Meaning Construction. A second prerequisite to advanced silent reading is facility in meaning construction. From a cognitive development point of view, reading comprehension is not a passive process of decoding written symbols. On the contrary, it must be regarded as a constructive activity analogous to creative writing.

The point is that meaning is not inherent in written or spoken words but rather that the words are given meaning by readers or listeners who interpret them within their own storehouse of knowledge. Silent readers give meaning to the words they read by relating these to the conceptual system they have constructed in the course of their development. The richness of meaning they derive from their reading will depend both upon the quality of the material they are reading and the breadth and depth of their conceptual understanding. Satisfaction in reading often derives, in part at least, from the degree of fit between the material being read and the conceptual level of the reader.

A recent doctoral dissertation supports this position. The author chose 33 books that had won Newbery awards for excellence. She then determined how frequently each had been checked out over the preceding three-year period in a number of libraries. On the basis of these data, she selected the five most frequently chosen books and the five least frequently chosen books from her original list. She then analyzed the books from the standpoint of their congruence with the conceptual systems of the age group for which they were written. She found that the five most frequently chosen books were congruent with the cognitive level of the children for whom they were written, while this was not true for the five least chosen books. Apparently, other things being equal, children prefer stories which have meaning within their own cognitive organization.

Comprehension, or the construction of meanings, is also helped by the children's own efforts at giving meaning to (i.e., representing) their own experiences. The more opportunity children have to experience the effort and satisfaction of representing their own thoughts verbally

and otherwise, the better prepared they will be for interpreting the representations of others.

In contemporary education, teachers often do not leave time for the children to write creatively or otherwise. But I believe that the more children write, the more they will get from their reading. Writing and reading are reciprocal processes of meaning construction which mutually reinforce one another.

Receptive Discipline. A third prerequisite to effective silent reading seems at first to be a contradiction to what has just been said about the reader being an active participant in the process. This prerequisite is that the reader have a receptive attitude, a willingness to respond to the representations of others. Good readers, like good listeners, have to be simultaneously passive (receptive to the representations of others) and active (interpreting those representations within their own conceptual framework).

Many young people are poor readers for the same reason that they are poor listeners: They are more interested in representing their own thoughts and ideas than they are in interpreting the thoughts and ideas of others. They lack what might be called receptive discipline.

Young people demonstrate receptive discipline when they attend fully to the representations of others and resist following their own free associations and tangents. Many so-called slow readers have problems with receptive discipline and not with rapid reading.

Receptive discipline is not innate and can be facilitated and taught. Text material that is of interest to readers and at their level of competence facilitates a receptive attitude. Another way to encourage receptive discipline is to have goals for non-recreational reading. When young people (or adults for that matter) know that they will have to present what they have read to a group, they are likely to be more attentive than if this were not so.

These are but a few examples of techniques that might be employed to encourage receptive discipline. Whatever techniques are used to instill it, receptive discipline seems to be an important ingredient for successful reading comprehension.

This article was adapted from Dr. Elkind's article, "Cognitive Development and Reading," Claremont Reading Conference 38th Yearbook, *Claremont (California) Graduate School, 1974.*

Take Only What You Want

Think of your reading speeds as analogous to car speeds. I read the first page of "We Can Teach Reading Better" at about 25 mph. The rest I read at 75 mph, after I decided how to manage the article. By managing how I'm going to read something first, I save enormous time because I only take what I want and whip through the rest to notice what is there.

"But I'm Missing So Much!"

"But I'm missing so much," you may be clamoring. Of course you are. We are always missing so much. The point is, when I want to cover vast quantities of material, I'd sometimes rather get the highlights, the main concepts, from more reading material than become an expert on an author's details and examples. This approach is especially helpful when material is disorganized and badly written.

The technical jargon and objective tone of this article make it seem much more complicated than it really is. With intimidating material, it is even more important to take control and decide what you want to get out of it. This may mean going in for specific information and leaving the jargon for later.

Remember that in the Thesis Pattern, proofs are the verifiable supporting evidence. The implication is the answer to "So what?" If the data supporting the thesis is verifiable, then what we can predict is the implication.

WHAT TO DO

In "Studying the Secrets of Childhood Memory" look for the thesis, proofs, and implication. Then answer the questions that follow.

READ:

STUDYING THE SECRETS OF CHILDHOOD MEMORY

by Daniel Goleman

Researchers find recollection may be linked to language.

When Rachel Hudson was 2, she recalled details about things she had done weeks and months before, prompted by her mother, a psychologist studying children's memories. But by the time she was 8, the only episode Rachel could recall from her first couple of years was a trip to Disneyland.

The old mystery of just why most people are unable to dredge up memories from the first years of life has a new solution, thanks to research like that of Rachel's mother, Dr. Judith Hudson of Rutgers University.

The ability to fix a childhood memory strongly enough to last into adulthood, psychologists now say, depends on the mastery of skills of attention, thought and language at the level of an average 3- or 4-year-old. People simply do not retain into adulthood memories of specific episodes that took place at 1 or 2, before these crucial abilities emerge, although research like that with Rachel shows that as young children they do, indeed, have such memories.

"Most adults have trouble remembering much, other than fragmentary impressions, before they were 3½," said Dr. Robyn Fivush, a psychologist at Emory University in Atlanta. "Yet we know that children as young as 2 can remember what happened to them even months before."

The new research, based largely on studies of the developing memories of young children, contradicts Freud's notion that "infantile amnesia," the inability of adults to remember the events of early infancy—is due to the later repression of perverse lusts and hatreds that seethe during the first years of life.

Instead, the findings suggest a more innocent end to life's early amnesia: that toddlers acquire the skills for remembering significant episodes in their lives only as they acquire the language skills necessary for later retrieval. As they have conversations with adults about past events, psychologists say, infants learn the art of shaping events into a story, the form that allows memories to be retrieved many years later.

"We have a whole new way of thinking about earliest memories, based on studies of what young kids actually remember," said Dr. Ulric Neisser, a psychologist at Emory. "At 2½ or 3, kids are not very interested in the past. You don't see a bunch of 3-year-olds sitting around talking about old times."

Dr. Neisser added, "But ask a 2-year-old about what happened on a visit to Grandma's months before, and she'll have some memories: 'saw a horsie.' The question is why, as adults, don't we remember those very episodes from life's first few years?"

Part of the answer, psychologists say, lies in distinguishing between three fundamentally different kinds of memory. One is a "generic" memory, in which the most general attributes of a familiar situation are stored, like what Grandma always served for lunch, or what color the rooms were in a childhood house.

Such general characteristics do not pertain to any single episode but are distilled from a series of repeated episodes, which Dr. Neisser has called repisodes, episodes that blend into a generic memory. When an event has occurred in a child's life about five or more times, it tends to be stored in memory in this general form.

A second kind of memory, "episodic," is for specific events, like a visit to Grandma's when a favorite, rarely seen, cousin was also there. Such memories are for a distinct event at a given time and place.

But few of these specific episodes—such as what was eaten for breakfast that morning—are significant enough to warrant remembering years later. Out of such specific episodes people selected and weaved together the particularly meaningful events that compose "autobiographical memory," the story of one's life.

These are the specific memories that last throughout a lifetime, beginning with what people call their earliest memory. As autobiographical memory begins, infantile amnesia ends.

THE POWER OF STORY

From the time children begin to talk, around age 2, they have both generic and episodic memories, researchers say. But they do not begin to weave together autobiographical memory until around age 3½, according to research reported by Dr. Katherine Nelson, a psychologist at the City University of New York, in the January issue of *Psychological Science*.

On the basis of research with young children, Dr. Nelson, as have others, concluded that although children as young as 1 or 2 do have episodic memories, these memories almost never last into later childhood, let alone adulthood. Autobiographical memory seems to take root only as children begin to have conversations with their parents or others about what has happened to them.

"Parents implicitly model for their young children how to piece together a story with a beginning, a middle and an end about what has happened," said Dr. Fivush. "Between 3½ and 4½, children reach a critical level of language ability, where words become the medium through which you represent the events of your life to yourself rather than, say, images. And years later, when you tell a story from your earliest years, language is the medium of retrieval."

The process of autobiographical memory seems to be given a great impetus by adults who review events with a young child. In Dr. Fivush's research, young children of parents who mulled over incidents with much embellishment of detail had at 4 years better memories for things that had happened to them than did children of parents who typically simply asked, "Do you remember the time we went to the circus?"

"At around 3 or 4, you find mothers talking a lot about past events to a kid," said Dr. Neisser. "Then a kid starts to value her memories and starts to tell stories about herself. The events you can easily remember as an adult are those you had, back then, put into a narrative, at least in your own mind."

At about the same period, children learn from talking to parents and others that a given event can be seen from multiple perspectives. "Around age 4 children seem to start to understand that people see things differently," said Dr. Fivush. "I might have gone to the circus and been scared by the big animals, while someone else loved it."

PHOTOS AS HINDRANCE

This cognitive ability to see an event from several points of view, some psychologists contend, may add to the thoroughness with which it is remembered, as a stronger net of associations is built. The onset of that ability also marks the point at which most people have their earliest lasting memory.

Still another capacity that ripens around age 4 is the ability to perceive the structure of events more as an adult would, highlighting the most salient points. Toddlers notice mostly what to adults seem to be trivial details, psychologists say.

Oddly, seeing an event in a photo frequently or discussing it often with others does not determine how well it is remembered, either in the short term or in later autobiographical memory. Dr. Fivush had parents keep track of distinctive events in the lives of children between the ages of 2 and 6 and also had them note how often the children talked over those events or looked at photos of them. There was no apparent effect on the children's memory.

Indeed, talking over an event with a very young child may somehow interfere with its being stored in memory, according to findings by Dr. Neisser, with JoNell Adair, a graduate student, that will be published in *The Journal of Experimental Psychology* later this year.

In a study of college students, in which their memories were verified by checking with their parents, Dr. Neisser and Ms. Adair found that events from the first four years of life that became enshrined in family stories or for which there were photos were remembered less well than events that had no such memory aids.

But they also found that those students who had been hospitalized or who had had a sibling born between their second and third birthday could usually still remember the event. "For such highly memorable events, people seem to have memories, though a bit fragmentary, as early as age 2, though that may mean closer to 3," said Dr. Neisser.

Other studies of adults' earliest memories have found that most date from around 3½. A few people report no memories of their childhood at all before age 8 or so.

The problem with studies that rely only on adults' recollections of earliest memories, of course, is that it is almost always impossible to date such memories exactly or to be sure that they are truly memories rather than imagined episodes.

For example, when Dr. Hudson began her research on children's early memories by intermittently quizzing 2-year-old Rachel on what she remembered about recent events, she found that in response to specific queries like, "Do you remember when we went to the aquarium?" Rachel could recall many details of what had happened up to 10 months before. But over the next several years, those memories faded.

When quizzed again at 4 years, Rachel remembered almost nothing. By age 8 when Dr. Hudson asked "What is your earliest memory?" Rachel replied with conviction that it was of a time just before her younger brother was born, when she crawled into his bassinet and pretended to be a baby herself. At that time, said Dr. Hudson, Rachel was thirty-three months old. The Disneyland trip was actually her earliest memory, although Rachel, now age 9, believed otherwise.

The New York Times

QUESTIONS

1. Circle the major THESIS the author gives in the article.
   a. If you have a poor memory, it's likely because your parents didn't talk to you enough at age three or four.
   b. By talking with their parents, and listening to what they say, children can learn that their point of view probably isn't the only right one.

     c. Even people who are smart enough to go to college don't correctly remember their own childhood.

     d. People have difficulty remembering events before age three because until then they don't have the language skills needed to create stories that can be recalled.

2. Circle FOUR of the PROOFS the author gives to support his opinions.

     a. Children at age three or earlier are not interested in the past, shown by the fact that they don't remember it.

     b. We tend not to remember specific episodes from early childhood unless they were dramatic, such as an illness, or were repeated many times so that they blend into a generic memory of attributes of a familiar situation, such as what Grandma always served for lunch.

     c. What few specific episodes we do remember, we weave together into meaningful events that compose our "autobiographical memory," or the story of our individual life.

     d. From age two, children remember both general attributes of people and places, as well as specific episodes, but they do not begin to form their personal autobiographical stories until around age three and a half.

     e. Children at age four whose parents review incidents in much detail with them remember more than children whose parents ask simple questions.

     f. The events you can easily remember as an adult are those you had, as a child, put into narrative form, at least in your mind.

     g. Seeing an event from several points of view may make it more memorable because this means you are more open-minded.

     h. Seeing an event from several points of view may make it more memorable because this builds a stronger net of associations.

     i. A study of college students found that they often don't tell the truth about their early family life.

3. Circle the ONE letter that best describes the IMPLICATION of the article.

     a. Most people don't remember the first three years of their life because they aren't really interested in it once they become adults.

     b. People have difficulty remembering events before age three because the higher centers of their brain have not developed enough.

c. People with devoted parents who talk with them a lot will become more intelligent than children who are left alone or ignored.

d. Children's memories fade before age three to four not because of Freudian repression, but because they do not have the language skills to turn events into stories they can recall. Parents who review events in detail with their children can help create strong early memories.

e. People forget most of what happened before they enter school as a way to deal with the pain of childhood.

Answers on page 163.

WHAT TO DO

Read the following article on slam dancing just looking for the theses and proofs. This time really push for speed. Only glance at the examples long enough to be satisfied they're there. Swoop up the proofs. Gear yourself up to move rapidly. Time yourself. Go!

READ:

SLAM DANCING MAY LITERALLY KNOCK YOUR CLOTHES OFF

by Eleanor Dugan

If the Harpo Hypothesis is correct, you may soon be wearing crash helmets and knee pads . . .

Archimedes was in a bathtub. Newton was under an apple tree. I conceived the Harpo Hypothesis at two in the morning one July night in a yellow bean bag chair while I watched a Marx Brothers movie on TV.

If my theory is correct, "Slam Dancing" may soon do more than provide chiropractors with a lucrative business. It may change the way you and I dress.

If you haven't participated in this new dance craze, you may have seen pictures of it on TV. The participants, cheeks full of safety pins and bolts, throw themselves at each other as hard as they can, trying to inflict bodily injury. If possible, they hurl themselves off raised platforms to crush those beneath them. These people, in turn, try to get out of the way in time to let the leaper crash ignominiously to the floor. It's very playful.

Back to Harpo. There he was, jitterbugging with a group of Black teenagers in a barnyard. It was a great number, but something seemed vaguely wrong. Then it hit me.

The girls were all wearing long, tight skirts and their braless chests were bouncing painfully as they leaped and kicked. The boys also seemed hindered by the tightness of their pants in their slithering crouches and flying splits. A look at the TV Guide told me why: the film was *A Day at the Races* and the year was 1935, a good seven years before jitterbugging in short, pleated skirts and baggy zoot-suit pants became the national norm.

Then I recalled the first TV news films in the 1950's of society folk doing the racy new dance, the Twist. How silly the women looked trying to shimmy in their tight, boned bodices and bouffant ballerina skirts. Within months the "sack" came on the fashion scene, scorned and ridiculed but just right for the writhing necessary to rock around the clock.

Could it be, I thought, that new dance steps cause fashion to change? After all, until the age of video villages, dancing was a characteristic of all major social interchanges: tournaments, coronations, weddings and barn raisings. These dances were the major source of sharing news from other places. Jane Austen heroines were always hoping that enough strangers would turn up in their part of the country to make it possible to hold a dance.

We've always associated distinctive costumes with distinctive folk dances. The bent-kneed leaps of Russia require sturdy boots and voluminous trousers. Spanish dancing would never be done barefoot or in wooden clogs. The hula would fail in a kimono. Picture any characteristic folk dance without the accompanying costumes. Won't work, will it? But, which came first, the dance or the costume?

A quick comparison of costume and dance histories shows that, throughout western civilization, fashions have changed to enhance new dance steps.

In the 14th century, lords and ladies alike wore long, loose gowns, great for keeping warm in drafty castles, but hard to do more than promenade in. Then the vigorous peasant galliard became fashionable at court. Instead of pacing side by side, men faced their partners, seized them by the waist and lifted them in the air. Try to do that when she's wearing a great, woolen muumuu. She'd slide right through your hands and you'd both end up on the floor engulfed in homespun.

In a very short time by Gothic standards, 20 years or so, women appeared in tight-fitted, boned bodices, perfect for giving their partners a good grip. Men's long gowns shortened and their shoes lost their long points, all the better for displaying their fast footwork.

Here we have two interesting, contradictory trends. Dance historians have long noted that dance styles are begun by the lowly and move upwards. Fashion, on the other hand, is generally conceded to start at the top and move down.

The courante, popular from the late 1500's into the 1700's, required men to kneel down a lot. If you remember your Shakespeare, you know that in the mid 16th century men wore tights. Not knit tights— Queen Elizabeth I had the first knit garments in England—but fitted leggings cut from woven fabrics. Imagine the baggy knees, the awkward up and down movements caused by binding fabric. Pants, until then worn by only the lowliest workmen, appeared at court.

In the 18th century, when the minuet advanced arm movements to an art in themselves, cuffs exploded with lace to show off the hands of the dancer. Elegantly posed feet stimulated an orgy of shoe bows and jeweled buckles for both men and women. The minuet, also descended from a peasant dance, was adopted by the French court in 1670 and remained popular until the French Revolution.

The scandalous waltz also presaged a major fashion change. Waistlines had risen and skirts dwindled in the Napoleonic era and women assumed the simple silhouette of a Greek statue. The dresses of the Empire had shirred fullness in back falling from just below the shoulder blades. For a brief, astonishing period, women even sported back bustles, giving them the appearance of feminine Quasimodos.

Then the waltz became popular. It was worse than anything that had gone before. Not only did the man stand facing his partner, he embraced her and held her close, hand firmly on her waist to turn her through the intricacies of the dance. But courtly hands encountered wire bustles and yards of fabric instead of waists. This back extension required the gentleman to advance the ladies' front even closer to his own so that his arm could reach around behind her. The new Victorian morality quickly banished the back protuberances, slimmed the waist and extended the skirt to keep men at a proper arm's length.

Besides, who could waltz effectively in a simple sheath dress? The boisterous rhythms begged for miles of ruffles to sweep across a dance floor and that's what women got: crinolines that belled the skirt to romantic excess as ballrooms blossomed with swirling varicolored human flowers.

When changing economics and the decline of the monarchies made enormous ballrooms less accessible, skirts grew smaller.

Do new dances cause fashions to change?

The polka, with its somewhat jerky leaps, made huge skirts look awkward and skirts flattened and pulled back into the slim bustle silhouette of the last quarter of the 19th century.

Fashions remained fairly static until the 20th century when new stirrings were felt. Isadora Duncan danced with scarves and Europe was disrupted by revolutions, impressionist painters and new dance steps. In America Vernon and Irene Castle shook the nation and then the world with their exhibitions of the turkey trot, the fox trot, the bunny hug and the grizzly bear. Utterly impossible to do in the heavy, corseted fashions of the Victorian era. Mrs. Castle designed her own costumes: a light bra instead of a long corset, mid-calf skirts and (a national scandal) bobbed hair.

The Charleston in the early 1920's caused other big changes. Skirts shortened rapidly to allow for the vigorous kicks and feminine knees appeared for the first time in 2500 years. Chests were tightly bound to prevent uncomfortable bouncing. Waistlines became loose because there was no need for men to grasp them. Men's trousers widened alarmingly to accommodate wild leg swings.

In the very late 20's and early 30's, rapid changes in American music forced a change in dancing. Gliding to the crooning of Crosby, Columbo and Vallee was best done in sinuous sheaths of bias-cut fabric. Even Ginger's lively dances with Fred in this period were sometimes hindered by the sleek lines of her clothes.

The 40's brought jitterbugging, the 50's the twist, the 60's the frug. Tightly fitted bodices for women vanished in the mid 50's when men no longer needed to steer their partners. Indeed, since there was no longer a "men's step" and a "women's step," clothing reflected this by becoming androgynous. In the 70's, disco was king and the clothing responded with disco jeans, disco purses and disco dresses, clothes to flash and flow in the 110-decibel theatrical settings.

Now slam dancing is turning young Americans into human projectiles. Will Seventh Avenue start turning out football shoulder guards, crash helmets and knee pads? Are pre-bloodstained shirts and pre-torn pants just around the corner?

Harpo may know, but wherever he is, he's not talking.

Write down your reading time in the blanks below. Then answer the questions and determine your comprehension level from your score, as calculated on p. 163.

Length of article: 1,382 words.

Mins. _____ Secs. _____ Words per minute _____

Comprehension _____%

QUESTIONS

1. Check the author's THESIS.
   a. Rock music promotes violence.
   b. Harpo Marx is the inspiration for a new style of dancing.
   c. Slam dancing is a symptom of the moral decay of our time.
   d. Many people enjoy dressing up as movie stars such as Harpo Marx.
   e. Changes in dance styles cause changes in fashion.
2. Check FIVE of the SUPPORTS offered by the author.
   a. Black teenagers found it hard to jitterbug in the long, tight skirts and fitted pants of the mid-1930s.
   b. Juvenile crime has increased in an almost exact proportion to the sale of rock records.
   c. Harpo was noted for his dancing.
   d. It would be impossible to hula in a kimono.
   e. Vigorous dancing requires unrestrictive clothing.
   f. Irene Castle had to design her own clothes in order to perform the vigorous turkey trot, fox trot, and bunny hug.
   g. Joan Crawford inspired several dances of the thirties and forties.
   h. Today's young people wear shabby clothes to honor Harpo.
   i. The waltz was regarded as very risqué when it was introduced.
   j. The galliard exposed women's knees for the first time in 2,500 years.
3. Check the ONE major SIGNIFICANCE of the author's theory.
   a. Rock music should be banned.
   b. Movie stars should run for public office.
   c. It may be possible to predict new dances by observing new fashions.
   d. It may be possible to predict new fashions by observing new dances.
   e. Harpo Marx has had a profound effect on twentieth-century culture.
   f. The sound level in public places should be limited to 90 decibels.
   g. Slam dancing should be outlawed.
   h. Twenty years is a short time in the course of history.
   i. Vernon and Irene Castle initiated most of the dances we do today.
   j. Folk dancing requires special clothing.

Answers on page 163.

DAY 4 ANSWERS

BOOKS ARE NOT FAST FOOD

Opinion:
   Speed-reading is not a good thing.
Reason:
   Slow reading creates time for thought and reflection.
Significance:
   Reading should be savored.

A CHINK IN THE WALL

1. a–e–f (Score 10 points each)
2. b–d–e–h–i (Score 10 points each)
3. c (Score 20 points)
100 points equals 100%.

OUTLINE OF "A CHINK IN THE WALL"

1. OPINIONS
   a. A white middle-class doctor can learn important medical and social lessons from a poor black patient once her "eyes are opened" by events.
   b. An unplanned pregnancy for a poor, unmarried black teenager with an extended family support network is not the life-changing crisis it would be for a middle-class, single white professional woman.
   c. A white middle-class doctor and an uneducated black teenage girl each have strengths that the other would benefit by learning.
   d. When the author decides to become pregnant, she will try to do it the way Darling did: as something comfortable and natural. She also wants to live her life with a "take it as it comes" attitude, rather than worrying so much.

2. REASONS
   a. The doctor saw pregnancy and child care as life-changing events, an awesome responsibility, preferably undertaken by choice. To Darling, it had "simply happened," and was not a burden or problem, nor forever life-changing.
   b. The doctor saw the pregnancy and child care as "something to worry about," while Darling had faith that everything would be all right. Darling also had child-care skills from past experience and supportive family to help her.
   c. Darling is a loving mother, showering pride and affection on her "little man."
   d. "Darling has taught me to view my own wisdom with a comforting skepticism, and to approach my patients with a lot more respect."

3. SIGNIFICANCE
   Well-educated, comfortable people can learn important lessons from poor, uneducated people when something happens to "open a chink in the wall" that separates them. Life wisdom is often where you don't expect to find it.

THE SEARCH

1. c (Score 20 points)
2. b–d–e–f–g (Score 10 points each)
3. a–d–e–g–h–j (Score 5 points each)
100 points equals 100%.

COMPUTE YOUR RATE FOR "THE SEARCH"
(Approximate number of words: 3,325)

Time	Wpm	Time	Wpm
1 min.	3325	5 min.	665
1 min. 15 sec.	2660	5 min. 15 sec.	633
1 min. 30 sec.	2217	5 min. 30 sec.	605
1 min. 45 sec.	1900	5 min. 45 sec.	578
2 min.	1663	6 min.	554
2 min. 15 sec.	1478	6 min. 15 sec.	532
2 min. 30 sec.	1330	6 min. 30 sec.	512
2 min. 45 sec.	1209	6 min. 45 sec.	493
3 min.	1108	7 min.	475
3 min. 15 sec.	1023	7 min. 15 sec.	459
3 min. 30 sec.	950	7 min. 30 sec.	443
3 min. 45 sec.	887	7 min. 45 sec.	429
4 min.	831	8 min.	416
4 min. 15 sec.	782	8 min. 15 sec.	403
4 min. 30 sec.	739	8 min. 30 sec.	391
4 min. 45 sec.	700	8 min. 45 sec.	380

Your rate is _____ wpm.
(Record this on page 224.)

WE CAN TEACH READING BETTER

Visual Independence. Rapid silent reading and comprehension require, at the very outset, that the visual verbal system become independent of the sensory motor system. Rapid reading involves fewer motor fixations and wider visual segments of scanning, and this in turn means less motor involvement and more conceptual inferential activity. In effect, in rapid silent reading, the brain does more work and the eyes do less. We have some recent evidence that supports the importance of visual independence in advanced. . . . Visual independence amounts to a kind of automatization of the visual aspect of reading in which the visual scanning process is relatively independent of tactile motor input.

Meaning Construction. A second prerequisite to advanced silent reading is facility in meaning construction. From a cognitive development point of view, reading comprehension is not a passive process of decoding written symbols. On the contrary, it must be regarded as a constructive activity analogous to creative writing.

The point is that meaning is not inherent in written or spoken words but rather that the words are given meaning by readers or listeners who interpret them within their own storehouse of knowledge. Silent readers give meaning to the words they read by relating these to the conceptual system they have constructed in the course of their development. The richness of meaning they derive from their reading will depend both upon the quality of the material they are reading and the breadth and depth of their conceptual understanding. Satisfaction in reading often derives, in part at least, from the degree of fit between the material being read and the conceptual level of the reader. . . .

Receptive Discipline. A third prerequisite to effective silent reading seems at first to be a contradiction to what has just been said about the reader being an active participant in the process. This prerequisite is that the reader have a receptive attitude, a willingness to respond to the representations of others. Good readers, like good listeners, have to be simultaneously passive (receptive to the representations of others) and active (interpreting those representations within their own conceptual framework).

Many young people are poor readers for the same reason that they are poor listeners: They are more interested in representing their own thoughts and ideas than they are in interpreting the thoughts and ideas of others. They lack what might be called receptive discipline.

STUDYING THE SECRETS OF CHILDHOOD MEMORY

1. d (Score 20 points)
2. b–e–f–h (Score 15 points each)
3. d (Score 20 points)
100 points equals 100%.

SLAM DANCING

1. e (Score 25 points)
2. a–d–e–f–i (Score 10 points each)
3. d (Score 25 points)
100 points equals 100%.

COMPUTE YOUR RATE FOR "SLAM DANCING"
(Approximate number of words: 1,382)

Time	Wpm	Time	Wpm
1 min.	1382	5 min.	276
1 min. 15 sec.	1105	5 min. 15 sec.	263
1 min. 30 sec.	921	5 min. 30 sec.	251
1 min. 45 sec.	789	5 min. 45 sec.	240
2 min.	690	6 min.	230
2 min. 15 sec.	614	6 min. 15 sec.	221
2 min. 30 sec.	552	6 min. 30 sec.	212
2 min. 45 sec.	502	6 min. 45 sec.	204
3 min.	460	7 min.	197
3 min. 15 sec.	425	7 min. 15 sec.	190
3 min. 30 sec.	394	7 min. 30 sec.	184
3 min. 45 sec.	368	7 min. 45 sec.	178
4 min.	345	8 min.	172
4 min. 15 sec.	325	8 min. 15 sec.	167
4 min. 30 sec.	307	8 min. 30 sec.	162
4 min. 45 sec.	290	8 min. 45 sec.	157

Your rate is _____ wpm.
(Record this on page 224.)

DAY 5

Review of Five Patterns of Organization
Skimming

THE PROBLEM PATTERN

To spark action

Problem
Effects
Causes
Solution

THE OPINION PATTERN

To persuade

Opinion
Reasons
Significance

THE INSTRUCTION PATTERN

To instruct

Materials
  (optional)
Step 1
Step 2
Step 3, etc.

THE THESIS PATTERN

To prove something

Thesis
Proofs
Implications

THE INFORMATION PATTERN

To share information

Facet 1
Facet 2
Facet 3, etc.

Each of the following five articles represents one of the basic nonfiction formats: problem, instruction, information, opinion, thesis. Decide which is which and fill in the blanks at the end of the five articles.

[A]
KING KONG VS. CON EDISON

by David Dugan

Each night as the sun goes down, the Empire State Building begins to glow with an orange and pale green light of its own. The 102 stories of grey Art Deco granite come alive with a fairy tale brilliance that can be seen for 30 miles. It's easy to see what captured the heart of King Kong.

But King Kong didn't have to reckon with Consolidated Edison. The cost of this night-lighting has risen 300% in the last five years and now the building's owners are threatening to douse the lights unless outside funds are found to cover the cost increase.

Cole Porter wrote: "Imagine Mr. Lord without a Taylor, imagine Central Park without a sailor" . . . possible, perhaps, but I defy you to imagine the skyline without old 350 Fifth Avenue glittering and glimmering in the night.

Since the Landmark Commission has declared the Empire State Building a historical landmark, the city ought to provide funds for maintaining this bright tower, a beacon for native and tourist alike. Maybe Frank Sinatra and Joan Baez could do Save the Arc Lights concerts and the mayor could get school children to send their pennies to old Con Ed.

There's no brighter light on Broadway, so don't let it flicker out.

[B]
CITY LIGHTS MAY ALTER MIGRATION PATTERNS

Each night as the sun goes down, the Empire State Building begins to glow with an orange and pale green light of its own. The 102 stories of grey Art Deco granite come alive with a fairy tale brilliance that can be seen for 30 miles. It's easy to see what captured the heart of King Kong.

But, the Empire State Building and other tall buildings are also luring migrating birds from their ancient routes and altering North American bird life, according to one scientist.

Prof. Charles Shibuk of the American Ornithological Assn. has recorded major deviations in traditional flight patterns.

The number of banded birds that overshoot their traditional feed grounds has risen during the past 20 years in direct proportion to the volume of buildings over 500 feet tall in the east coast and west coast metropolitan areas, says Prof. Shibuk. Studies done in 1990, 1992, 1994 and 1996 show a 302% increase in bird dislocation while the cubic volume of buildings above 500 feet in the Boston-Washington corridor has risen 311% in the same period.

Even the swallows of Capistrano may be in danger. If Prof. Shibuk's theory is correct, within 20 years, the famous birds will be landing in Newark.

[C]
BIRDS ARE CRASHING INTO EMPIRE STATE BUILDING

Each night as the sun goes down, the Empire State Building begins to glow with an orange and pale green light of its own. The 102 stories of grey Art Deco granite come alive with a fairy tale brilliance that can be seen for 30 miles.

Unfortunately, the birds are also attracted to the Empire State Building and this year they are perishing in record numbers.

Maintenance Superintendent John Cocchi, who is in charge of cleaning up the dead birds, reports that the "body count" is up 300% from last year.

The cause may be the new ultra-high frequency scanning equipment that was installed last December on the 101st floor. Prof. Charles Shibuk of the American Ornithological Assn. speculates that these frequencies are disrupting the birds' natural sonar navigation.

Scientists from the Fish and Game Department have already developed a way to broadcast complementary frequencies to override the fatal signals given off by airport traffic control towers. Now they are trying to adapt this equipment to neutralize the scanning equipment. In the meantime, federal officials have ordered the equipment shut down until after migration season, to get the birds back on course.

[D]
NO LONGER THE HIGHEST, "EMPIRE" CELEBRATES ITS 75TH BIRTHDAY

Each night as the sun goes down, the Empire State Building begins to glow with an orange and pale green light of its own. The 102 stories of grey Art Deco granite come alive with a fairy tale brilliance that can be seen for 30 miles. It's easy to see what captured the heart of King Kong.

This week old "Empire" is celebrating its 75th birthday and the stars will be turning out to celebrate at a big party on the observation deck. Frank Sinatra, Ella Fitzgerald, Itzhak Perlman, Donny and Marie, and Luciano Pavarotti are scheduled to perform at a $1,000-a-head benefit for the Children's Fund.

Toodles Galloway, whose father played in the orchestra of the old Waldorf Hotel, which once stood on the site, will provide dance music for the occasion.

The 1,462-foot building stood supreme as the world's tallest structure for 35 years until it was surpassed by the World Trade Center here in New York, which in turn was surpassed by the Sears Tower in Chicago.

The building has long held the affection of New Yorkers and Americans. Even the remake of *King Kong*, changing the site of the ape's climb to the World Trade Center, hasn't changed the association of building and monkey in the public's mind.

[E]
THE SUN NEVER SETS ON THIS EMPIRE

Each night as the sun goes down, the Empire State Building begins to glow with an orange and pale green light of its own. The 102 stories of grey Art Deco granite come alive with a fairy tale brilliance that can be seen for 30 miles.

This month the U.S. Postal Service is commemorating the 75th birthday of this beloved landmark by issuing two three-color stamps. Two different first day covers will also be issued.

To get your surface mail cover, send a self-addressed unstamped envelope, plus $1 to Postmaster, Empire Station, NYC 10001. These covers will be stamped on August 14th and returned by surface mail.

A special airmail cover will also be available. These may be obtained by sending an unstamped, self-addressed envelope and $2 to Air Services, U.S. Postmaster, Main Station, NYC 10003. All mail received by August 10th will be hand stamped by astronauts aboard the Uranus 7 and returned to Earth by satellite shuttle on August 15th.

Mail may be hand delivered to the Main Post Office up to 10:00 a.m. on the morning of August 10th for airmail and up to noon at the Empire substation on August 14th for surface mail.

PROBLEM: _____

The problem is _____

_____

The effect(s) _____

_____

The cause(s) _____

_____

The solution(s) _____

_____

THESIS: _____

The thesis is _____

_____

The proof is _____

_____

The implication is _____

OPINION: _____

The opinion is _____

_____

Reasons are _____

_____

The significance is _____

_____

INSTRUCTION: _____

Step 1 _____

Step 2 _____

Step 3, etc. _____

INFORMATION: _____

Facet 1 _____

Facet 2 _____

Facet 3, etc. _____

Answers on page 193.

SKIMMING

You started skimming back under Previewing—flying high, looking for just the bit you want. It's like looking for the nearest plumber in the Yellow Pages while ignoring all the rest. You use this skill every day, probably without realizing it. For instance, how long would it take you to look up a phone number? Find a TV listing? Skim a theater section? Let's practice.

WHAT TO DO

Here's a section from the Hong Kong phone book. How quickly can you find the Mocambo Mahjong/Tinkau School?

Mahjong Schools

Chan Kai Choi 68 Tai Sun St 5-981-8018
Cheung Shing Co 198 Matauwei Rd 3-623140
  Do 3-625968
Cheung Shing & Co
  3 Yee Pei Sq 12-422827
Chui Lok Co 3 Temple St 3-840892
Chung Po Sang
  3 Spring Garden Lane 5-727865
Chung Wah Majong Co
  486 Shanghai St 3-316479
Double Won 3 Sau Fu St 12-760002
Fat Choi Co 33 Lung Kong Rd ..3-822040
Feder Co 23 Kam Wing St 3-215491
Good Luck Co 223 Temple St ...3-847208
  Do 3-847767
  225 Temple St 3-306485
Great China Entertainment Co The
  390 Lockhart Rd 5-735993 5-735995
Hing Lee Co 8 Wu Nam St ...5-526521
Ho Ho Fat Tat Co
  160 Temple St 3-858056
Ho Lee Mahjohn Gaming Hse Co
  361 Ngautaukok Rd ..3-898988 3-895589
Ho-Shun Lei Mahjong Co
  119 Woosung St ...3-316256 3-316693
  Do 3-316911 3-885361 3-885694
H K Majong Co 320 Lockhart Rd 5-745746
  Do 5-725874
Hop Shing Co 87 Shekpaiwan Rd ..5-535185
Hop Shing Entertainment Co
  87 Shekpaiwan Rd 5-520952
Kai Kee 72 South Wall Rd 3-821858
Kai Kee 48 Temple St 3-844466
Kai Kee Co 27 Kam Wing St ...3-226523
  Do 3-226522
Kai Kee Fun Den 15 Yan Oi Wai 3-890873
  Do 3-896060
Keung Kee Co 120 Temple St ...3-851052
Kin Marjoh Co 164 Portland St ..3-844685
  Do 3-844653 3-844691
Kung Fat Co 111 Wuhu St 3-624051
Kwok Pao Entertainment Co
  78 Java Rd 5-623811
Kwok Po Entertainment Co
  16 Tong Shui Rd 5-627079
Kwong Gut Bun 335 Ngautaukok Rd 3-892238
Lam Shui Lin
  42 Temple St 3-857679 3-857625

Lau Wei 390 Lockhart Rd 5-730281
Li Yuen Co 13 Larch St 3-920449
Loong Chu Majong Co
  3 Ivy St ..3-955523 3-955729 3-955936
Lucky 18 Pau Chung St 12-760322
Lucky & Win Majhong & Tinkau Common
  Gaming Hse 20 Pau Cheung St 12-760842
Lui Woon Sum 111 Wuhu St 3-623952
Man Hing 13A Pokfulam Village ..5-510011
Man Po Loy (Fook Kee)
  296 Lockhart Rd 5-751250
  Do 5-728598 5-721791
Mocambo Mah Joing Tin Kau School
  19 Peel St 5-453032 5-453025
Mocambo Mahjong/Tinkau School
  19 Peel St 5-435187
Nam Shing 385 Castle Peak Rd ..3-860333
Nam Shing Majong School
  385 Castle Peak Rd 3-784858
New World Co 240 Shaukeiwan Rd 5-602068
Pak Lok Majong Co 15 Un Chau St 3-867316
Sam Lee Co
  37 Tak Ching Circuit 12-822288
Shin Hing Co The
  187 Portland St 3-843007
Shing Hing Ma-Jong Co
  582 Shanghai St 3-961956 3-961980
  Do 3-961552 3-962378
Shui Cheong Marjok Co
  410 Shanghai St 3-841747
Shui Hing 187 Portland St 3-881321
  Do 3-881322 3-881323
Shun Lee Co
  93 Nam Cheong St 3-863849
Shun Lee (Kung Kee) Co
  93 Nam Cheong St 3-865521
Sing Kee Mar-Jong
  59 Ho Bui St 12-422274
Sui Cheong Mahjong Co
  410 Shanghai St 3-842040 3-884334
Sum Hoi Lee 44 Gillies Ave 3-622360
Sun Fat Choi 33 Lung Kong Rd ..3-820558
Sun King Cheung 36 Hau Wo St ..5-460963
Sun Kong Nam Co 79 Taipo Rd ..3-615962
Sun Lok Co 51 South Wall Rd ..3-821676
Sun Tai Fat Majong Amusement
  8 Tai Por Fong 12-426952
Sun Yat Loi
  150 Castle Peak Rd 3-782840

Sun Yuit Loy 150 Castle Peak Rd 3-865786
Tai Bo Lee Entertainment Co
  11 Wu Nam St 5-535676
  14 Chengtu Rd 5-531079
Tai Cheong Ho 199 Portland St ..3-885824
  Do 3-844156
Tai Choy Lee 15 Kam Wing St ..3-215493
Tai Fat Co 133 Temple St 3-857218
Tai Fat Ma Jong Schl
  133 Temple St 3-855546
Tai Fat Mahjong Schl
  25 Yi Pei Square 12-423160
Tai Fuk Lee Co 26 Mut Wah St ..3-895059
  Do 3-418813
Tai Hei Ma-Jong Co
  6 Boundary St 3-957465 3-962281
Tai Hing Mah Jong Entertainment Co
  23 Centre St 5-403716 5-403730
Tai Ho Choi Co 131 Temple St ..3-855804
  Do 3-843266
Tai Ka Lok 7 Fuk Ting St 12-760766
Tai Kam Lung 2 Spring Grdn Lne 5-721379
Tai Kar Fat Co 396 Lockhart Rd ..5-721178
  Do 5-732470 5-721189 5-721186
Tai Koon Yuen Yiu Kee
  123 Thomson Rd 5-724909
Tai Kwong Ming
  106 Wellington St 5-443994
Tai Loi Majong Co
  194 Matauwei Rd 3-659611
Tai Loong Wah Majong Amusement Co
  481 Jaffe Rd ...5-7908620 5-7902069
  Do 5-7908374 5-7908305
Tai Lung Fung Mah Jong Co
  393 Castle Peak Rd 3-7410205
Tai Po Loi Ma-Jhong Entertainment Co
  35 Spring Gdn Lne 5-727390
Tai Sam Yuen 219 Castle Peak Rd 3-864863
  Do 3-866701
Tai Seng Co 497 Jaffe Rd 5-7906654
  Do 5-7906658
Tai Tung Co 237 Portland St 3-313749
  235 Portland St 3-852854
Tai Wah 42A Pak Tai St 3-026180
Tai Wing Wah Co 32 Bute St ...3-945856
Tai Yau Lee Co 79 Hip Wo St ..3-426480
  Do 3-419488
Tak Shing & Co 3 Pau Cheung St 12-762541
Tak Sing 299 Shaukiwan Rd 5-602692

You probably did that in two or three seconds because you went right to the "M's." You used a framework you already know, the alphabet, to find what you didn't know, just as you use the nonfiction structures to find what you want to know. Now skim again and find a mah-jongg school at 111 Wuhu St.

WHAT TO DO

Quickly find the answers to the questions below as you skim the following *New York Times* theater directory.

1. At what theater is *Guys and Dolls* playing?_____
2. Lynn Redgrave is appearing in which production?_____
3. Which play is at a theater on 52nd Street?_____
4. Which street has the most theaters?_____
5. Which play won the 1993 Pulitzer Prize?_____
6. Who wrote the music for *Kiss of the Spider Woman*?_____
7. Which play starts at 8:30 P.M.?_____
8. Which Gershwin musical is playing?_____
9. Which play have over 30 million people seen?_____
10. Which play is listed as a new comedy?_____

Answers on pages 193–94.

Celebrating 100 Years of Broadway

BROADWAY

NOW THRU SEPT. 25
Thurs. & Fri. at 8, Sat. at 2 & 8
PART 1: MILLENNIUM APPROACHES

ANGELS IN AMERICA

Beginning October 4,
PART 2: PERESTROIKA
will join MILLENNIUM APPROACHES in
repertory. Both plays on sale now.

WINNER! 4 TONY AWARDS
including BEST PLAY!
1993 Pulitzer Prize
Tele-Charge 212-239-6200 (24hrs/7dys)
GROUPTIX 212-302-7000
Walter Kerr Theatre(+) 219 West 48th St.

TONIGHT AT 8PM
"UNMISSABLE AND UNBEATABLE!"
—Sheridan Morley, Int'l Herald Trib.
PERFORMANCES: 145
STANDING OVATIONS: 145

DAVID   PETULA   SHAUN
CASSIDY   CLARK   CASSIDY
in

BLOOD BROTHERS

Book, Music & Lyrics by
WILLY RUSSELL

Eves Mon-Sat at 8, Mats Wed & Sat at 2
Tele-Charge:(212)239-6200(24hrs/7dys)
Groups:(212)398-8383/(800)223-7565
MUSIC BOX THEA.(+) 239 W. 45th St.

Tomorrow at 8pm
THE ANDREW LLOYD WEBBER/
T.S.ELIOT INTERNATIONAL AWARD
WINNING MUSICAL

CATS

Mon-Wed,Fri,Sat8;MatsWed,Sat2;Sun.3
Tele-Charge (212)239-6200(24hrs/7dys)
Outside Metro N.Y.: (800) 432-7250
Groups (212) 239-6262
Winter Garden Thea(+) 50 St.& B'way

Tonight & Tom'w at 8, Sat. at 2 & 8
Sunday Matinees begin Sept. 12 at 3pm
BEST MUSICAL
1993 OLIVIER AWARD
1992 TONY AWARD
1992 DRAMA DESK AWARD
1992 OUTER CRITICS CIRCLE AWARD
"A FIRECRACKER OF A SHOW!"
—David Patrick Stearns, USA Today

HARRY   JODI
GROENER   BENSON
in
The new GERSHWIN musical comedy

CRAZY FOR YOU

Eves Mon-Sat at 8, Mats Wed & Sat at 2
Tele-Charge (212)239-6200(24hrs/7dys)
Outside NY, NJ, CT: (800) 432-7250
Groups: (212)398-8383/(800)223-7565
Shubert Theatre(+) 225 W. 44th Street

FINAL WEEKS! MUST END SEPT. 5!
Tonight & Tomorrow at 8
"THE FUNNIEST SHOW ON B'WAY!
IRWIN AND SHINER ARE A
TRIUMPH!"—Raidy, Newhouse Syn.
DAVID SHINER   BILL IRWIN

FOOL MOON

A New Comedy
with THE RED CLAY RAMBLERS
Mon-Sat 8, Mats: Wed & Sat 2
Call TicketMaster Now! (212) 307-4100
Richard Rodgers Th. (+) 226 W.46th St.

Tonight at 8
"YOU MUST NOT MISS THIS
'GUYS AND DOLLS'!"
—Frank Rich, The New York Times

GUYS AND DOLLS

Eves Mon-Sat at 8, Mats Wed & Sat at 2
Telecharge:(212)239-6200(24hrs/7dys)
Outside NY, NJ, CT: (800) 432-7250
Groups:(212)398-8383/(800)223-7565
Martin Beck Thea.(+) 302 W. 45 St.

(+)

THIS SIGN, WHEN FOLLOWING THE
NAME OF A THEATER, INDICATES
THAT A SHOW IS EQUIPPED WITH AN
INFRARED LISTENING SYSTEM

LAST 3 WEEKS!
FINAL PERFORMANCE SEPT. 5
TONIGHT AT 8PM

"THE BEST NEW MUSICAL OF THE
SEASON. A DAZZLING, FRESH AND
ORIGINAL WINNER!"
—Stewart Klein, WNYW-TV

JELLY'S LAST JAM

A New Musical
with

BRIAN   BEN
MITCHELL   VEREEN
PHYLICIA
RASHAD

Tue-Sat at 8, Wed & Sat at 2, Sun at 3
Tele-Charge (212)239-6200(24hrs/7dys)
Outside NY, NJ, CT: (800) 432-7250
Groups: (212)398-8383/(800)223-7565
Virginia Theatre (+) 245 W. 52nd St.

TONIGHT at 8
WINNER! 7 TONY AWARDS
incl. BEST MUSICAL
WINNER! NY DRAMA CRITICS' AWARD
BEST MUSICAL
WINNER! 5 DRAMA DESK AWARDS
incl. BEST MUSICAL

CHITA RIVERA
BRENT CARVER ANTHONY CRIVELLO
in

KISS OF THE SPIDER WOMAN

The Musical
Book by   Music by   Lyrics by
Terrence   John   Fred
McNally   Kander   Ebb
Directed by Harold Prince
Mon-Sat at 8; Mats: Wed & Sat at 2
TELE-CHARGE: (212) 239-6200
Groups: 997-KISS or 239-6262
Broadhurst Thea.(+) 44 St. W. of B'Way

THEATER DIRECTORY

TONIGHT AT 8PM
Good Seats Available!
Sunday Mats. resume Sept. 12 at 3pm
TICKETS FROM ONLY $15
Tele-charge(212)239-6200(24hrs/7dys)
Outside NY/NJ/CT: (800)432-7250
Over 30 Million People Have Seen

LES MISERABLES

Mon.-Sat. 8pm, Mats: Wed. & Sat. 2pm
GROUP SALES: (212) 398-8383 or
(800) 223-7565; (212) 239-6262
Latecomers Will Only Be Seated At A
Suitable Break In The Performance.
Imperial Theatre(+) 249 W. 45th St.

Good Seats Available!
THE CLASSIC LOVE STORY
OF OUR TIME
TONIGHT AT 8PM
TICKETS FROM ONLY $15
Tele-charge(212)239-6200(24hrs/7dys)
Outside NY/NJ/CT: (800)432-7250

MISS SAIGON

Mon.-Sat. 8PM, Mats: Wed. & Sat. 2PM
GROUPS 20 OR MORE:
Group Sales Box Office (212) 398-8383
or (800) 223-7565; TDI: (212)541-8457;
Shubert Groups:(212)239-6262
Broadway Theatre(+) 53rd & Broadway

5th Smash Month!
Still With Original Cast
HOW MANY TIMES HAVE YOU SEEN
BROADWAY'S NEW CULT HIT?
TONIGHT & TOMORROW at 8
"THE SLEEPER HIT OF THE SEASON!"
—William A. Raidy, Newhouse Nwsprs.
LYNN REDGRAVE in

SHAKESPEARE FOR MY FATHER

conceived & written by Lynn Redgrave
produced & directed by John Clark
TicketMaster:307-4100/Group:398-8383
$15 Student Tkts ½ hr. prior to any perf.
Tue.-Sat. 8; Mats: Wed. & Sat. 2, Sun. 3
Helen Hayes Theatre (+) 240 W.44th St.

Performances Resume Sept. 28
CALL TICKETMASTER NOW: 307-4100
"AN EVENING OF SHEER
ENCHANTMENT!" —Rich, NY Times

SHE LOVES ME

The Musical Hit
Tue-Sat at 8; Mats:Wed & Sat at 2, Sun 3
Grps:398-8383, 765-8058, 800 223-7565
Brooks Atkinson (+), 47 St W. of B'Way

TONIGHT AT 8
TICKETS FROM ONLY $15
Tele-charge(212)239-6200(24hrs/7dys)
Outside NY/NJ/CT: (800)432-7250

THE PHANTOM OF THE OPERA

Shubert Groups: (212) 239-6262
or TDI (212) 541-8457
MAJESTIC THEATRE(+) 247 W.44th St.

Tonight at 8
WINNER! 5 TONY AWARDS
WINNER! BEST MUSICAL
Outer Critics Circle Award
WINNER! 6 DRAMA DESK AWARDS
"BRILLIANT, BLOODY BRILLIANT!"
—Clive Barnes, New York Post
THE WHO'S

TOMMY

Music and Lyrics by Pete Townshend
Book by
Pete Townshend & Des McAnuff
Mon-Sat at 8, Mats. Wed & Sat at 2
Telecharge (212) 239-6200(24hrs/7dys)
Outside NY, NJ, CT: (800) 432-7250
Groups: (212)398-8383/(800)223-7565
St. James Theatre(+), 246 W.44th St.

COMEDY TONIGHT at 8—$20 Rush Tix
Today 5:30-6:30 at B.O. with this ad
Winner! 1993 Word-of-Mouth Award
"NON-STOP BELLY LAUGH"-Liz Smith
2nd Laugh-Smash Comedy Hit Year!

BEAU JEST

Mon,Wed-Sat.8;Mats.Wed.2,Sat,Sun.3
Telecharge 239-6200/Groups 496-5710
Lambs Theatre, 130 W. 44, 997-1780

TONIGHT & TOMORROW AT 8:30
"MORE BITE AND BETTER THAN
EVER!" —WQXR Radio
NY's ever-changing mega-musical hit!

FORBIDDEN BROADWAY 1993

Tue-Fri 8:30; Sat 7 & 10; Sun 3:30 & 7:30
BOX OFFICE (212) 838-9090
Ticketmaster307-4100/Groups398-8383
Dinner/Theatre Package Available!
THEATRE EAST, 211 East 60th St.

TONIGHT at 8
"SCREAMINGLY FUNNY!"-NY Post
4th "HILARIOUS" YEAR !

FOREVER PLAID

The Heavenly Musical Hit
Tue-Fri 8; Sat 7:30 & 10:30; Sun 3 & 7:30;
Mat Wed: 2:30. Food/drink avail, No Min.
PLAID-TIX: 595-7400/Grps: 719-9566
STEVE McGRAW'S, 158 W. 72nd St.

TONIGHT & TOMORROW at 8
2 Outer Critics Circle & 3 Obie Awards
including BEST OFF-B'WAY PLAY!

JEFFREY

by Paul Rudnick
directed by Christopher Ashley
Call TicketMaster now: (212) 307-4100
Groups:302-7000/Box Office:420-8000
Tue.-Fri. 8, Sat. 7 & 10, Sun. 3 & 7
Minetta Lane Theatre, 18 Minetta Lane

TONIGHT AT 8
"A CUNNING LITTLE WHODUNIT"
-New Yorker

PERFECT CRIME

Mon., Thurs.-Sat. 8PM; Sun. 7PM
Mats. Wed. & Sat. 2, Sun. 3PM
All Seats $30   Mail Orders Now
B.O. 695-3401   Ticketmaster 307-4100
Theatre Four   424 West 55th Street

Skimming Sprint #1

Put a pencil slash through the word that means almost the SAME as the
first word in each line. Go as fast as you can, timing yourself. See if you
can do them all in ninety seconds. If you do them all in one minute, great.
If you can do them in less than forty-five seconds, you are a pro.

1. **grab**   grapple grin snatch hatch hutch such
2. **book**   tome tame take sake sack sock
3. **wish**   destroy display desire dessert desert
4. **fly**   pair pour soar sour soap sole single
5. **cat**   puddle pudgy puppy pussy fussy fancy
6. **fog**   mist missed mast mass moss money magic
7. **gun**   preferred permanent perfect paper pistol
8. **number**   static statistic stamina stepping stationary
9. **wash**   client clamor clay clap clean clip class
10. **boat**   basket bed shed ship sheet heat happy
11. **snicker**   love leg little long laugh linger longer
12. **stove**   open oven even ever aver after alter
13. **shoe**   boot foot fool tool toil soil song sag
14. **vision**   plight flight sight might night nibble
15. **renegade**   outside outdone outlaw in-law indigestion
16. **perhaps**   minute mackerel mayhem maybe mayor
17. **shine**   polish politic polite police poetic paranoid
18. **vicious**   vacuous vehement vibrant cruel crazy cracked
19. **elegant**   sinful sumptuous satisfying silly solid tepid
20. **glitter**   thin thank spank sparkle spilled splashed
21. **unusual**   slender piquant finicky listen laugh rare
22. **bitter**   sour slippery sandy soft sulky slipper slap
23. **leap**   found sound pound round bound hound
24. **box**   cart crate crack track trait plait please tease
25. **hidden**   disgusting dangerous cautious concealed careful

Time ————————

Answers on page 194.

SKIMMING SPRINT #2

Put a pencil slash through the word that means about the OPPOSITE of the first word in each line. Go as fast as you can, timing yourself. See if you can do them all in ninety seconds. If you do them all in one minute, great. If you do them in less than forty-five seconds, you are a pro.

1. **rough**   ragged raging sage smooth smell small
2. **dirty**   clear clean cling claim clam clumsy calm
3. **finger**   finish famish tarnish tingle toe top tap
4. **ceiling**   floor flood flute flop flip flue blue flub
5. **casual**   dismal normal formal fortunate fortitude fatuous
6. **day**   naught narrow naughty night nickel never nuts
7. **alive**   dazed dazzled double deceased depressed deed
8. **happy**   miserable miserly masterful mink muddy mopped
9. **silly**   sailing sinful solemn sapped sunny safe
10. **wonderful** awl anvil apple ant anatomy ask awful
11. **awake**   slippery slap slush slim sleeping weeping
12. **dark**   late light last lint loft left lift laugh
13. **little**   bag bug beg bog hog huge hag hug
14. **icy**   hat hit hot cot got gold fold hold
15. **wealth**   walking waiting parting poverty paltry
16. **dismal**   chair chore cheerful chase chaise chafe
17. **sweet**   sweat swindle wine sour spine
18. **laugh**   care car carry cry try tray tarry tar
19. **cautious** cartful colorful careless careworn candy
20. **go**   step staple stipple stop stump stupid steps
21. **stale**   frigid fragile frost frantic fresh frump
22. **lazy**   easy evil every energetic engine eat
23. **always**   niece nimble noise nice never nuts
24. **end**   beg big bargain beginning between bud
25. **luminous** bull hull gull dull full pull null

Time_____

Answers on page 194.

WHAT TO DO

Set your timer for 2 minutes. Grab your pencil and skim the following article, putting pencil strokes (not a check—that takes two slashes, therefore too much time) through any place names such as "France" or "Rome" and also through any name that describes a language or people of a particular region, such as "French" or "Roman." Zip through at maximum speed. Go.

SKIM:

"A LILAC LUKE-WARM SEA"

THE WANDERINGS OF LAFCADIO HEARN

by Paul Collins

He was born in 1850 on the Greek island of Santa Maura, the ancient "Lefcadia" for which he was named, and died in Japan in 1904. His father was a military doctor from an old Dorsetshire family in England which had settled in Ireland at the end of the 17th century. His mother was from Malta with Phoenician, Arab, Norman, Spanish and Italian ancestors. In later years Lafcadio liked to think he had a touch of Romany from his father's side, a fitting predisposer to his gypsy wanderings.

His childhood language was Italian and he said his prayers in Demotic Greek. His parents soon returned to Ireland where his mother tired of the climate or her husband and departed when Lafcadio was only six. His father remarried and sent the boy to live with a great aunt. Hearn never saw either of them again.

His aunt had him educated by private tutors in Dublin and at Catholic schools in England and France. He remained a British subject until he became a naturalized Japanese citizen at the age of forty-six. At various times he lived in Martinique, the Windward Islands and British Guiana and made a meager living translating many of the great writers of France. Yet he is universally regarded as an American writer.

"Yes," he said in a letter to an English friend in Japan, "I have got out of touch with Europe altogether and think of America when I make comparisons (with Japan). At nineteen years of age, after my people had been reduced from riches to poverty by an adventurer,—and before I had seen anything of the world except in a year of London among the common folk,—I was dropped moneyless on the pavement of an American city to begin life. Often slept in the street, etc."

He was a small man, five feet three inches tall, and nearly blind. One eye had been injured in a childhood accident and it stared white and opaque at the world. The other, myopic to the point of endangering his life when he tried to cross the street, bulged like that of a beetle. He used a magnifying glass for close work, a telescope for distance; otherwise his world consisted of the few feet in front of him. He was also, as one biographer said, "shy as an African pygmy and as quick to take offense as the king's musketeers."

His limited classical education left him with a love of language and no way to earn a living. In New York and later in Cincinnati he existed mainly through the kindness of acquaintances who fed him and gave him warm places to sleep as one would a stray animal.

When he sought the warmth of the Cincinnati Public Library, the librarian took pity and found him odd jobs to do. A Syrian peddler gave him work and he slept in a box of paper shavings behind a print shop where the printer, Henry Watkins, offered to teach him the trade. Watkins called him "The Raven" and their correspondence was later collected into *Letters from the Raven*.

For Watkins, he worked as a proofreader, poring over the galleys with his one myopic eye six inches from the page. At night he wrote newspaper articles that he didn't have the courage to submit.

Then in 1872 he crept into the office of Colonel John A. Cockerill, the editor of the *Cincinnati Enquirer*. "Do you pay for contributions?" he whispered. Cockerill replied in the affirmative. Hearn handed over a manuscript with trembling hands "and stole away," Cockerill said, "like a distorted brownie, leaving behind him an impression that was uncanny and indescribable."

The *Cincinnati Enquirer* used that manuscript and almost everything that Hearn brought them. The Sunday editions frequently had 14 or 15 pages of his writing and it soon became cheaper to have him on the payroll as an employee.

It is difficult to associate his rather rococo pronouncements of this period with the clean, spare prose of his Japanese years. Yet much of his later style clearly evolved in Cincinnati. The romance and lush descriptions tempered by sheer horror were characteristic of American journalism of the period. Unlike 19th-century books and magazines, newspapers appealed to a popular male taste and could comfortably explore the sordid, the cruel and the shocking in an embellished literary style that would have made even Victorian authors blush.

The wages were low—$10 a week for cub reporters and perhaps $30 for a top name—but newspaper employees ate regularly, unlike their more esteemed brethren. Writers like Bierce, Crane, Phillips and Dreiser fed themselves while they defied "loftier" literary traditions.

Hearn's work in this period embodied every virtue and vice of the era. His employers even encouraged his excesses. He described a visit to a hospital during a yellow fever epidemic thus: "The grizzled watcher of the inner gate extended his pallid palm for that eleemosynary contribution exacted from all visitors;— and it seemed to me that I beheld the gray Ferryman of Shadows himself, silently awaiting his obolus from me, also a Shadow."

He used his knowledge of French to present translations of the more dazzling and controversial French authors, probably without royalty payments, and drew on his childhood readings of classical literature to weave vivid recreations of the folk tales of Arabia and India for his Ohio readers. Later in Japan he recalled, "My first work was awfully florid. I should like now to go through many paragraphs written years ago and sober them down."

Hearn wrote of a spider "repairing her web of elfin silk" and then in turn described a murdered, burnt corpse into which he had curiously thrust his fingers to learn the consistency of a boiled human brain. This same mixture of poetry and horror, infiltrated with his love of the exotic, was the hallmark of his later work.

"I would give anything," he wrote in 1883, "to be a literary Columbus—to discover a Romantic America in some West Indian or North African or Oriental region. . . . If I could only become a Consul at Bagdad, Algiers, Isphahan, Benares, Samarkand, Nippo, Bangkok, Ninh-Binh—or any part of the world where ordinary Christians do not like to go!"

In Cincinnati Hearn married a black woman named Alethea Foley and lived with her in a shanty next door to a stable. If he had been in almost any other profession, the resulting scandal would have left him jobless immediately, but newspapers were a law unto themselves and it was probably his contentious nature, not his marriage, that caused his discharge from the *Cincinnati Enquirer* a year later. He quickly found employment with the *Cincinnati Commercial*, albeit at a lower salary.

In 1877 Hearn left Alethea—no divorce was necessary for mixed marriages were not legally recognized in Ohio—and went to Memphis before moving on to New Orleans. There an attack of dengue or breakbone fever nearly killed him. After months of starvation, he found work on the *New Orleans Item* at $10 a week.

It was easier to live in the soothing warmth of New Orleans on such a small salary, and the sensual heat of his writing seemed more at home here. The occasional scandals about his private life, possibly based more on the tone of his writings than actual misdeeds, may have helped his rise or at least did not hinder it, for four years later the *New Orleans Times-Democrat* was paying him $30 a week.

New Orleans might be regarded as his first step toward his ultimate destiny, Japan. Here he wrote "Some Chinese Ghosts" and realized his affinity for the tropics. He visited Grande Isle in the Gulf of Mexico in 1884 and thereafter wrote of nature, "nude, warm, savage and amorous."

He got a commission from Messrs. Harper to write travel articles and departed for the Windward Islands and British Guiana in 1887. He settled in St. Pierre in Martinique, but dreamed of going on to the Latin countries, "to haunt the crumbling Portuguese and Spanish cities and steam up the Amazon or Orinoco and get romances nobody else could find." Here he wrote *Two Years in the French West Indies.*

In 1889 he spent an unhappy summer in Philadelphia and an unhappier winter in New York where he wrote of wanting to be back "among the monkeys and the parrots, under a violet sky among green peaks and an eternally lilac and luke-warm sea . . . the rich, divine, moist, life-sapping and life-giving heat of the tropics."

He accepted another commission from Harper for a travel book and left for Japan in 1890. In Tokyo, he predictably quarreled with Harper, lost the commission and again faced starvation. This time he found employment as a professor of English at a government school in Matsue, the capital of a feudal province on the Sea of Japan. His salary of $45 a month made him one of the richer inhabitants of the little city.

Unlike the rest of the world that Hearn had encountered, the Japanese did not regard him as small and ugly. He was taller than many of them and as for his face, well, all foreigners looked odd to the Japanese, Hearn no more so than others. Hearn loved Matsue and the people returned his affection.

His first winter there saw unusually severe weather, and, after suffering through several freezing nights, Hearn took the advice of friends and married. His bride, Setsu Koizumi, was the daughter of an impoverished samurai family, plump and plain, polite and conscientious. Hearn acquired a devoted bride and also a large hungry family of in-laws and relatives. He supported them all and amazingly they were loyal and devoted in return.

They kept his working hours free of interruptions, prepared European meals for him, managed his money scrupulously and taught him Japanese customs. His wife read him classic Japanese stories, translated into their own private language that they called "Mr. Hearn dialect," Herun-san Kotoba. He became a Japanese citizen in 1896 after the Koizumis legally adopted him as their son.

Hearn's first son, Kazuo, was the light of his life. At Kazuo's birth, Hearn had knelt by Setsu's bed praying in broken Japanese, "Come into the world with good eyes." Though three other children followed, it was Kazuo, accompanied by Setsu, who would always recall his father when the ghosts and demons of his creativity seized him. With the birth of "Great treasure child," Hearn became Papa-san, the leader and insulated center of a large, warm family.

"There are nearly twelve here to whom I am Life and Food and other things. However intolerable anything else is at home, I enter into my little smiling world of old ways and thoughts and courtesies; where all is soft and gentle as something seen in sleep." This pleasing domesticity sustained him when the family was forced to move to Kumamoto, then Kobe, and then Tokyo, as the Ministry of Education transferred him, capriciously he thought, from school to school.

It was here that Hearn's writing obtained the simplicity and power that would characterize his remaining work: *At that instant Hoichi felt his ears gripped by fingers of iron and torn off. Great as the pain was, he gave no cry. The heavy footfalls receded along the veranda, descended into the garden, passed out to the roadway, ceased. From either side of his head, the blind man felt a thick warm trickling; but he dared not lift his hands.*

Of the sixteen books he published in his lifetime, only one, *Japan: An Attempt at Interpretation*, is a book properly speaking. The others are either loose novelettes like *Chita* and *Youma* or else they are collections of shorter pieces that appeared in magazines. Some of his students took down his lectures word for word and after his death a whole series of volumes—four in America, five in Japan—was compiled and published from his notes.

Cornell University in Ithaca, N.Y. invited Hearn to lecture, and for a while he thought he would take his son, Kazuo, to visit the United States and attend school there. But Cornell changed its mind and the trip was never made.

He worked constantly, concerned with providing for his family even though the doctors warned him that he had a weak heart. The Japanese winter was torture and he dreamed of visiting warm, tropical Manila, but he dared not leave his writing desk. "Money, money, money" he would murmur as he worked.

He died in Tokyo in 1904. His last words were in Japanese, "Ah, Byoki no tame"—ah, on account of illness. A Buddhist archbishop presided at the cremation and his ashes were returned to a place of honor in Papasan's study. There his children, descended from Japanese and Greek warriors, English and Irish landowners, Arab and Italian traders, gathered twice a day to recite prayers before his photograph.

Count your pencil strokes. If you found over 100, you did very well. There are 117 place names and languages mentioned.

WHAT TO DO

Get a pencil and go through this article, putting a pencil stroke through the names of inventions. Read nothing else, only their names. Notice how you resist the temptation to read more thoroughly. Remember, this is skimming! Find 13 in one minute. Go.

SKIM:

AUSTRALIANS LIKE *THE INVENTORS* ON TV BOTH FOR FUN AND COMMERCIAL REASONS

by William D. Hartley

Staff Reporter *of* The Wall Street Journal

SYDNEY—Don't try to reach an Australian corporate research director or marketing official at 8 p.m. on Wednesdays. He'll be busy watching television.

The program attracting so many eyes is an Australian Broadcasting Commission show called *The Inventors,* and it is watched by more people in Australia than any other show. Most just see it as entertainment, but many viewers watch for commercial reasons.

"I watch that show every week without fail," says Colin Payne, a marketing man for a big hardware maker. "It's almost a directive from my managing director."

The format is simple. Four amateur inventors appear, demonstrate their inventions and are judged by a panel. The complications arise the following morning as company after company tries to reach the previous evening's inventor. Telephoning the show's producer, Beverly Gledhill, on Thursday morning is, as a magazine noted, "rather like trying to get through to God."

Miss Gledhill estimates that about 60% of the inventions that have appeared since the show began seven years ago have reached the market.

ROTATING BRUSH

For example, a rotating carwashing brush that appeared during the show's first year is widely sold throughout Australia by Mr. Payne's company, Sylon International Ltd. The brush is attached to a hose, water hits vanes and spins the brush. Another salable device was a simple pineapple peeler that produces slices of fresh pineapple.

"The two men on the panel weren't impressed, but the panel's woman thought it was marvelous," recalls Miss Gledhill.

"Unless you've tried to peel a pineapple, you don't know what a yucky job it is." A local company makes the peeler and recently shipped 1,000 units to a distributor in Hawaii to see if it would sell there.

Mostly the show is a lot of gadgetry, but serious industrial inventions do appear. Named best invention last year was a machine and process to make steel-reinforced concrete panels in any shape by using steel fibers instead of bare mesh. Another invention came from a man who was badly jolted in an ambulance on the way to a hospital. Later he invented a six-wheel suspension system that an ambulance service here uses.

A German immigrant who sells plants was angered when a cardboard-pot supplier raised prices, so he devised a technique and machine to make pots out of cow dung and straw. "The environment people went ape on that one," Miss Gledhill says. A big advantage is that the pot can be planted with the plant and provides fertilizer. A big garden-equipment maker, Hortico Ltd., is negotiating with the inventor. Hortico also is giving a prize this year for the best gardening invention. "Maybe the winner will come to us for production and selling," says John Hill, state manager for the company.

BEST-KNOWN INVENTION

Probably the invention from the show that is best known to Australians is the orbital engine. A backyard inventor, Ralph Sarich, showed it in 1972. Mr. Sarich currently is in a joint venture with Broken Hill Pty., Australia's largest industrial concern, to develop it.

Broken Hill has spent the equivalent of $1.9 million annually on the engine. "We believe we have sufficient evidence to test whether the world is interested in it," says Russell J. Fynmore, a senior company executive. "In the next six months, we'll be seeking to sell development licenses [to] companies in the big engine business from motor bikes up to autos."

The popularity of *The Inventors* apparently stems from the propensity of Australians to tinker. It was long an isolated country and in parts of the West and North, the feeling of isolation still is strong. A disproportionate number of inventions, in fact, come from those sparsely settled areas. "The remoteness breeds into Australians the idea that if you want something, you don't go to a store but you make it," Miss Gledhill believes.

Farmers are big contributors to the show because they are usually in remote areas, and when a problem arises they must solve it as best they can. In the north of the state of Queensland, for example, farmers make temporary grain silos by lining huge tubes of chicken wire with cloth. But it's difficult to climb the mesh, so one farmer invented a pair of boots that grip the wire so easily that he can run up the silo.

HOME AND YARD GADGETS

Other areas of Australia tend to produce more home and yard gadgets for the show. Above-ground swimming pools are popular in the nation, but their small size prevents much exercise. So a man developed a harness and tension device that a swimmer can fight against, and by the time he has traveled 10 feet, he has swum the equivalent of a 500-yard race. A device to be shown this year is a car-top luggage rack that converts to a covered bed.

The show runs 18 weeks a year, but long before the first airing Miss Gledhill and her assistant, Paul Belfanti, begin reducing the 500 or so entries they get each year to about 80. They haunt shops to make sure something they've accepted isn't already being produced. Some entries seem to be hardy perennials, like step ladders with adjustable legs for uneven ground, heated toilet seats and mailboxes that signal automatically when a letter is inserted. "People are kinky about letter boxes," sighs Miss Gledhill.

One woman who failed to make the show designed raincoats for tomato plants. "She thought the little dears wouldn't like to get wet," the producer laughs.

Some inventors come back several times. Stanley Blakeway, who invented the spinning car-washing brush, returned with a technique to build a swimming pool in a day by using a roll of steel plate that springs into the proper shape. This year he wants to demonstrate what he calls a pack-away-box trailer, and although the show's staff isn't sure what it is, he'll probably appear.

Count your pencil strokes. If you found all 13 in under forty-five seconds, you did very well. Ready for another?

WHAT TO DO

Read through this article, putting a pencil slash through each and every mention of a place where the author, Jan Morris, has been able to write. Go as fast as you can. Try to find more than 16 in ninety seconds or less.

SKIM:

A Welcome in the Hillsides

by Jan Morris

Jan Morris describes a writer's habitat

"OH, I WON'T interrupt you," they always say, "I didn't realise you were . . ."—but I have pounced on them by then. I suppose there are writers who dislike being interrupted, but I am not among them. "Come in, come in," I fulsomely cry. "Coffee? Biscuits? A glass of wine?": and so for half an hour or so I can get away from my typewriter, and behave like a normal person.

For writing, wherever you do it, is like a kind of drug, of varying effects.

I myself write a book three times, and each successive draft influences me differently. The first, which is a sort of stream-of-consciousness affair, drains me of all feeling, numbs me, rather like that soothing but distinctly debilitating shot they give you before you leave for the operating theatre. The second draft is a sensible, no-nonsense, tidying-up process, and is more like a wholesome medicinal corrective—vitamin pills, perhaps, or some anti-migraine extract.

But the third draft, that's pure hallucination! That's when I try to make it sing and flow—bother the facts, stick the melody!—and when people interrupt me then they often eye me strangely, as though I really am hooked on some secret stimulant.

These inner medications, I find, operate wherever I am. It is the work, not the setting, that triggers them. I began my professional life as a foreign correspondent, and this taught me to write anywhere, at any time: there is no room for artistic temperament, no yearning for compatible vibrations, when you have to cable a thousand words in half-an-hour's time. I have written in the backs of lorries, on the decks of warships, in Arab tents, in Afrikaan kraals, in a saloon bar in the Yukon, in a Moroccan hospital, in an anteroom of Yves St. Laurent's salon, on a Mississippi towboat, in a Central American secret police chief's bunker, in a Las Vegas wedding chapel, on the steps of a just-opened 12th Dynasty tomb, beside a camp fire in the Omani desert, and in a damp cold tent on the Himalayan slopes.

The product varied in quality, though, I have to admit, and in some places I do seem to write better than in others. I find it hard, for instance, in public libraries. Many of my colleagues do their best work in the silent rooms of the London Library, that haven of civilised efficiency in St. James's Square. Not me. The scratching of competitive pens inhibits me. The hush deadens my spirit. The presence of more scholarly contemporaries makes me feel I ought to be verifying my references. The words do not exactly dry up inside me, but they are no longer quite themselves: besides, I am never absolutely certain that I have paid my subscription.

On the other hand noisy, raffish public places suit me well. Nobody is going to shrivel my purple passages in an airport lounge, for example (though I have more than once been asked, at airports here and there, if I am a demonstrator for Olympia typewriters). I love the constant variety of distractions, the shifting cosmopolitan scene, the muffled loudspeaker voices in the background, the ever-present possibility of seeing somebody I know and the very good chance that somebody may engage me in conversation, if only to ask if that particular model is available on extended credit.

Mobile places, too, seem to suit my Muse—perhaps she wants to remind me that however hard I try to be historian or essayist, I am only a wandering reporter really. In the days when aircraft were noisier (and I was brasher, perhaps) I often used to type chapters in mid-air. I wrote the whole of a book about Oxford in the back of a Volkswagen microbus, sometimes static, sometimes on the move, and there are few more creative postures, for my tastes, than feet-up in an American railroad sleeperette, with your typewriter on your lap and the great brown prairie landscape rolling by outside.

People often commiserate with me about the hotel life. How can you stand it, they always say? But I have stayed in 32 different hotels so far this year, and in one way or another have enjoyed them all. Some have been lavish, some spartan, but from a literary point of view there is no denying that the more luxurious a hostelry is, the better. Nothing speeds the paragraphs like the possibility of unlimited coffee. Nothing colours the adjectives like a bottle of Chablis on its way. The writer's task is infinitely easier, I find, when you know that whenever you like you can ring for an omelette, take a hot bath, consult the Gideon Bible, switch on the TV or book a phone call home to Wales. . . .

For yes, when all is said, for the travel writer especially, perhaps, home is where the inspiration is. There are advantages, it is true, in writing about a foreign place when you are still there: the experience is fresher, the emotions are hotter, and you can always walk down to Pennsylvania Avenue to make sure you got that inscription right, or pay one more visit to Red Square to catch a last cold baleful nuance.

But there is nowhere like home, for a writer like me. Wales is the land of my fathers and since I came back to live here 20 years ago I have never wanted to settle anywhere else. For one thing the people I love are here in Wales, and that keeps the spirits bubbling. For another Wales itself lies all around me like a benediction, whispering poetic voices through the rain. And for a third, my house beside the Dwyfor River, between Snowdon and Cardigan Bay, is a sort of literary machine, geared, greased, fuelled and fitted out with just one purpose, the writing of books.

So you may imagine me now, as I type this essay, in the happiest environment of all. I have taken time off, to do it, from writing a book about India. All around my desk on the floor, on the window-sill, are the maps and pamphlets and postcards and multitudinous notebooks that are the raw material of my craft. Downstairs the library to which I have devoted 25 years of affection and overdraft stands ready for my every need.

There is a telephone beside my left hand, a cup of tea at my right, and I have put a bottle of Puligny-Montrachet in the fridge for supper. My cat Solomon is asleep on the sofa. *Ain't Misbehavin'* is on the record-player.

Perfect! And with any luck—ah, there they are now! Come in, come in, I *love* to be interrupted!

WHAT TO DO

This is your last timed test. Look aggressively for the problem, effects, causes, and solutions. Ignore everything else. Really push for speed. Time yourself. Go.

SKIM:

GOOD-BYE, NANCY DREW

by E. R. Knowles

As Acid-Based Paper Decomposes, the Twentieth Century Is Fast Becoming a "Lost Civilization"

Imagine trying to write a history of this century without any newspapers to refer to, without any maps or photographs, without magazines or text books, business records, phone directories, census statistics, personal letters, diaries, popular literature or any of the trivia of everyday life: match book covers, record jackets, theater programs, cereal boxes, railroad timetables, menus or sheet music. It would be nearly impossible, right? Yet this is the task that may face historians only 50 years from now.

We are in danger of losing more than a century of human records and the culprit is modern paper-making technology. Ironically, while we are making throw-away packaging out of seemingly indestructible plastics, the world's knowledge is stored on materials that may not last another 30 years.

Since the late 1800s paper manufacturers have routinely used processes that leave acid residues in paper. When light, heat and moisture react with these acids, paper becomes brittle and eventually self-destructs, often in only a few years. While paper made 200 or 2000 years ago remains fresh and resilient, a five-year-old newspaper can turn to crumbs in your hands.

Evidence of this potential catastrophe was recently presented by the Council of Library Resources (CLR), through its Committee on Production Guidelines for Book Longevity.

At the Library of Congress in Washington, they reported, a 1972 sampling indicated "perhaps a million books in the total collection are in advanced stages of deterioration. In thousands of instances, the paper has become so brittle that to turn a page is to break it off."

At the University of Michigan Library, a study showed that 45% of the Western European Literature collection required immediate attention if it was to be saved.

France's national library, the Bibliotheque Nationale, reports similar difficulties:

90,000 volumes are in extremely poor condition. 7,000,000 pages of periodicals have deteriorated to the point where they can no longer be consulted while 36,000 maps, 375,000 prints and 300,000 photographs together with manuscripts and musical documents are in critical condition. The major factors blamed for this situation all relate to the poor quality of modern paper.

Libraries have been the first to suffer from this wave of destruction. The short life of contemporary paper means that they must constantly replace or try to rescue disintegrating materials instead of adding to their collections.

But all areas of our civilization will soon feel the effects. In addition to our literary and cultural heritage, business and legal records and scientific data are in danger. History itself may be drastically altered, because, as Santayana notes, "those who cannot remember the past are condemned to repeat it." Without paper, the twentieth century may be represented by a few Frisbees, toothpaste tubes and battered Formica TV cabinets.

The effect of this "paper death" on future generations is almost incalculable. We smugly regard our century as the most important 100 years since ancient Greece, featuring tremendous advances in technology, medicine and human rights.

THE LOST CENTURY

Yet future generations may regard the twentieth century as lost to them, as elusive and enigmatic as the civilizations of the Etruscans and Minoans. Most of the creative work of our best minds is turning to dust as you read this.

Of course, outstanding work will be preserved. Our descendants will certainly have access to the books of Hemingway and Faulkner, the manuscripts of Stravinsky and Ravel, the sketches of Picasso and Renoir. But what about the plays of Neil Simon and Herb Gardner, the songs of Richard Whiting and Harold Arlen, the sketches of Charles Schulz and Shel Silverstein, the newspaper wit-and-wisdom of Art Buchwald, Walt Lippman, Max Lerner and William F. Buckley? Can anyone understand us without at least a reference to our popular culture?

No Dear Abby or Ripley's Believe It Or Not.

No Katzenjammer Kids, Gasoline Alley, Li'l Abner, Mary Worth, Garfield or Doonesbury.

No *Harper's* or *Hustler*, *Life* or *Liberty*, *TV Guide* or *Variety*.

No *Modern Romances*, *Popular Mechanics*, Harlequin novels or *National Enquirer.*

No *True, Screw, Cue* or *National Review.*

When they talk about saving the

really important literature of this century, will they be able to budget something for Little Lulu and Felix the Cat? The Bobbsey Twins and Nancy Drew? Aren't they what we were really reading when our parents were pushing Winnie-the-Pooh and Peter Rabbit? Didn't Dick Tracy and Captain Midnight do more to form us as citizens of this century than any "Great Books"? Can anyone truly understand us without them?

And what should we save? What do we try to thrust into the lifeboat for our descendants? So many fragments of our civilization go unvalued until another puzzle piece comes along to show their worth.

Creating standards for preservation might defy even a Solomon. Some works, regarded as masterpieces today, received little attention when they first appeared or fell out of favor in the intervening years.

How It Began

How did we get in this mess? The destruction of the twentieth century began quite innocently in the late nineteenth century when the ever-expanding world population and higher literacy rate increased the demand for cheap paper to print on. Until then paper had been made by a rather slow process from rags or, less frequently, wood fibers.

By breaking down the rag or wood fibers with acids, paper-makers discovered that they could produce huge quantities of paper at much lower cost. They could now fill the demand not met by the old process.

But the vigorous processes so degraded the fibers that it is no wonder they have a short life. The new chemical processes separated wood fibers from the gluey lignin that bound them. The lignin is dissolved and washed away from the cellulose fibers of the wood. Wood can then be ground directly into low-grade ligno-cellulose fiber for newsprint and the fibers are bleached, further weakening them.

The most serious mistake seems to be adding alum sizing to the beaten fibers. Paper made from pure cellulose fiber is like a blotter, absorbing water and causing ink to feather out in an alarming way. The early paper-makers of Italy corrected this by "sizing" the paper in dilute gelatin solutions. This made paper like vellum and parchment, and was much more acceptable to the scribes; thus gelatin-sized paper became the standard for centuries. Then in the early nineteenth century, paper-makers found that adding rosin soap and alum to the fibers eliminated the sizing step. Thereafter paper made by this method could be made conveniently and directly on the paper machine without an extra step.

Unfortunately this alum leaves the paper acid, and acid cellulose becomes brittle within twenty-five to fifty years. Most people believe that wood-based papers uniformly undergo quick deterioration while rag-based are long-lasting, but studies have shown that this isn't true.

To predict aging, a heat test was developed in the 1950s. It determined that seventy-two hours at 100 degrees are approximately equal to twenty-five years at ambivalent conditions.

This relation has been used to predict the life of tested paper.

Good quality alkaline paper lasts over a thousand years while highly acidic paper is brittle in fifty years, according to their studies. While not everyone agrees with these conclusions, the procedure gives reasonable and conservative predictions which are in accord with what we know about the acidity or alkalinity of papers of the past.

That acid is the villain was demonstrated in an experiment by an American paper manufacturer. He set aside five acid-paper samples and one alkaline paper in 1901. When the samples were examined in 1929, the acid papers were badly discolored and weak. The calcium carbonate paper had remained white and seemed as strong as when it was made. In this experiment the rag papers failed and the refined wood fiber paper lasted.

A 1576 physics text provided final proof. Some of its pages were brown and weak while others were white and strong. In a study by the Institute of Paper Chemistry, the papers were found to be identical in every way but one. The white pages had been treated with an alkaline sizing while the brown pages were acid-sized.

Now manufacturers and paper users are trying to reverse the destruction of our paper heritage. Studies by several major organizations and new specifications by paper users like the Library of Congress have called attention to the problem.

Two steps are necessary if we are to pass on our technology, culture, hopes and dreams to our grandchildren. Both must be taken immediately before it is too late.

First, material printed on old acid papers needs to be preserved. This may involve using special chemical deacidification procedures or reprinting the material on acid-free paper.

To deacidify paper that has not yet lost its strength and flexibility, several processes have been developed. A liquid alkaline solution can be applied to the paper. The book is taken apart and the pages supported on screens through a series of immersions. The book is reassembled. This may cost two or three hundred dollars per book and care must be taken that the soaking itself doesn't damage the material. Other experimental processes expose the whole book to vapor or gas.

Another way to maintain existing acid-paper materials is to keep them cool. A consistent temperature of 65-85 degrees and a low relative humidity of 40-45 percent is recommended. Humidity above 70 percent is quite dangerous because it permits mold growth. Very low humidities stiffen papers but extend their life.

ALKALINE PAPER IS CHEAPER

The second major step that must be taken is to end the production of acid paper entirely or restrict it to use in packaging materials. It is estimated that paper made according to new specifications would have a life expectancy of more than four hundred years.

Some European manufacturers have already given up the use of acid-producing agents in papermaking. Neutral-sized, calcium-carbonate-loaded papers are now firmly established in the European market, not only, as was originally thought, for specialty lines, but competing successfully in the popular lines of lithography, industrial papers, chart papers, stationery and photocopying papers.

But the major portion of the American paper industry has not responded to the simple production solutions. They continue to make rosin-alum-sized acid impermanent paper. Why they do so in the face of mounting evidence of the poor survival and extra cost of producing their product can only be explained by ignorance, inertia or lack of funds to make the initial change-over.

It is actually cheaper to make alkaline papers. A German paper mill changed over to the alkaline system and now makes 250,000 metric tons of paper a year with a substantial drop in energy and water requirements. Major mills report that alkaline paper-making not only pays off in material costs, but in hidden benefits such as cleanliness, reduced down-time, improved runability and lower energy and effluent costs.

Good paper can be recycled, reason enough for the paper makers themselves to be interested in permanence. Acid paper degrades so rapidly that it is not worth recycling. Since fifty percent of the garbage taken from American cities is fiber, this would be a valuable resource if the paper were made from strong fibers in the first place.

When more purchasers specify acid-free papers, American manufacturers may be motivated to produce them. The Library of Congress now specifies alkaline paper for file folders, film jackets, film boxes, etc. Vendors are featuring alkaline paper in their catalogues and dwelling on its virtues. We need to change acid-free paper from a novelty to a standard.

So we begin the race with time to save our century. Much will be lost. Some materials will be pulled back from the edge of destruction just in time, to survive and show future generations what we did and how we lived. I'm rooting for Nancy Drew.

Write down your reading time in the blanks below. Then answer the questions and determine your comprehension level from your score, as calculated on p. 195.

Length of article: 2,100 words.

Mins. _____ Secs. _____ Words per minute _____

Comprehension _____%

QUESTIONS

Circle the appropriate answers.

1. The major PROBLEM described in the article is:
   a. The Library of Congress is spending too much money to preserve old books.
   b. We don't appreciate the importance of popular literature.
   c. The entire cultural and scientific output of the twentieth century may disappear.
   d. Children are watching too much TV and not reading.
2. THREE of the EFFECTS are:
   a. Loss of maps, photos, documents, and books
   b. Lower reading scores in school
   c. Loss of major forested areas for parks
   d. The high cost of paper
   e. American dominance of the paper market
   f. Loss of invaluable materials for future historians
   g. Shorter library hours and smaller staffs
   h. Banning books like the Nancy Drew series from library shelves
   i. Higher rate of adult illiteracy
   j. Loss of the popular literature that will help future generations understand us
3. The main CAUSE is:
   a. Poor parental supervision
   b. The short life of acid papers
   c. Using wood to make paper
   d. Low library budgets
   e. Poor preservation techniques
4. The TWO suggested SOLUTIONS are:
   a. Special libraries for popular literature
   b. Licensing TV sets

      c. Preserving books and materials now on acid paper

      d. Requiring more educational broadcasting

      e. Banning wood-based papers

      f. Encouraging the manufacture of alkaline papers

      g. Buying only American paper

      h. Setting aside more parkland

      i. Using books like the Nancy Drew series in the classroom

      j. Decreasing the Library of Congress budget

5. Check whether the following are True, False, or IRrelevant to the article.

T F IR   a. No paper exists that is over two hundred years old.

T F IR   b. Soaking paper in alum extends its life.

T F IR   c. Children learn faster when they read comic books.

T F IR   d. Environmentalists are losing the struggle to save our forests.

T F IR   e. Japan exports the most paper.

T F IR   f. Carolyn Keene, the author of the Nancy Drew books, was actually a man.

T F IR   g. Wood-fiber papers always deteriorate quickly.

T F IR   h. Parents' associations are uniting to fight inappropriate TV programs.

T F IR   i. Paper manufacturers deliberately set out to make a self-destructing product.

T F IR   j. It is actually cheaper to make alkaline papers.

Answers on page 195.

If you made a huge leap in your reading speed, consider what you may have done without realizing it. You have been set up in the skimming exercises to look for one thing, ignoring everything else. You were asked to skim for only the problem, effects, causes, and solution. You were probably so busy skimming for those that you went very fast (because you thought you were only skimming).

But anytime you are looking for main ideas you are more reading than skimming. From your experience with this last exercise you now know what it feels like to read rapidly, more hearing the words of your questions ("What's the problem?" etc.) and the answers to your questions as you find them than hearing word-for-word in your head.

DAY 5 ANSWERS

EMPIRE STATE BUILDING

Problem—C
   Problem: Birds are crashing into Empire State Building.
   Effect: Death rate is up 300%.
   Cause: Scanning equipment disrupts birds' natural navigation sys-
        tems.
   Solution: Adapt equipment. Shut down during migration.
Thesis—B
   Thesis: City lights alter migration patterns.
   Proof: Studies that show dislocation is increasing in proportion to
        number of tall buildings
   Implication: Within twenty years, the swallows of Capistrano may
        land in Newark.
Opinion—A
   Opinion: The city should help pay the building's electricity bill.
   Reason: Empire State Building, a major tourist attraction, can't afford
        night lighting at higher electric rates.
   Implication: Lights may go out, a loss to all.
Instruction—E
   Step 1: Send self-addressed envelope and money.
   Step 2: Meet specifications and August 10 or August 14 deadline.
Information—D
   Facet 1: Empire State Building is now seventy-five years old.
   Facet 2: A big party is being held.
   Facet 3: It is no longer the world's tallest building.
   Facet 4: The Waldorf Hotel once stood on the site.

THEATER LISTING

1. Martin Beck Theater
2. *Shakespeare for My Father*
3. *Jelly's Last Jam*

4. 44th Street
5. *Angels in America*
6. John Kander
7. *Forbidden Broadway 1993*
8. *Crazy for You*
9. *Les Misérables*
10. *Fool Moon*

SKIMMING SPRINT #1

1. grab — *snatch*
2. book — *tome*
3. wish — *desire*
4. fly — *soar*
5. cat — *pussy*
6. fog — *mist*
7. gun — *pistol*
8. number — *statistic*
9. wash — *clean*
10. boat — *ship*
11. snicker — *laugh*
12. stove — *oven*
13. shoe — *boot*
14. vision — *sight*
15. renegade — *outlaw*
16. perhaps — *maybe*
17. shine — *polish*
18. vicious — *cruel*
19. elegant — *sumptuous*
20. glitter — *sparkle*
21. unusual — *rare*
22. bitter — *sour*
23. leap — *bound*
24. box — *crate*
25. hidden — *concealed*

SKIMMING SPRINT #2

1. rough — *smooth*
2. dirty — *clean*
3. finger — *toe*
4. ceiling — *floor*
5. casual — *formal*
6. day — *night*
7. alive — *deceased*
8. happy — *miserable*
9. silly — *solemn*
10. wonderful — *awful*
11. awake — *sleeping*
12. dark — *light*
13. little — *huge*
14. icy — *hot*
15. wealth — *poverty*
16. dismal — *cheerful*
17. sweet — *sour*
18. laugh — *cry*
19. cautious — *careless*
20. go — *stop*
21. stale — *fresh*
22. lazy — *energetic*
23. always — *never*
24. end — *beginning*
25. luminous — *dull*

Score 4 for each correct answer. 100 points equals 100%.

GOOD-BYE, NANCY DREW

1. c (Score 20 points)
2. a–f–j (Score 10 points each)
3. b (Score 10 points)
4. c–f (Score 10 points each)
5. (Score 2 points each)

a–F	f–IR
b–F	g–F
c–IR	h–IR
d–IR	i–F
e–IR	j–T

100 points equals 100%.

COMPUTE YOUR RATE FOR "GOOD-BYE, NANCY DREW"
(Approximate number of words: 2,100)

Time	Wpm	Time	Wpm
1 min.	2100	5 min.	420
1 min. 15 sec.	1680	5 min. 15 sec.	400
1 min. 30 sec.	1400	5 min. 30 sec.	382
1 min. 45 sec.	1200	5 min. 45 sec.	365
2 min.	1050	6 min.	350
2 min. 15 sec.	933	6 min. 15 sec.	336
2 min. 30 sec.	840	6 min. 30 sec.	323
2 min. 45 sec.	764	6 min. 45 sec.	311
3 min.	700	7 min.	300
3 min. 15 sec.	646	7 min. 15 sec.	290
3 min. 30 sec.	600	7 min. 30 sec.	280
3 min. 45 sec.	560	7 min. 45 sec.	271
4 min.	525	8 min.	263
4 min. 15 sec.	494	8 min. 15 sec.	255
4 min. 30 sec.	467	8 min. 30 sec.	247
4 min. 45 sec.	442	8 min. 45 sec.	240

Your rate is _____ wpm.
(Record this on page 224.)

STRUCTURING BUSINESS WRITING FOR RAPID READING

Moving through your in-box competently and quickly is a breeze when business writers tell you their purpose immediately. This means they clearly ask for an action, decision, or recommendation up front or that they tell you why they are sending you information. If, in addition, they provide headings arranged for *your* convenience, they have probably turned you into a rapid reader. Do not read anything until you locate the purpose. You may need to skim a bit until you find it.

Good structure promotes good substance. As you go through your in-box, you may want to have that motto inscribed on a rubber stamp and release your frustrations occasionally by going *thunk, thunk, thunk* on the more obtuse, meandering, and unreadable missives you find there.

Don't Play Brer Rabbit

When you don't find the purpose up front in a business communication, imagine that the author is muttering and doodling in front of you before talking directly to you. Think: "Here we go with 'Once upon a time.'" Then skip over the disorganized preamble.

If you remember the story of Brer Rabbit, Brer Fox, and the Tar Baby, think of letters and memos without a purpose up front as Tar Babies and avoid getting stuck. Don't let a bad writer take you the long way round the block. Start reading where the purpose begins, notice what you need to know, read it wherever it is, and dump the rest.

Why Do Writers Write That Way?

Business writers often organize their ideas in a once-upon-a-time fashion, starting with how they first noticed the subject and then going on to a full history before they reach the conclusion, way down at the bottom of the last page. Meanwhile you are asking impatiently or groggily, "Why are you telling me all this?" As readers, we want to be positioned to know the writer's PURPOSE.

The Business Pattern

Business writers usually write for one of the following purposes.

1. To ask for action
2. To ask for decisions
3. To give information

Surviving Your In-Box

It's the writer's job to write for your convenience. Here is a Reader-Ready Checklist.

[ ] *Clear Subject*
Is the subject title helpful to the reader?

[ ] *Purpose Up Front*
For: Action   Decision   Information

[ ] *Conclusion Up Front*
What has the writer decided or recommended?

[ ] *Headings*
Are similar issues or tasks bunched together with useful headings to announce them?

[ ] *Verbs*
Were action verbs used when making requests?

[ ] *Short Paragraphs and Sentences*
Is the writing easy to read?

[ ] *Attachments*

Were background information, schedules, instructions, charts, etc., in attachments with headings?

When the writer fails these criteria, there are still some things you can do.

First of all, much of what you have been practicing in the information section—making headings and turning them into questions—will speed you on your way. The following samples of real (but disguised) business writing are ideal for you to practice what you already know: *how to find what you need to know quickly*.

WHAT TO DO

Scan the following two memos, looking only for REQUESTED AC-TIONS. As soon as you find them, underline them and move on to the next memo. After each memo you will see a crafted version that will represent how you can mentally reorganize others' writing so the purpose is up-front.

You are probably noticing that such active reading requires more effort than just starting at the beginning and risking all the distractions that can overtake us when our purpose is vague or hidden. By ruthlessly insisting on reading the purpose first and creating headings where you find daunting chunks of narrative prose you *will* read rapidly. But do tolerate this new behavior, knowing you can make it a habit.

SPECTOR CORPORATION—INTEROFFICE CORRESPONDENCE

TO: S. S. Van Dyne

FROM: P. Vance

DATE: April 1, 1998

SUBJECT: Dutch Shoe Floor Products

Your memo 3/29/98

I concur with your observation that their slip resistant floor treatment product does indeed work effectively. You raised a question in your memo of potential drawbacks regarding the use of plastic gloves, deterioration of shoes, cart wheels, etc., which may be valid; however, I would think that if we found a product strong enough to do a like job, it would undoubtedly have the same drawbacks. The question you raise on a price justification of $15.00 per gallon may indeed be a valid one. I would definitely encourage your attempts to renegotiate with Dutch Shoe a reduced price for their product along with your continued attempts to identify another product that could do a comparable job at a reduced price.

Crafted version of page 198.

SPECTOR CORPORATION—INTEROFFICE CORRESPONDENCE

TO: S. S. Van Dyne   DATE: April 1, 1998

DEPT: Purchasing   PLEASE RESPOND BY:

FROM: P. Vance   CC:

DEPT: Controller   EXT:

SUBJECT: EVALUATION OF DUTCH SHOE FLOOR PRODUCTS

FOR: ACTION ☒   DECISION ☐   INFORMATION ☐

<u>You should definitely renegotiate with Dutch Shoe for a lower price on their slip-resistant floor treatment as well as search for another product that could do a comparable job at a lower price.</u> $15 a gallon for Dutch Shoe may be too high.

I agree with you that the Dutch Shoe product does a good job. Your point about potential drawbacks—use of plastic gloves, deterioration of shoes and cart wheels, etc.—may be valid. However, if we find a product strong enough to do the job, it would undoubtedly have the same draw-backs.

PV:bg

SPECTOR CORPORATION

To: Distribution

From: Pat Davis   ext.

Date: July 24, 1992

Subject: TRAVEL RESERVATIONS

Jean Charles will be located in the Boston Thomas Cook office on Monday, July 27. Due to a power shutdown at the Beverly Spector plant for the entire day on 7/27, Jean will not have computer capability. Jean can be reached at 617-723-4567 but will be unable to send tickets to Greenwich from this office. Should you need tickets for 7/27, or early travel on 7/28, we will need to prepay these tickets in this unusual emergency. Please call me if there is a problem.

Jean will be on vacation from August 3–7 but another agent assigned to the Beverly office will accommodate us.

Here is how the memo would look if the writer organized the material for rapid reading. Note how even the change in subject title positions the reader. Fortunately, you can unscramble the original and reformulate it in your mind to approximate the organization of the rewritten version.

Crafted version of page 199.

TO: Distribution   DATE: July 24, 1992

FROM: Pat Davis

SUBJECT: Changes in travel arrangement procedures

FOR: ACTION ☐   DECISION ☐   INFORMATION ☒

If you need tickets Monday, 7/27 or early Tuesday, 7/28:

> You will need to prepay and be reimbursed, due to an unusual combination of emergency circumstances.
>
> During this brief time period you can reach Jean Charles at the number below, but she will be unable to send out any tickets. Please call me at ext. 1234 if you have a problem.

For reservations after Tuesday noon, 7/28:

Update your directory to:

> TRAVEL RESERVATIONS
> Jean Charles
> Thomas Cook, Boston office
> 1-617-723-4567

(Jean will be on vacation August 3–7, but another agent will be assigned to accommodate Beverly Spector.)

WHAT TO DO

Preview "Quality Control" on the next page, looking for the answers to the following questions.

	YES	NO
1. Is the purpose up front?	___	___
2. Are there convenient headings?	___	___
3. In the next five seconds, find out:		
Is the writer asking for action?	___	___
Is the writer asking for a decision?	___	___
Is the writer writing primarily to give information?	___	___

Now set your timer for one minute. Within that time, SCAN this memo to find out what the writer is proposing and underline each recommendation.

SPECTOR CORPORATION—INTEROFFICE CORRESPONDENCE

TO: John Dunne   April 17, 1998

FROM: Bob Lytle

RE: Quality Control

This note is to give you the current status of Quality Control and the CPN group. Accounts Receivable is another subject which I want to go over also because of its deep impact on Quality Control.

I will go over the functions mentioned in the last decentralization plans memo. As Bill very well covered, the functions are basically clerical. I would like to add, that after analyzing the section, functions performed, including reconciliation of MQCRs, I have come to the conclusion that it is impossible to keep it running as is.

There are several reasons why I can say this is so:

1) We have taken three persons from Maintenance head count, temporarily covered with temp, and two positions from Production Control head count.

2) We need these five persons in order to be able to develop or hire enough cost accountants to feed the future Departmental organizations.

3) Even if we could keep these five persons in Quality Control temporarily, the kind of people we have hired or plan to develop won't stand more than one or two months of the purely clerical work.

We need then a totally different approach to the problem, and the one I have used is basically a zero budgeting approach. After going through it I came out with the following things we can live without.

MQCR reconciliations:
I have not been able to find one person who could tell me why we had to do these reconciliations. Some of the justifications I have heard in this last year were: for the sake of accuracy, for the sake of control, for goodness sake. There is only one reason I consider strong enough to invest the time and effort it takes to reconcile an approximate 4500 MQCR's; that is to control the payment cycle and be able to prove that what we have billed for we have sent out.

We even considered the possibility of requesting that all offices send in their shipping reports to be able to match them to the invoices and POs for the future Accounts Receivable organization. The one thing that worries me most is that if we rely on the MQCR reconciliation to determine our sales, we are actually doing a poor job and untimely. As a general average, we reconcile over a month after the fact.

With our hopes for Office Systems partially shattered and very worried because of our poor controls, I went to three of the QC&P managers to discuss the problem. Much to my surprise I discovered that no one was holding us responsible for that kind of control. It was explained to me that the normal procedures of QC&P cover this control. Of course the persons who explained it to me did not call it part of the sales cycle or the accounts receivable matching function.

Nevertheless, I found that in these three departments, a shipping bill at a given location is allowed through a PO detail called plant release. At the same time I found that the clerks who stamp the authorization on the bills, do so first matching it to the PO detail. The shipments are reported daily by the locations on the JBAG TWX which makes it timely. This TWX is, at the same time, the source of information for operational decisions. This makes the information much more reliable, the reason being that you can derive a quality control negative and worry about the reason later. That is the kind of thing you cannot do with the daily operational data.

This is why I propose that:

1) We do away with the MQCR reconciliations as part of the normal and monthly procedures.

2) Reinforce the controls necessary to ensure that all transactions get processed through the system.

3) Invest the time saved by not reconciling MQCRs in controlling the quality and consistency of the information we receive from the field, and avoiding our own clerical errors.

4) Put more effort into processing all shipping activity in the corresponding month using any means of communication available: telephone, TWX, Express Mail.

I also propose we make this effective as from this month.

This decision will not only relieve Quality Control of its biggest nightmare, but will also reduce substantially the workload of the future accounts receivable organization and probably very strongly impact its scope and volume.

When we manage to communicate with Automotive we will probably find that they follow the same procedures as the other departments and the same concepts will be applicable to them.

Production Control

As I already mentioned, we are using part of this section's head count for other purposes rather than just production control. On top of this, the workload is growing more than significantly. An example of this is Housewares which is constantly adding new contractors and has now decided to move from the buy back system into the controlled (that is Spector-owned) inventory at contractor locations. The initial move involves 20 contractors, a combination of old and new. This initial move adds an approximate 5 to 15% workload to the section.

The conclusion is very simple. We cannot any longer do this job the same way we were doing it. On this part of the Company's inventory I have not been able to find yet a clear definition of which way we have to go and what would be eliminated either because it is redundant or because it is meaningless.

Nevertheless I find that the THCPP to invoice reconciliation which is currently being performed by Production personnel is definitely part of what we call the Accounts Receivable function. This being so it seems to me that the obvious way to go is to train the Payment Processing group in this function and have the function transferred immediately. Of course this means that their function would be upgraded and so would their positions.

We will also drop the reconciliation of shipping bills for anything that is controlled as parts, as we have already acknowledged that this control is being performed by QC&P. I also recognize a problem area in the payment reconciliation being performed by Production personnel. I'm talking about office generated purchases. There is no reason why, if the office generates the invoice and receives the payment, they cannot approve the payment reconciliation, and either credit it to office income or forward it to the home office for credit. Anyway, before making any changes outside Controller's, I think we can achieve a lot and gain a better workload balance by making these in-house changes.

cc: A. Lyons
      T. Farrow
      G. Dellmack

Attachment A: Use of Plant Release
Attachment B: Staffing Requirements

The answers are underlined in a crafted version on the next page. It is organized to demonstrate how the writer could have written for your convenience. In the original version he is talking to himself in front of the reader instead of to the reader. By refusing to read anything until you find the purpose (here in the form of recommendations) you will save time and energy.

Crafted version of pages 201–203.

SPECTOR CORPORATION—INTEROFFICE CORRESPONDENCE

TO: John Dunne   DATE: April 17, 1994

DEPT: Operations   PLEASE RESPOND BY: April 25th

FROM: Bob Lytle   cc: A. Lyons
                                             T. Farrow

DEPT: Quality Control   EXT: 3442

SUBJECT: RECOMMENDED CHANGES IN QUALITY CONTROL
         PROCEDURES

FOR: ACTION ☐   DECISION ☒   INFORMATION ☐

The purpose of this memo is to recommend changes to enable Quality Control to handle its increased workload without additional personnel.

—Eliminate MQCR Reconciliations

My investigation establishes that reconciling 4500 MQCR's each month is a monstrous clerical workload which serves no productive purpose. Adequate controls to insure we are paid for what we ship are maintained through a PO detail called "Plant Release" which is what the QC&P managers actually rely on. See Attachment A for further detail.

—Transfer the THCPP-to-Invoice Reconciliation from Production Control to the Payment Processing Group in Accounts Receivable

Production Control is understaffed and switching Housewares to a controlled inventory system at 20 plants will increase workload 5-15%. THCPP-to-invoice reconciliation is both an Accounts Receivable function and a Production group function and should be transferred. See Attachment B for details.

—Invest the time saved in intensified quality control within our group

—Put more effort into processing all shipping activity in the corresponding month using any means available: telephone, TWX, Express Mail

—Implement these recommendations this month

WHAT TO DO

Read the following looking for five complaints. When you find them underline them. Then compare yours with those in the rewrite. You are using the same label-making skill you practiced in the Information Pattern.

SPECTOR CORPORATION

June 5, 1996

Ms. Carmen Miranda
Sales Manager
The Tropicana
1234 Tropical Avenue
Miami, FL 30000

Dear Carmen:

As we discussed, below are my comments regarding The Tropicana's handling of Spector's recent annual conference, "Improving Lender Performance '86," which was held at your hotel from May 4-7. (Thanks again for preparing the first draft from my tape.)

I thought, as did our attendees and speakers, that the hotel has beautiful facilities. The meeting rooms worked well for our group, as well. The meals at the hotel were very good. And, most importantly, despite problems which I encountered, the conference appeared to run smoothly to the participants.

As the on-site manager of the conference, however, I did encounter fairly consistent flaws within the hotel's organization. There is no single person to hold responsible—nor is that the purpose of my feedback. I hope the information provided below assists you in tightening your shop.

Shortly after arriving at the hotel, I discovered that the VIP list which I had created for the conference had been seriously disregarded. Not only were our Advisory Board members asked to produce their credit cards in order to check in (I had specifically requested their bills be put on Spector's master account), they were assigned less desirable rooms (I had expected they would be upgraded a bit). Even the Chairman and co-owner of Spector, John Beta, was put into a standard room. For Spector's conference, in which we do not pay our speakers and board members, it is very important to give whatever "perks" we can. I was very dissatisfied with and embarrassed by this situation.

On Monday morning, the first day of the conference, the audiovisual equipment was not set up until immediately prior to the start of the breakout sessions. This naturally posed a problem for our speakers, since many of them wanted to acquaint themselves with the equipment and rooms before their sessions met. Additionally, I had problems with having the breakout rooms refreshed in between session offerings. I had to stay on the hotel staff during the entire run of our conference to see that these things were done. I am quite critical of this situation since at our previous conference hotel things like this ran smoothly enough to allow me to tend to other matters surrounding the conference.

On the second day of the conference, Sam Smith had the day off. Understandably, I had already come to rely on him, and no effort was made to let me know of the "changing of the guard." On this day, especially, I had trouble getting the staff to refresh our breakout rooms. As a matter of fact, I had to pitch in to see that it was done.

Beginning as early as Saturday, and continuing through Monday and Tuesday, I was hunting for several envelopes/packages which were shipped to me via Federal Express. Robin in Conference Services put a lot of effort into locating these items, to no avail. On Wednesday morning, the final day of any conference activities, four items were brought out to me. They had been sitting somewhere in the hotel since <u>Saturday</u>.

On a positive note, The Tropicana's staff, as people, were all very nice. For the most part, when I encountered problems, everyone was quick to respond.

As I reflect on what happened during our conference, I realize that part of the problem can be attributed to the newness of the hotel. Part of it may be attributable to the hotel being understaffed. Part of it may simply be a lack of organization. Regardless of the combination of causes, I would hesitate holding another conference at the hotel. At least, let me say I would not do so unless the hotel received some very high praise from groups you've had in there in the interim.

Carmen, I trust that you'll distribute copies of this letter to anyone who can learn from it.

Again, I want to personally thank you for your own outstanding work. You have been a professional from the beginning to the end, and I think you are an invaluable member of the Tropicana's staff.

Hope to speak to you in the not-too-distant future.

Sincerely,

Barbara Murphy
Conference Coordinator

/bm

Crafted version of pages 205–206.

SPECTOR CORPORATION

June 5, 1996

Ms. Carmen Miranda
Sales Manager
The Tropicana
1234 Tropical Avenue
Miami, FL 30000

Dear Carmen:

As we discussed, here are my comments regarding The Tropicana's handling of Spector's recent annual conference, "Improving Lender Performance '86," which was held at your hotel from May 4-7.

POSITIVE COMMENTS

Beautiful facilities: I thought, as did our attendees and speakers, that the hotel has beautiful facilities. The meeting rooms worked well for our group. The meals at the hotel were very good. And, most important, despite the problems which I encountered, the participants viewed the conference as running smoothly.

Helpful staff: The Tropicana's staff, as people, were all very nice. For the most part, when I encountered problems, everyone was quick to respond.

PROBLEMS

As the on-site manager of the conference, I encountered fairly consistent flaws within the hotel's organization. There is no one person to hold responsible—nor is that the purpose of my feedback. I hope this information assists you in tightening your ship.

Major check-in errors: Our VIP list was seriously disregarded. I had requested that the bills for our Advisory Board members be put on Spector's master account and that they be assigned desirable rooms. Instead, they were each required to produce their own credit cards at check in, and were assigned less desirable rooms. Even the Chairman and co-owner of Spector, John Beta, was put into a standard room. Since we do not pay our speakers and board members, it is very important to give whatever "perks" we can. I was very dissatisfied with and embarrassed by this situation.

Last-minute AV setup: On Monday morning, the first day of the conference, the audio-visual equipment was not set up until immediately prior to the start of the breakout sessions. This naturally posed a problem for our speakers, since many of them wanted to acquaint themselves with the equipment and rooms before their sessions met.

Difficulty with maintaining meeting rooms: I had problems with having the breakout rooms refreshed between sessions. I had to stay on top of the hotel staff during the entire run of our conference to see these things were done. I am quite critical of this situation since, at our previous conference hotel, things like this ran smoothly enough to allow me to tend to other conference matters. On Tuesday, I actually had to pitch in and help refresh the rooms myself!

Misplaced packages: Beginning on Saturday, I hunted for several envelopes and packages which had been shipped to me via Federal Express. Robin in Conference Services tried hard to locate these items, to no avail. On Wednesday morning, the last day of conference activities, four items were brought to me. They had been sitting somewhere in the hotel since Saturday.

No notification of contact change: On the second day of the conference, Ricky Ricardo had the day off. Understandably, I had come to rely on him, but no effort was made to let me know of the "changing of the guard." (This was the day that I had to help clean out the breakout rooms myself.)

I would hesitate holding another conference at the hotel, and would not do so unless the hotel received some very high praise from groups who had used it in the interim. As I reflect on what happened during our conference, I realize that part of the problem can be attributed to the newness of the hotel. Part of it may be that the hotel is understaffed. And part of it may simply be a lack of organization.

Carmen, I trust that you'll distribute copies of this letter to anyone who can learn from it. Again, I want to thank you personally for your own outstanding work. You have been a professional from the beginning to the end, and I think you are an invaluable member of The Tropicana's staff.

Thanks again for preparing the first draft from my tape. Hope to speak to you in the not-too-distant future.

Sincerely,

Barbara Murphy
Conference Coordinator

/bm

WHAT TO DO

This time underline the actions the reader is asked to take, then jot them below. Begin each direction with an active verb.

_____

_____

_____

_____

Now create two more headings for the remaining information in the memo.

_____

_____

SPECTOR CORPORATION

October 22, 1994

TO: EXECUTIVES, DIRECTORS & MANAGERS

FROM: Jeanette Furth, Manager, Publications

SUBJ: Release of the Interim Operator's Manual

As you may know, the Operator's Manual is being revised. The existing volumes (II, III, IV, V) are being replaced with a full set (I-V). This set is code named the "Interim Manual" because we are in the process of redesigning the entire Operator's Manual from start to finish. This Interim Manual will provide stores with updated information and will meet the requirements set forth in the current Franchise Agreement. The Interim Manual will be in use through April 1995, when we plan to release the new Operator's Manual.

We request your cooperation in helping to make the transition as smooth as possible. C/L U.S. will receive the Interim Manual via UPS the week of October 19, 1994. We are asking that they destroy the old contents of the manuals. (Saving the binders and tabs.) By destroying the old volumes they can insure that they are using the most up-to-date information available. If store owners ask you about these new volumes please remind them to destroy the old contents.

Volume I is a completely new volume, titled Owner's File. We have suggested that they familiarize themselves with it as soon as possible.

Please direct your questions or comments to me at extension 44-33 (x3997).

NOTE: International Stores will receive these volumes with a cover memo explaining that these were written for U.S. stores. The redesign will include the first International Edition of the Operator's Manual.

Crafted version of pages 209–210.

October 22, 1994

TO: EXECUTIVES, DIRECTORS & MANAGERS

From: Jeanette Furth, Manager, Publications

Re: Release of the Interim Operator's Manual

FOR: ACTION ☒   DECISION ☐   INFORMATION ☒

You will receive your copy of the new "Interim Manual" this week. When you do, please:

Destroy the contents of outdated existing volumes II, III, IV and V of the current Operator's Manual.

Retain the binders and tabs for later use.

Read Volume I, "Owner's File," which is completely new.

Remind store owners to do these three things.

New Operator's Manual Due in April

The Interim Manual will be in effect until April 1995, when we plan to release the entirely new Operator's Manual. The Interim Manual will provide stores with updated informataion and will meet the requirements in the current Franchise Agreement.

International Stores will receive the Interim Manual volumes with a cover memo explaining that they were written for U.S. Stores. The first International Edition of the Operator's Manual will be issued in April also.

Please call me at extension 44-33 (x3997) with any questions or comments.

WHAT TO DO

Create a heading for each of the four paragraphs in the Spectorville Project Evaluation below. Then check your headings against those in the rewritten version that follows it.

SPECTORVILLE PROJECT EVALUATION

The proposal to subdivide this 3.7 acre parcel into three lots is not in conformance with established General Plan goals and policies. The General Open Space designation for the site provides for the protection of ridges. The existing 29% slopes on the site exceed the slopes recommended for conventional pad grading.

Significant modification to the hillside would be necessary in order to construct three dwellings on the site. The 2:1 cut slopes necessary in order to establish building pads violates General Plan goals for maintenance of natural areas and avoiding development in particularly vulnerable areas. The Preliminary Soils Investigation report submitted by the applicant suggests that expansive soils exist on the site. The avoidance of slope instability is stressed in the General Plan.

The finished floor elevations of the proposed three lots is 50 feet above the adjacent homes to the south. The existing home south of lot one is two-story, while the other two are one-story homes. The elevation of the proposed private drive will be approximately 30 feet above the finished floor elevations of the existing homes and will be supported by a 6 foot cribwall on the south side. The orientation and elevations of the proposed lots would have a negative impact on the adjacent lots to the south and violate the General Plan goal of maintaining the visual quality of open space areas.

This site is extremely difficult to develop and is visually prominent within the adjacent neighborhood. The property should more appropriately be developed in a manner similar to the adjacent subdivision along Santiago Lane. While zoned R-100, this area is developed with lots which average in areas of five acres in size. Similarly, the adjacent Robinson property which is seven acres in size will ultimately be developed with one residential unit. While zoned R-15, the site represents extremely difficult terrain which cannot be developed in a manner which is consistent with the general plan and compatible with existing residences to the south. Because of the terrain, this site more logically relates to the adjacent development along Santiago Lane rather than that along Richard Lane, Christine Court and Gwen Court.

Crafted version of pages 210–211.

<u>Violates General Plan</u>: The proposal to subdivide this 3.7 acre parcel into three lots is not in conformance with established General Plan goals and policies. The General Open Space designation for the site provides for the protection of ridges. The existing 29% slopes on the site exceed the slopes recommended for conventional pad grading.

<u>Slope too steep</u>: Significant modification to the hillside would be necessary in order to construct three dwellings on the site. The 2:1 cut slopes necessary to establish building pads violate General Plan goals for maintenance of natural areas and avoiding development in particularly vulnerable areas. The preliminary Soils Investigation report submitted by the applicant suggests that expansive soils exist on the site. The avoidance of slope instability is stressed in the General Plan.

<u>Negative visual impact:</u> The finished floor elevations of the proposed three lots are 50 feet above the adjacent homes to the south. The existing home south of lot one is two-story, while the other two are one-story homes. The elevation of the proposed private drive will be approximately 30 feet above the finished floor elevations of the south side. The orientation and elevations of the proposed lots would have a negative impact on the adjacent lots to the south and violates the General Plan goal of maintaining the visual quality of open space areas.

<u>Develop like Santiago Lane:</u> This site is extremely difficult to develop and is visually prominent within the adjacent neighborhood. The property should more appropriately be developed in a manner similar to the adjacent subdivision along Santiago Lane. While zoned R-100, this area is developed with lots which average in areas of five acres in size. Similarly, the adjacent Robinson property which is seven acres in size will ultimately be developed with one residential unit. While zoned R-15, the site represents extremely difficult terrain which cannot be developed in a manner consistent with the general plan and compatible with the existing residences to the south. Because of the terrain, this site more logically relates to the adjacent development along Santiago Lane rather than that along Richard Lane, Christine Court and Gwen Court.

WHAT TO DO

Scan the following memo in less than one minute, and underline what the writer is asking the reader to do.

SPECTOR CORPORATION

April 23, 1988

To: All Supervisory Staff—Health Division

From: Arthur Marx, Director

Re: Request for Staff Input

The past two years have brought about a number of modifications to our practices and procedures. Most have been the result of automation, legislative mandates, judicial direction, increasing workload, and fiscal constraints. Differences in management perspective and style have added a share to changes we've incorporated. Equitable distribution of workload and delivery of services are areas of continuing concern. Doing more with the same, and in some cases with less, has been the watch word not only in Tudor County health services, but with other departments and counties throughout the state and nation as well.

We've all felt the impact of recession/inflation at home as well as at work. It's required changing some old notions, stepping off of familiar paths, and shifting gears at a fairly rapid clip. All of which adds to our burden, to not only keep pace, but learn more and varying aspects to our job functioning as we try to keep abreast of it all. This has been difficult at times for all of us, at all levels, and we continue to go through these changes, which hopefully are growing pains, there is an increasing need to work closer together in a team effort with a positive spirit, sharing our collective expertise to get the job done together.

We all have a stake in the organization and take pride in the quality of our work product. None of us want to compromise quality for expedience sake. However, reality demands creative approaches to deal with the numerous issues that confront us, e.g., increased referrals, more patients, more paper work, to mention a few. Policy decisions regarding staffing patterns, work assignments, standards for both clerical and supervision, accommodating personal preference for assignment, will have to be formulated over the next several months. Management has an obligation to wrestle with such issues and formulate policy.

An open-policy, which encourages input from supervisors and line staff as well, working in concert, promotes a more effective style to accomplish meaningful, progressive improvements. We have evolved over the past several years to a group of specialists where no one person has it all intact. The operation has grown and diversified at both supervisory and clerical levels. We need collective ideas, input, suggestions, and we need to be able to sit together, objectively with a divisional perspective, sharing and willing to help resolve problems.

To that end, and with that purpose in mind, we are asking each unit supervisor as you meet with your respective unit staff to solicit their input as well as offering your own, to identify specific work related issues which need to be addressed in the Health Division, in supervision, clerical, special programs, control of workload, paper work, and other areas of concern.

For organizational purposes, and to prevent indiscriminate offerings from 140 staff, the following format is to be used:

1) A one page memo to the Division Director.

2) The memo is to be typed and submitted by a supervisor, either medical or clerical.

3) The memo is to be constructed as follows:

    a) Subject: suggestion for change.

    b) Paragraphs should be brief and entitled:

       Problem—(definition of what the problem, issue, concern is).

       Current practice—(what are we doing now).

       Suggestion—(what are you recommending be changed, added, deleted).

Implementation—(how do you envision this change being made).

Results—(what will be the results, value, benefit, of doing this).

4) The Director will consider each proposal submitted, determining fiscal impact, feasibility, divisional/departmental effect, time-lines, staffing, and any other areas of import and will do so with consultation of other divisional management staff. Submitters may be requested to participate in discussions.

5) Suitable proposals will then be presented to all supervisors for review and discussion prior to implementation.

This procedure while at first blush looks bureaucratic and cumbersome, is designed to offer a vehicle, organized format. The Division Director will provide a written response to each proposal.

It is hoped that this practice will be accepted by all staff as an opportunity to participate actively in divisional decisions.

Do you find it amazing the author takes over two pages to ask his staff to write one page?

Crafted version of pages 212–214.

April 23, 1998

To: All Supervisory Staff—Health Division

From: Arthur Marx, Director

Subject: Request for Staff Input on Policy Changes

FOR: ACTION ☒   DECISION ☐   INFORMATION ☐

Reply by: May 15

I need your help.

Please meet with your unit staff to ask for their input. We want to hear from you before we begin making policy decisions on such issues as staffing patterns, caseload sizes, standards for investigation and supervision, special programs, paper work, and accommodating personal preference in assignment.

Need for New Policies: We have had a lot of changes in the past two years from automation, legislation, increased workload and new budgets. We have also grown so specialized that no one person is aware of everything going on. Now we need to pull all the loose ends together, solve problems, and rethink policy.

How to Respond: This is a chance for everyone to participate in divisional decisions. Although it may seem bureaucratic, I can handle your responses more efficiently if you use the attached form.

My Follow-up: I will consider each proposal and respond to it in writing. I may want to discuss some of them further with the submitters. Suitable proposals will then be presented to all supervisors for review and discussion prior to implementation.

Attachment: sample Survey Form

To: All Clerical and Medical Personnel   April 23, 1998

SURVEY

What policy changes would you like to see?

(Please type your suggestions.)

Problem—definition of problem, issue, concern

Current practice—what are we doing now?

Suggestions—what should be changed?

Implementation—how do you see this change being made?

Results—what will be the result, value or benefit?

Your Name_____

Submitted by_____
                (Probation or Clerical Supervisor)

Return to Arthur Marx, Director, by May 15, 1998. He may wish to talk to you further about your ideas. THANK YOU!

WHAT TO DO

Read the following memo looking for the three pieces of news it answers. Underline them as you find them.

INTRA-OFFICE COMMUNICATION

Sheriff's Office, Windsorville

DATE: _____

TO: Lt. William Burleigh

FROM: Anne Bullen, Accounting

SUBJECT: Accounting Procedures at the Women's Correctional Center

This will confirm our meeting of January 23rd pertaining to the procedures for the fiscal record keeping and cash transactions at the Women's Correctional Center.

Beginning February 1st, the shift envelopes will be forwarded to the Sheriff's Administration Division on a daily basis. Envelopes will be forwarded subsequent to the close of "A" and "B" shifts and will total 24 hours. They must contain all cash receipts, disbursements, machine tape and any other pertinent data.

In an effort to keep to a minimum the amount of money orders, cashier's checks, etc., that are returned from the bank marked "payment stopped," it is prudent to consider a $100 maximum amount for such funds that are to be used for commissary activities. It is understood that funds received at the time of booking are uncontrollable.

Per our discussion, new disbursement forms are on order and will be forwarded to the respective facilities, including the Women's Correctional Center, when received. At that time, any old forms may not be used and should be discarded.

Questions regarding the above mentioned procedures should be directed to Tom Moore on ext. 1749.

Your continuing co-operation is appreciated.

_____
                                                    Anne Bullen

cc: Walter Raleigh, Administrative Service Officer
      Francis Drake, Accountant

[x]   For your information

[ ]   Reply requested within _____ days

[ ]   Note, forward and return to _____

Crafted version of pages 215–216.

INTRA-OFFICE COMMUNICATION
Sheriff's Office, Windsorville

DATE: _____

TO: Lt. William Burleigh

FROM: Anne Bullen, Accounting

SUBJECT: Accounting Procedures at the Women's Correctional Center

FOR: ACTION ☐   DECISION ☐   INFORMATION ☒

Shift Envelopes Will be Forwarded Daily

Beginning February 1st, [name/s] will forward shift envelopes to the

Sheriff's Administration Division daily. S/he will do this after the close of the "A" and "B" shifts. The envelopes must contain:

All cash receipts
Disbursements
Machine tape
Any other pertinent data

$100 Maximum for Money Orders

Too many money orders and cashier's checks are being returned by the bank marked "payment stopped." We recommend that you set a $100 maximum for such funds that are to be used for commissary activities. (We understand that funds received at the time of booking are uncontrollable.)

New Disbursement Forms

You will get these soon. When they come, discard all old forms.

This memo confirms our discussions at the January 23rd meeting. If you have any questions, please contact Tom Moore at ext. 1749. Your continuing cooperation is appreciated.

Anne Bullen

cc: Walter Raleigh, Administrative Services Officer
     Francis Drake, Accountant

[ ] reply requested by _____

[ ] Note, forward, and return to _____

How to Remember What You Read

Before Marlene began Rapid Reading she wrote, "I'm afraid I'll forget, fail the test, and feel stupid because I don't think I have a good memory." But these were her feelings from school.

Having learned to perceive patterns of organization, you and Marlene now have structures on which to hang key ideas. Once you've broken down your reading into its pattern parts, as you have been doing throughout this book, all you need to do is rehearse the material you want to remember. Look at your outline, say it out loud, cover it up, and repeat what you remember. Keep repeating this behavior until you are fluently remembering. If you are like most readers, you will succeed more with frequent short periods of review than with larger time chunks spaced far apart. Fifteen minutes a day for a week is usually more effective than a total of one hour and forty-five minutes of review at one time.

The steps to remembering are:

Registration—picking out pattern parts
Retention—storing them in a structure
Retrieval—recognizing or recalling what you need

When we are excited about what we want to remember, the images to be stored are more vivid. It seems our excitement is accompanied by a burst of adrenaline enhancing our chances of retrieval. The more senses you use to embellish or simplify what you choose to remember, the more places it is stored in your mind. The more associations you make around your desired memory, the more success you can expect.

Index of Articles

Skimming

Structuring Business Writing for Rapid Reading

TABLE OF READING RATES

Words Per Minute	SOS	Our Shocking	Overland Journey	The Search	Slam Dancing	Goodbye Nancy Drew
2000						
1950						
1900						
1850						
1800						
1750						
1700						
1650						
1600						
1550						
1500						
1450						
1400						
1350						
1300						
1250						
1200						
1150						
1100						
1050						
1000						
950						
900						
850						
800						
750						
700						
650						
600						
550						
500						
450						
400						
350						
300						
250						
200						
Comprehension						